DRAGON'S BREATH

A BLACK BEACONS MURDER MYSTERY

DCI EVAN WARLOW CRIME THRILLER # 14

RHYS DYLAN

COPYRIGHT

Print ISBN 978-1-915185-35-8
eBook ISBN 978-1-915185-34-1

Published by Wyrmwood Books.
An imprint of Wyrmwood Media.

EXCLUSIVE OFFER

Please look out for the link near the end of the book for your chance to sign up to the no-spam guaranteed VIP Reader's Club and receive a FREE DCI Warlow novella as well as news of upcoming releases.

Or you can go direct to my website: https://rhysdylan.com and sign up now.
Remember, you can unsubscribe at any time and I promise I won't send you any spam. Ever.

OTHER DCI WARLOW NOVELS

THE ENGINE HOUSE
CAUTION DEATH AT WORK
ICE COLD MALICE
SUFFER THE DEAD
GRAVELY CONCERNED
A MARK OF IMPERFECTION
BURNT ECHO
A BODY OF WATER
LINES OF INQUIRY
NO ONE NEAR

THE LIGHT REMAINS
A MATTER OF EVIDENCE
THE LAST THROW

CHAPTER ONE

November in the West.

Summer had long gone, winter shivered on the horizon. Only a few days after the clocks were turned back an hour for daylight saving, an Atlantic storm came calling. And there was no light to save on this night. A pitch-black, wet, windswept night all over the South and West of Wales.

And nowhere blacker, wetter, or windier than where the Brecon Mountain Rescue Team were searching. They had a location from the last phone message. The control vehicle had sent a text and got a reply. That allowed the software to pinpoint the caller. GPS coordinates placed them on the bottom of the slope of Fan Hir, a little behind the lake of Llyn y Fan Fawr in the heart of the Black Mountains.

Inhospitable was an understatement.

It was not yet midnight, but soon would be, and they were already two hours into this hunt. Four hours since the 999 call to the police. Time was not on their side.

They'd driven the long-wheelbase Land Rover rescue vehicle up to the shores of Llyn y Fan Fach, the smaller of the two lakes at an elevation of five hundred metres. From there the team had stayed on the lower elevations, heading east below the escarpments of Fan Brycheiniog and the

Carmarthenshire Fans before rounding Fan Foel and heading south towards the lake.

They were at this point now, in the teeth of the gale that howled up from the southwest. The gale accompanying the third Atlantic storm of the season, this one christened innocuously Ciaran.

Rhydian Humphries, one of the four from the "hasty" party sent out as the first response, always thought they should give these storms proper names. Something mythical that fed into their fury and strength. Cerberus or Charybdis might have suited better. It certainly felt like they were experiencing the wrath of a monster now.

He signalled to his partner, Lydia Stephens. No point trying to talk in this weather.

They made up half of the four from the hasty party. The decision was to trek east or west of the lake, looking for someone who'd given his name as Emyr Dobbs, pronounced the Welsh way, Em-irr. They did not know why he was up here. The message they'd got through was confusing, and that had as much to do with the conditions as anything. Comms in this kind of weather were always bad.

They took the east side of the lake where there was a path. They knew from old that there were a few gulleys. Places where someone might find a little bit of shelter out of the wind and rain.

Rhydian saw the light flickering, as someone stood up to attract their attention, fifty yards ahead. They bent into the wind and hurried along the winding path. When they reached him, the walker, Emyr, could barely manage a weak entreaty. Pale, cold, and wet.

'I tried…'

'We need to get him warmed up fast,' Lydia shouted over the wind, pulling out emergency blankets from her backpack.

Rhydian bent to the second figure, motionless on the floor, wrapped in a silver blanket and a coat but hardly anything else, his face a deathly white. He ripped off gloves and felt for a neck pulse.

'I'm not feeling anything, Lydia. Wait, yes, maybe…'

'We're not walking off here,' she shouted back. 'That's for certain.'

Rhydian stood up and reached for his radio, the wind whipping around him, fingers numbed from the cold already. He pressed a button and called it in.

'Both found,' he said. 'One, severely hypothermic with a very weak pulse. And the second man is hypothermic but talking.'

The coordinator was also a volunteer, but ex-military. Used to making decisions. 'Speed an issue, then?'

'It is.'

'Chopper, then?'

'Definitely.'

'Okay, I'll call it in.' By that, he meant the coastguard at St Athan. Not exactly in the job description, but their Leonardo AW189s were a frequent sight over the hinterland when mountain rescues needed assistance.

Rhydian bent to the hunched-over walker who was on his feet. 'We're getting the helicopter in… Twenty minutes. Let's get some hot drink inside you.'

'No, my brother…'

'Help is coming.'

Lights approached from the east where the other two members of the hasty party were hurrying to join them. 'We'll get your brother dry and more insulated. But you need some warm tea. Come on.'

Rhydian turned to his backpack. He didn't ask what they were doing out here at this time of night. That would all come later. One of these men was near death, and Rhydian's job was to make sure not to let this second man get anywhere near that state.

'What's his name?' Lydia called up from where she was hunched over the prostrate man.

'Marc. Marc Dobbs,' Emyr said. 'He's my brother.'

More help arrived. Dry clothing, a box tent to keep off the rain and the worst of the wind, more blankets, and an insulated mat for him to lie on while they got Marc into the casualty bag – an Arctic-rated sleeping bag.

The people administering the aid were all volunteers. Highly trained and experienced. But Marc needed to be in a hospital.

Every heart on that mountainside lifted when the distant hum of the drone reached them, carried on the coattails of the howling wind, and followed by the unmistakable glow of the Coastguard helicopter's search beam slicing through the pitch-black sky. Emerging from the east, its lights were a lifeline, cutting through the darkness and offering hope in the cold, bitter, unforgiving night.

CHAPTER TWO

DCI Evan Warlow looked out at the driving rain through the front-room window of his cottage, Ffau'r Blaidd, and wrinkled his nose. At his side, Cadi, his black Labrador, looked up at him imploringly.

'We both know there is no point in me even opening the door. You won't want to go out.'

The dog's tail swept the flagstone floor like a drummer's brush.

'Don't give me that look.' Warlow pulled the door open, and Cadi lifted her nose to sniff the wet air. But she did not move from the spot.

'*Glaw, glaw a mwy o law,*' Warlow muttered in his native Welsh. Incessant rain indeed.

Cadi was not a dog who enjoyed the rain. At least not this kind of rain. The kind that pummelled and stung your skin like a mad acupuncturist with a hangover. There'd been no let up for twenty-four hours. A wet West Wales weekend if ever there was one. Cadi braved the elements only for a bathroom break and even then, reluctantly.

'Won't last forever, eh, girl?'

Of course, it would not. It only felt like it would. And was it not always the same come autumn once the clocks went back for daylight saving? Dark November mornings, darker evenings. And never-ending bloody damp.

Warlow and Cadi much preferred proper winter. Cold, dry days like you got in January and February, the true winter months, with the ground iron-hard from frost and your breath a plume of water vapour. But they were months away from that in early November.

Nothing for it but to take what mama nature dished out. Warlow shut the door.

'Maybe Marjorie and Bouncer will take you out tomorrow.' He referenced Cadi's human sitter and her canine pal. Both names triggered a keen, intelligent head tilt from the dog.

Warlow scratched the dog's head, marvelling, as he always did, at the dog's ability to see the bright side of things. At least, that was how it always struck him. They were a bloody miracle, dogs. Lacking that self-awareness that dragged so many humans down. She lived in the moment, and one magic word from him would have her up and raring to go in a heartbeat.

He gave her head an extra rub which she tolerated for a minute, until he stopped, at which point she got up and turned to walk stoically to her basket.

Warlow glanced at the sheeting rain one last time, horizontal in the porch light's glow, which opening the door had triggered. Where the hell had the summer gone?

Since rescuing Sergeant Catrin Richards from an underground bunker and dealing with the fallout that came with the death of her kidnapper, someone pressed the fast-forward button on Warlow's life. Many times, he'd wondered if he'd been transported into the body of one of those toy rabbits the advertisers favoured for demonstrating the power of alkaline batteries.

First, there'd been the inevitable hand-wringing internal inquiry into Catrin's abduction and the killer who'd almost left her for dead. His deadly pipe-bomb attack in a sleepy

Pembrokeshire village had made international headlines. Headlines that Warlow made every effort not to be part of.

There would also be an external review by another Force, as always in these situations. But he and his team had nothing to fear. His molars were far too long to worry about such things, and he'd made it clear to the team they should not either. The same could not be said of his superiors who'd unwittingly facilitated DS Richards's abduction and, ultimately, the bombings.

It would all come out in the wash, as DS Gil Jones was wont to say: "So long as they use plenty of that biological detergent, the kind that gets rid of really nasty stains and dog-dirt."

After that, the summer seemed to run away from Warlow. His son Tom and partner Jodie had come for a few weeks, having borrowed Jodie's dad's RV. The plan had been to use the RV to go places, but the places had all ended up being within a day's drive of Nevern. And why not, since the Welsh coast and the mountains behind it were relatively unknown to Jodie. A chance for Tom to show her what she'd been missing all these years. And when they came back to Ffau'r Blaidd, they used the RV to sleep in, which meant no juggling of sleeping arrangements. Warlow stayed in his garden room, Jess Allanby in one bedroom and Molly Allanby, Jess's daughter, in the other. Molly and Jodie hit it off really well, even though Jess expressed her discomfort at Tom having to share the cottage with her and her daughter.

A discomfort that Warlow waved away as unnecessary.

Before he knew it, August came and went, bringing Molly Allanby a crop of excellent exam results. September followed on and, for Molly, university. For the first few weeks, she commuted, but by the end of October she'd made friends, and a move into a rented room in a house, vacated by a student who'd decided university was not for her, followed.

Meanwhile, Jess, now that Molly was settled, travelled to and from Manchester to complete the extraction of the remaining items she and Molly left at the house they'd previously lived in when Jess was married to Molly's father. In a stroke of stunning inconvenience, Rick Allanby had broken a bone in his ankle attempting a tough mudder event.

'Half of me thinks he's done it deliberately.' Jess sighed on hearing the news. 'But at least he'll be well out of the sodding way while I sort through things.'

Her eyes glinted with challenge as she'd said this. Rick Allanby finally found the funding to buy Jess out of the house they'd shared, rather than selling it. Warlow suspected Jess had been secretly glad and wanted to stay busy, too, now that Molly was officially out of her hair. At least for term time. She denied it, but empty nest syndrome was a real thing.

And so, on this Sunday, with houseguests Molly in Swansea, and Jess in Manchester, Warlow found himself alone for the first time in a while.

And he wasn't sure how he felt about that.

He did not relish reflection. Some people, he realised, never married or had children, and experienced a lifetime with little or no connection with close family in other places. Warlow did not consider that to be a healthy existence.

Humans were social animals. Men and women were programmed to make more men and women, like every other living thing on the planet. That primal urge, the one that got so many people in trouble these days and such bad press to boot, was a Darwinian fact of natural life. You could rail about it with all the pseudoscience you liked, but biology was biology. At least it was for the vast majority of the population who viewed the new century's self-destructive ideological battles with quiet bewilderment.

So, as old-fashioned, triggering, and privileged as no doubt some vociferous minority would claim it was, Warlow believed in family.

And how ironic that was, as the one he'd began had not lasted the distance as a unit. But the fruits of the effort he and Denise put in before vodka and the job skewered it were an inextricable part of Warlow's life.

He'd spoken to Tom, his youngest son, that morning

whilst he and Jodie, his fiancée – sheltered in London by distance and time from the excesses of the day's storms in West Wales – walked across Hampstead Heath on the way to a pub lunch. And very nice too. He also Facetimed his other son, Alun, and his wife, Reba, their son Leo and little Eva, Warlow's granddaughter in Perth, Western Australia. Alun took great pleasure in showing Warlow the wall-to-wall sunshine outside the window, and Leo had insisted that he join in a chorus of *The Wheels On The Bus* playing incessantly on a loop from the speaker of a toy phone. Meanwhile, Eva, now eleven months old, scrambled all over Alun for the whole of the duration of the call.

'I thought girls were supposed to be less active than boys,' Alun moaned plaintively.

'You'll have to book her into gymnastic lessons, I can see that.' Warlow's grin was wide.

'So, when are you coming out next, Dad?'

Though it hadn't been voiced, the silent end of that sentence had "to help" tagged onto it in invisible words.

'I was thinking perhaps New Year again.'

'You can come business class next time. Spend some of Denise's money.'

Alun's reference to his deceased mother by her first name harboured no insult. The boys often called Warlow Evan and always had.

'Make a trip of it, Dad. Stop off in Singapore or Bali on the way.'

An interesting idea, that one. And Alun was right about the money. Denise, after being aggressively acrimonious and small-minded during their divorce, had capitulated when illness and a face-to-face meeting with her own mortality in an ITU bed drove her to change her will. In it, she had been very generous, effectively reversing all the things that she took such pleasure in removing when she was alive. The boys, naturally, benefitted much more than he had.

Warlow took thoughts of another trip to Australia to bed with him. Thoughts of tropical sun and iced coffee, both wonderful counter points to the hammering rain against the window. He'd gone with Tom and Jodie last time, but they were planning a much longer trip in six months' time, using Perth as a stopping off place with New Zealand in their sights.

But there was nothing preventing Warlow from going on his own, of course.

Or even asking someone else to go with him…

He let that idea linger as he shut his eyes. But when he opened them again at 5.10 am the following morning in response to the sound of his phone, dreams of Australia and the Far East evaporated as DS Gil Jones's voice came over loud and clear, the storm having at last abated.

'Morning,' Gil said. 'Did I wake you?'

'Not to worry. Only just got back from clubbing in Little Haven,' Warlow said. Little Haven being a sleepy fishing village not renowned for its nightlife.

Gil snorted. 'There is a very tasteless joke involving seals in there somewhere, but I will forego the humour to get to the point.'

'I am, as always, grateful for small mercies.'

'Brecon Mountain Rescue and the Coast Guard airlifted two men off the Black Mountains in the early hours. One didn't make it, at which point they kindly let us know.'

Warlow rubbed the sleep from his eyes. 'Tragic as that sounds, how does it involve us?'

A fair enough question from a Detective Chief Inspector tasked with running a rapid response team for the Dyfed Powys Police Force. A team that dealt mainly with serious crimes.

'Right. Thought you'd ask that. Are you sitting comfortably?'

'I've put the light on and shifted my teddy bear to one side, so I've said goodbye to sleep.'

'Tidy. Then I'll begin.'

CHAPTER THREE

Jess Allanby left the house she'd shared with her ex, Rick, the house that Molly had grown up in on Northleigh Road in Stretford, at six sharp. Rick was at his partner's house – his new partner's house – and Jess's car was laden with clothes neither she nor Molly were likely to wear again, but which she'd had no time to offload to a charity shop. Besides, knowing Molly, she'd want to hang on to one or two things. Like the party dress from when she was seven. Nostalgia as opposed to practicality.

Jess had shared a cup of tea with her ex-neighbour, Mrs Sharma, who'd tearfully expressed her sorrow for how things had turned out and said she missed their chats. Most of which revolved around Mrs Sharma's kids, a diaspora now spread all over the country.

The car was packed the night before to allow a quick getaway after posting the keys through the letterbox. That she now did, knowing a four-hour drive to work faced her that morning, lingering on the doorstep of her house, the first and only one she'd actually owned, with surprisingly few regrets.

When she'd upped sticks, angry and hurt by the breakup of her marriage and wanting, more than anything, to lash out at Rick by distancing herself and their daughter from him, she'd done so half expecting to come back to this city at some point.

But Molly had settled remarkably well in West Wales. Much better than Jess had dared hope, and to her surprise, her own career as a DI had blossomed in a different place with a very different crime rate, helped by Evan Warlow and the Force's approach to major crimes in such a huge and spread-out geographical area.

She was part of a Rapid Response Major Crimes team, had qualified as a senior investigator, and was now considering buying her own property with a view to developing it. Either to live in or rent. Evan had suggested that.

Second homes were now being charged double the council tax in parts of Wales. A law that some considered punitive bigotry, but others saw as significant opportunity as it might lead some people to sell.

But now she had a daughter at university. So, this trip, this clearing out, was more a cathartic final step than she thought it would be. Though quite what she was driving away from, and to, was still something she had not yet settled on.

Still, she had a four-hour drive ahead of her to ponder that.

Ninety minutes of that four hours had gone by when her phone rang and DS Catrin Richards's voice came through the speaker.

'Morning, ma'am. Okay to talk? Sounds like you're in the car.'

'Approaching Oswestry.'

'Oh, I won't ask how much fun that is.'

'At least it's stopped raining. You're up early.'

'Only went to the loo six times last night, ma'am. I was up when Gil called.'

Catrin Richards was heavily pregnant and approaching maternity leave at a rate of knots. Literally with days to go. As good as her word, she had determined to work until as near as damn it to maximise her leave, post-delivery.

'Poor you,' Jess said.

'No, it's all good. Other than looking, and feeling, like a rhinoceros, I am well.'

'I bet you Craig doesn't believe that.'

'Funny you should say that ma'am. Craig says I look… attractive. Not one of his usual words, but it'll do. Men are funny, aren't they?'

'Hysterical.'

The line went quiet for several seconds. 'If you're in Oswestry, you must be coming from Manchester, ma'am. I forgot you were going up there and there's me banging on about men.'

'Forget it, Catrin. And anyway, there's funny ha ha and funny in the head.'

'There is, ma'am. Shall I get to the point? Mountain Rescue took two men off the Beacons in the early hours and one of them didn't make it. I know little more than that except that there's something very off about it. Mr Warlow wanted us all in this morning.'

'That does sound odd.'

'Gil said we'd have a full briefing once everyone was in. He asked me to give you a heads up.'

'I doubt I'll be there much before 10.30.'

'That's okay, ma'am. DCI Warlow is at the hospital as we speak.'

'Okay, kettle on for 10.15, brews at 10.30.'

'Sounds good, ma'am.'

Catrin rang off, leaving Jess to contemplate the gradual lightening of the sky, remembering the weather of the night before, which had reached Manchester in the early hours, and wondering why on earth anyone would have wanted to be out on a mountain in that storm. Of course, you got die hards who considered braving the elements a challenge. And good luck to them. But when it then put the lives of the rescue services at risk when they were forced to secure the idiots' safety, all sympathy and understanding flew right out the window at Mach 2.

But involving Warlow's team meant that there must be another story here.

Not far ahead, there were a couple of garages that would do coffee. She'd grab one of those and then not stop. The road from Oswestry down through the heart of Powys and Carmarthenshire was a single lane with few opportunities to overtake, though that never seemed to put off the lunatics. Either way, she'd need to concentrate, and a coffee would help that.

As plans went, it seemed as good as any on this dark and dismal morning.

DETECTIVE CONSTABLE RHYS HARRIES sat at his desk in the unusually quiet Incident Room at Dyfed Powys Police HQ, watching Sergeant Catrin Richards set up two boards. One suitable for posting images, the so-called Gallery, and another, the Job Centre, a magnetic whiteboard for jottings and actions when they were required. He did so with the honest wonder of a man who had never worked closely with a pregnant colleague before.

'Does it feel odd, sarge? I mean, heavy, like you're carrying a kettle bell under your jumper?'

Catrin, well used to this sort of intrusive, but completely innocent line of questioning from her younger colleague, took no offence. Rhys's interest hid no snide subtext. The world remained full of wonder for the man.

She put down the tissue she'd soaked in surgical alcohol for cleaning the board and turned her face towards him over her right shoulder.

'Yes, it is heavy. No, it's not like a kettle bell. This has no handle.'

'I read some countries encourage partners to wear weighted strap-on abdomens so that they can experience what you're going through.'

'Craig does that with a lamb bhuna, rice, and a Peshwari

naan every Saturday night,' Catrin muttered. 'Not quite the whole nine yards, though, is it, tying a weight around your midriff?' The DS's smile never reached her eyes. 'You're missing out the heartburn and constipation for a start.'

'Two vital ingredients that make it a stereo surround-sound experience.' Gil, who had been busy at his monitor, spoke without looking around.

'How would you know?' Catrin asked.

'You may not have noticed, but in the right light, and with a wig on, I could pass for someone in the second trimester with ease.'

Rhys laughed, Catrin simply stared.

'But,' Gil continued his monologue without engaging his fellow sergeant in eye contact. 'I also have two daughters, and I am married to the woman who carried those two daughters to term. Therefore, I have some inside information.'

'Pregnancy is amazing, mind.' Rhys had a slightly dreamy look on his face when he said all this. 'I mean, seeing you get bigger has made me think of it long and hard.'

'Isn't that Viagra's new catchphrase?' Catrin said.

This time, Gil turned around. 'Wowbles, as my grand-daughter frequently says. Has anyone ever told you that pregnancy can cause disinhibition and feistiness?'

Catrin relaxed her shoulders. 'It's me 'ormones, according to Dr Craig. He says they are making me interesting and a bit crankier.'

'And a lot more entertaining, if I might add,' Gil muttered, hand, palm open, against his mouth in a theatrical aside.

Rhys was not about to be put off. 'But it is staggering, though. The thought that you push it out and, hey presto, you're back, like, the way you were.' He looked from Catrin to Gil for affirmation.

'It's childbirth, Rhys, not a Barbra Streisand song,' Gil said.

'Who?' Rhys asked.

'Let's hope he runs out of magic words after, hey presto,'

Catrin muttered. 'You're describing the Blue Peter version of childbirth.' She rolled her eyes.

'I'm not dissing it, sarge. It's just gobsmacking.' Rhys's eyes fell on Catrin's belly again, wide with wonderment. 'It's the circle of life, isn't it?'

'*Bois bach*, he's gone Disney on us.' Gil swivelled his seat around. 'Surely, you can come up with something better to go with childbirth?'

'You mean songs or films, sarge?' One side of Rhys's face crumpled in concentration.

'A little less conversation, a little more contraction,' Catrin offered.

'Bloody hell, she's on fire.' Gil grinned.

'I've got one. It's a film my mother watches on Sunday afternoons. From Here to Maternity.'

'Not bad, Rhys.' Gil nodded.

'Let's get Umbilical, Olivia Newton-John,' Catrin said.

'You've obviously thought about this.' Gil sent her a leery glance. 'Let's see, Womb-ours, Fleetwood Mac, and Meconium, Robbie Williams.'

Catrin winced.

'I've got one.' Rhys looked pleased with himself. Always a worrying sign. 'Shotgun, George Ezra.'

Gil sucked in air through whistle-shaped lips. 'Uncalled for, Rhys.'

The DC's grin froze when he got stony stares from the sergeants.

Catrin appeared highly unamused, until her face broke into a smile. 'I'll have to tell Craig that one.'

The light entertainment got no further as the door opened and Warlow walked in. 'What have I missed? An open mic night?'

'A far-reaching discussion of pregnancy, if you must know,' Gil said. 'And film or song titles appropriate to the same.'

Warlow didn't hesitate. 'Surely, there is only one. Salt n

Peppa's *Push It*. That's what my son played to my daughter-in-law in the labour suite.'

'Did she enjoy that?' Catrin asked.

'No. Of course not. He thought it was funny. Reba did not. He's never played it since. Right, kettle on. DI Allanby is fifteen minutes out.'

'You've got something you can tell us, sir?' Rhys asked.

'I have indeed. But first, warm brown liquid.'

CHAPTER FOUR

ONCE JESS ARRIVED, and she accepted a mug of the tea from Rhys with a smile that made the DC's day, Warlow stood up to address the team.

'I've come from the hospital. The deceased has been identified by his wife as Marc Dobbs, aged thirty-six, married to Leah Dobbs. They have a daughter aged four and half called Beca.'

Catrin took notes. 'Is that the Welsh spelling, sir, just the hard c and no k.'

'Yes,' Warlow said. 'Beca Dobbs.' Warlow paused then, as if repeating the little girl's name deserved that quiet pause to make everyone aware that Beca had just lost a father. 'His brother, Emyr Dobbs, is also in the hospital. I haven't spoken to him because he's still being treated for hypothermia. What I can tell you is that Emyr Dobbs was on the mountain, looking for his brother, and had found him. That was when the call to Mountain Rescue came in at about ten last night. The coastguard airlifted both men from an area in the Beacons known as Llyn y Fan Fawr. Some of you will know it. We'll get a map up.'

He nodded at Gil. 'Whether Marc Dobbs was alive when his brother found him, we have yet to find out. But the reason we are here talking about all of this is to do with a conversation Emyr Dobbs had with the coastguard winch operator who airlifted the two men to hospital.'

He had everyone's attention. No one had mugs in their hands or tea to their lips.

'I spoke to the winch operator this morning. Her name is Amy Reid. She said that Marc had no pulse when they got him on board. But that Emyr, who was also in a bad way, told her he'd gone to the mountain to pick up his brother after he'd got lost when the men who kidnapped him released him there.'

The four faces staring back at Warlow all shared the same shocked expression.

'Kidnapped, sir?' Catrin asked.

'Exactly. So, we're looking at all kinds of eventualities here. First things first, I've asked that DC Mellings be the Family Liaison Officer for Mrs Dobbs. She's on the way there now. And she will be our point of contact.'

'Excellent,' Jess said. 'What about the body?'

'On the way to Cardiff for Tiernon this afternoon at four.' Warlow threw an involuntary glance at his watch.

'Rhys and I can go to the postmortem.' Jess read the glance.

'No, you've just had a four-hour drive.'

'Then I'll go with Rhys,' Gil said. 'Catrin can run the Room.'

No one argued. But Rhys looked delighted with the prospect of yet more dissection.

'Starsky and Hutch, sarge. You and me.' Rhys looked delighted.

'More like Morecambe and Wise,' Jess muttered.

'And, for the first time in a while, there's no scene of crime,' Warlow added. 'The body having been removed from where Dobbs died.'

'How does that work, sir?' Rhys asked.

'If he was left on a mountainside deliberately, that might

do for malicious intent, don't you think? If the cause of death was exposure.'

'If there's no scene, are you saying you won't want us to tramp all over the Fans looking for clues?' Gil asked.

'I did not say that, but there is no point sending Povey up there. At least not until we get more intel. For now, let's get background checks sorted out on Dobbs. Phone records, the usual.'

'Not much to go on yet, is there?' Jess said.

'No, but I thought Rhys and I could go talk to the widow. Catrin can get the boards sorted out.' He glanced at his watch and then at Jess again. 'If you and Gil can start the background stuff rolling, we'll be back well before two, and Rhys and Gil can then shoot off to Cardiff.'

'Sounds like a plan,' Jess said.

WARLOW LET Rhys drive the job Audi, which would keep him happy and avoid extraneous noise from crisp packets and the plastic wrappings of chocolate bars. It also gave Warlow a chance to re-evaluate what little information he had. Of course, his thought processes were interspersed by the usual smattering of conversational gems from his junior officer.

'It's Cardigan you said we were heading for, is it, sir?'

'It is.'

'Funny name, isn't it, Cardigan? I mean, it isn't anything like the Welsh name. Aberteifi means the mouth of the River Teifi, but Cardigan…'

'Because of Cardigan Bay, presumably, not linked to the woollen overshirt or the bloke with questionable military judgement at the Charge of the Light Brigade.'

'Ah, yes, sir, but Cardigan is another English corruption. We did all this in school, sir.'

Warlow looked up from the papers on his knees. 'Go on. I'm all ears.'

'The name actually comes from Caredig who was the son

of Cynedda in the fifth century. I think he was Cumbric, you know, from Cumbria, which you may know is allied to Cymru, the Welsh for Wales. Ancient Welsh was spoken all over the north of Britain then. Cynedda came to help his cousins repel the Irish Scots. As a reward, they gave him land, and he called that Caredigion after his son, now Ceredigion, the Welsh for the county of Cardiganshire.'

'Bloody hell, Rhys.'

'Lots of "c" words there, sir. You don't like those.'

'I don't mind when they're nouns. But I am impressed.'

Rhys, though, looked troubled. 'I can remember all kinds of stuff like that, but then I'll forget to call in for milk and eggs on the way home ten minutes after Gina has asked me to do it.'

Warlow chuckled.

'Did Dobbs die from exposure, sir?'

'Good question. I hope you'll be able to answer that one for me this afternoon.'

Rhys drove on, with Warlow well aware that a question was brewing.

'How was he dressed, sir?'

'What?'

'The dead man. How was he dressed?'

'I didn't ask. Why?'

'I've got a mate who does potholing. He's been on a few cave rescues, and he told me once that a lot of hypothermia deaths are associated with paradoxical undressing.'

Warlow waited, knowing full well that Rhys would continue.

'Apparently, when people get hypothermic, they get disorientated and confused and sometimes, they take off their clothes. Weird, I know, but it's a fact.'

'Right, make sure you ask that question. If Tiernon doesn't have the answer, you can ask the Mountain Rescue Team. Put that on your list.'

'Will do, sir.'

Warlow scrolled through his phone. 'I have Dobbs's address here somewhere. I need to google it.'

'No need, sir. Gina dropped me a pin. She's already there. I put it into the Satnav before we set off.'

Another reason, apart from Rhys's mostly entertaining when not irritating non-sequiturs, for having him along, was his tech fluency.

'Did I ever tell you Gina was a keeper, Rhys?'

'You did, sir. But that's the first time today.'

It was only thirty miles from HQ, but about almost an hour's run on these roads. Rhys had taken a route through the town and out into the open countryside. A nice enough run, but not when you wanted to get there quickly.

'What's going to happen when DS Richards takes her maternity leave, sir?'

'I expect she'll be putting her feet up and doing the crossword every day.'

'Really? I thought looking after a baby was intense.'

'It is. She'll be exhausted. But I expect, knowing Catrin and Craig, they'll whip it into shape in no time.'

Rhys sent Warlow a side-eyed glance. 'You're having me on, sir.'

'Very likely. Your world becomes tiny when there is a baby in the house.'

'You had two, sir. How did you cope?'

That was a question he had asked himself many times. In those days, paternal leave was not a thing. He'd taken annual leave to be with Denise and both Alun and Tom in their turn. 'You do. Simple as that. And I am firmly believing that babies actually hypnotise you. If you asked me what I did for those first four years, I honestly do not know. You go from one minute to the next because if there is one thing babies are, it's unpredictable. Apart from the job, you, as a person or a couple, take second fiddle. The kids are number one. And if that happens to the man, it must happen even more so to the woman who is breastfeeding that infant. It's a kind of consensual brainwashing. Not sure how it happens in same-sex parenting, but the principle applies, I'm sure.'

'Sounds strange, being hypnotised by babies. And knackering.'

'It is. But while you're doing it, you would not swap it for the world.' Warlow threw Rhys a knowing glance. 'You and Gina had this conversation, Rhys?'

'Not really. But seeing DS Richards puts it into your head. I mean, you can't exactly miss it, can you? She has to go through doors sideways these days.'

'And some people have two, or even three in there.'

Rhys nodded. 'I can't get my head around that, sir. But DS Richards is only having the one, right?'

'So she says.'

Rhys chortled. 'Ha, what if they went in expecting one and ended up with two? That would—'

'Probably result in the ultrasound technician and the obstetrician being struck off,' Warlow said.

'Yeah, things like that don't happen. Except in horror films. Like *Rosemary's Baby*. You've seen that one, sir? It's the one about the baby being possessed and at the end, she looks into the baby's face and—'

'Yes, I've seen it, but perhaps best not to mention *Rosemary's Baby* until Catrin has had hers.'

'Oh, yes, right. Sergeant Jones says I need to take time before giving my opinion.'

'Did he now? That from a man untroubled by too much verbal circumspection. And before you say anything, no, I have not had the operation.'

'That's something Sergeant Jones would say sir.'

'Really?'

'Ha, I see what you did there, sir. But DS Jones also told me to always remember that discretion is the better part of Merthyr.'

'What?'

'Exactly, sir. I didn't understand it, either.'

'He means discretion is the better part of valour.'

Rhys's lower jaw shifted a centimetre to the left. 'No wonder people look a bit confused when I've said that.'

Warlow let his head drop but allowed himself a small exhalation of mirth. He sighed when he looked back up. 'Have you got an energy bar you can eat?'

'Yes, sir. Only I can't unwrap it while I drive.'

'Let me do the honours,' Warlow said. 'You eat while I find something on the radio to distract us.'

CHAPTER FIVE

THE DOBBS's property sat on an estate to the north of the town of Cardigan. Semi-detached, with the attachment as a garage at the front of the house. Thirty or more identical, white-rendered houses with grey stone around the front doors and in a horizontal line between the main bedroom and living room. All within a stone's throw of a B&M superstore.

This was not a large estate and every house had at least one car. Green recycling bins and black bin bags stood sentinel on the pavement. A refuse collection must be due.

When Rhys pulled up in the Audi, Warlow instructed him to park on the pavement.

'That's Gina's car, sir. The Corsa.' He nodded towards a silver Vauxhall outside the house.

Warlow made no move to get out. Even after Rhys switched off the engine. He was no stranger to houses of mourning, and his visits always came with the added need of questions that needed answers from people already psychologically traumatised.

He had a lot of experience. Not his first roundabout, as Gil would undoubtedly have said.

That did not make it any easier.

When Warlow eventually exited the car, Rhys followed. He did not need to ring the bell as PC Gina Mellings opened the door with her eyebrows raised above a half smile of acknowledgement. She took them through to a small living room with faux-leaded windows, a grey carpet, and black sofas. An open-plan dining room stretched behind. On a table in the corner sat a little girl with an older woman helping her put stickers in a book. The older woman looked up but said nothing. Warlow read a dull anger which disappeared once the little girl asked her a question.

Another woman sat on the sofa, though woman seemed to be stretching it a bit. She could not have been much over five-one, slight and pale in a baggy jumper and jeans, sitting hunched up, knees together, sleeves dangling off the ends of her arms. She had blonde hair with dark roots and a face devoid of any makeup and any proper expression. Only a blank emptiness that didn't change when Warlow walked in.

'These are the officers I told you about, Leah.' Gina sat next to the woman. One glance around the space told Warlow that this had been very much a family home. Nothing expensive, not much in the way of knick-knacks, but lots of photos of baby Beca, toddler Beca, and little girl Beca. Most of them included a man that Warlow surmised must have been Marc Dobbs.

Warlow found an armchair and sat. Rhys levered himself into its twin.

'I'm sorry to trouble you at a time like this, Mrs Dobbs,' Warlow launched straight in.

Leah nodded, but her lower lip quivered. As if Warlow's sympathy might tip her over at any moment.

'Some facts about the case have been brought to our attention, and the sooner we understand the situation better, the sooner we might do something about it.'

'Mam,' Beca spoke from the table she was playing at. 'Can I have juice?'

'Yes, darling. *Mamgu* will get it for you.'

'Maybe best to have it in the kitchen,' Gina said.

The older woman sitting next to Beca frowned.

'*Mamgu*,' Beca said. 'Please.'

The older woman got up reluctantly and held out her hand for Beca. The little girl held it and walked through the door. Gina followed.

'My mother, she's…'

'Only trying to help,' Warlow said. 'But it's probably for the best that this is between us for now, eh?'

Leah nodded.

'Marc's brother said something troubling in the helicopter.'

'How is he?'

'He is going to be fine. Hypothermia, but he is going to be fine.'

'Did he say something about the kidnapping?'

Warlow had not been expecting Leah to lead on this. But why not? He kept quiet and simply nodded.

Leah's lower lip wobbled once more.

'You must think I am so stupid,' she said and ratcheted in an inhalation. 'To not say anything, to not contact you, but they were… they were hurting him, Marc. It was real. Like a horror film. They said if I told you, they'd…'

Her words broke there, and a noise replaced it. A long drawn out, 'Noooo. Noooo, noooo.'

Warlow thought she might lose it, but she sucked in another two gulps of air, squeezed her eyes shut, and brought her hands together, invisible in the gloving sleeves.

'Tell us about this kidnapping, Leah,' Warlow urged.

'They said they'd let him go. They said that they'd made a mistake. One of them said that … but the other one told him to shut up. They wanted money. We didn't have that kind of money. I knew they'd got the wrong man.' Leah's words were now pitiful, a singsong version of abject misery. 'Marc had nothing to do with drugs.'

Rhys caught Warlow's eye. The DCI mouthed back. 'Record it.'

Rhys took out his phone. 'We're going to record this, Mrs Dobbs.'

She responded with a nod.

'You say the kidnappers said they had the wrong man?'

Leah nodded. 'Not at first, but then on Sunday, they said they were letting him go.'

'When was the last time you saw Marc, Leah?' Warlow asked.

It took a while, but eventually, Warlow and Rhys learned that Marc Dobbs worked as a self-employed electrician. He'd gone to work as normal on Friday. He was busy with domestic customers but sometimes worked with a builder as and when they needed him on bigger projects like wiring a house. But, on Friday, he'd told his wife that he'd be going to a house in Temple Bar and then to a farmhouse further north. He'd probably make it there after lunch.

He usually rang when a job was finished or in his van because he liked to know what Beca was doing. On Friday, he rang on the way to the farmhouse, but then he didn't ring again. Leah hadn't been too worried, not really, because sometimes he got caught up in his job. If he was in an attic or somewhere out of the way. But he never worked later than six if inside and with the light the way it was, he'd clock off at 4.30 on outside work.

When she hadn't heard from him by 6.30, Leah had wondered if he'd broken down. And then she'd had a call at 6.45. Not a number she recognised. But it had not been Marc on the phone. It had been someone else. Someone with a heavy accent that she hadn't recognised.

'What did he say?' Warlow asked. 'A male, was it?'

'Yes. They said that it was time to pay up now. If I wanted to see him again, I needed to pay up.' Leah's face had paled at the recollection.

'Pay up for what?'

'I don't know. I honestly don't know.'

'What happened afterwards?'

'They put Marc on. He sounded odd, muffled. I did hear a hum like they were in a car.'

'What did Marc say?'

Gina came back into the room. Leah looked up and

sobbed. Gina went to her and sat on the sofa, her arm around the woman's shoulders. 'It's okay, Leah,' Gina whispered. 'It's okay.'

Again, Leah keened quietly until she recovered enough to speak. This time, the words emerged in a low rumble. 'Marc said to listen to what the man said. I don't know what this is about, he said. But they want money. I need to transfer money.' She stared miserably up at Warlow, her face full of pleading. 'I don't… I didn't deal with any of that. Marc did it all. It sounds pathetic, but he was in charge of all of that.'

Warlow nodded encouragement.

'And then I heard Marc scream. Genuine pain. They must have done something to him in the car. The voice came back on. The man's voice. He said they'd hurt him and kill him if I didn't get it. Seventy k, they said. What they were owed.'

'What they were owed. They said that?' Warlow asked. An odd number. A very specific number.

Leah nodded. 'And if I told the police, they would kill Marc.' Her voice had gone up a register again, on the verge of more crying. 'I didn't know what to do. I rang Emyr. He's a paramedic. I thought he would know what to do. He came over, and I told him what had happened. I thought he could help me get the money.'

'He didn't ring the police?' Rhys asked.

'I wouldn't let him. I was too scared. Marc's phone was off. We had no idea where he could be.'

'Did the man ring again?'

'Yes, at ten that night. A different number again. The man asked if I'd got the money. I said no. I didn't know how. I needed more time to get money from the bank. The man said money or gear. I thought he meant tools, Marc's tools. But Emyr whispered they meant drugs. I didn't even know. Then Marc spoke. He said he'd told them they had the wrong bloke. That this was about drugs, and he had nothing to do with any drugs. That's all he said because his words cut off. It sounded like they'd hit him.'

Leah's head dropped to between her knees. Gina looked

imploringly at Warlow. 'Okay,' he said. 'One more thing. Leah, I'm sorry. I'm sorry to put you through all of this, but it is important. How did Marc and Emyr end up on the mountain?'

'I lost it on the phone. After Emyr said this was about drugs. I started screaming. I said that Marc knew nothing about drugs. That they'd made a mistake. They had the wrong man. I must have screamed and shouted because the phone went dead. But I heard nothing else from anyone. Not from the man or from Marc. I didn't sleep on Friday night. Emyr took Beca over to my mother's and told her I had the flu so that I could stay home. They rang again on Saturday and said that this was the last chance. But I lost it again. I screamed at them again. I told them Marc was an electrician, and we never had that kind of money. And then, on Sunday afternoon, Marc phoned. I spoke to him. Emyr was here. Marc said he'd been hurt and that they'd dropped him off somewhere with no shoes or a coat. He sounded odd. Not quite with it.' Her words came out in a torrent now. Like an unstoppable vomit.

'It was raining, and he didn't know where he was. But Emyr said I could trace his phone on an app and we did and it showed him in the middle of nowhere. Emyr said he'd go and get him there and then. But when he got there to the phone, Marc wasn't there. Oh God, oh god. Emyr said he'd start looking and found the phone. Kept ringing it and even in the storm, he found the phone, but not Marc until later … much later. He said Marc had been in the lake, soaked through. It was Emyr who phoned the police and rescue because Marc was in a terrible way.'

She looked up at Warlow imploringly. 'I should have rung you. I should have told you before, but they said they would inject him with drugs and throw him into a quarry. They said such horrible things.'

'It's okay, Leah,' Gina said. 'No one knows what the best thing to do is in those situations. You must have been beside yourself.'

Warlow sensed they'd pushed things as far as they could for now. 'Leah, I will want to talk to you again, but not now. Whatever's happened here, we'll get to the bottom of it, I promise you that.' He got up and Rhys followed. Leah did not make eye contact.

On the way out to the front door, Leah's mother and Beca stood to watch them leave, their expressions full of grief and mistrust. But all Warlow could do was nod in sympathy.

CHAPTER SIX

RHYS DROVE them back to HQ and stayed quiet for the first seven miles. No radio, just the Audi's smooth hum as a backdrop.

'Think she's telling the truth?' Warlow's question broke the silence, but the DC responded almost immediately.

'If she isn't, sir, she should be on *EastEnders.*'

'Did sound too bizarre to be made up, I have to agree. The brother, Emyr, should be able to corroborate. If he does, then this is bad. Kidnapping, torture, extortion.'

'Worst Christmas list ever, sir.'

'Indeed.'

Rhys waited a beat and then asked, 'Could they have got it wrong, sir? The kidnappers, I mean?'

'It's happened. Organised crime use shock troops, and they are not the most subtle or necessarily the most discriminatory. They do as they're told and ask questions later. How many drive-by shootings end up hitting the wrong person?'

'Where do we start, then, sir?'

Warlow pondered the question and decided that a quick phone call to a colleague in the drugs squad would not go amiss. He looked up DS Dai Vetch's number and made the call.

Vetch must have recognised the caller immediately because he opened with, 'DCI Warlow, how can I be of help?'

Warlow had worked with Vetch more than once in drugs-related cases and had concluded that, as a motive for the worst kind of chaos and cruelty, drug-related crimes took some beating. The men and women who worked in this field often dealt with the very dregs of society in the users and suppliers of drugs they encountered. He had nothing but admiration for the work they did.

'An odd one,' Warlow explained, and then outlined the story as related to him by Leah Dobbs.

'Hmm,' was Vetch's laconic response.

'Is that the best you can do?'

'Off the top of my head, yes. But let me do some digging and get back to you. And the wife seems genuine?'

'My DC and I think so.' Warlow's mind was made up on that score and unusually so. Leah Dobbs believed wholeheartedly that her husband had been abducted and that an attempt at extortion had taken place. That was her truth in the matter. Digging through the layers of crud to get to the facts was going to take some time. Vetch was but one port of call.

'You never disappoint whenever you contact me, sir,' Vetch said.

'I do my best,' was Warlow's dry reply.

In the Incident Room, Warlow led the catch up.

'We have a timeline supplied by Leah Dobbs. According to her, she spoke to her husband at 18.45 on Friday whilst he was under duress and travelling in a vehicle. After that, she next heard from him on his own mobile yesterday sometime around 1400 hours. In between, it appears his phone was switched off.'

Gil wrote the details down on the board.

'Where was he for the forty-eight hours in between?' Catrin asked.

Warlow's phone pinged a notification. He slid his glasses on and read the text.

'Gina has an address for the last call Dobbs made on Friday. He was an electrician by trade and liked to check in with his wife. Sounds a real family man.'

Warlow showed Gil his phone, and the sergeant added the address to the board.

'I'll get records for Dobbs,' Jess said. 'My guess is his phone has been turned off, as you say. But if it was used to contact Leah that first time, it might give us some kind of direction of travel.'

Another text came through for Warlow.

This time, he grinned. 'And she's got the address of the first call out Dobbs made on Friday morning. That should give us an indication of when he left for the second job.' He glanced up at Rhys. 'Had two Weetabix for breakfast, did she?'

'She's a toast and Marmite peanut butter girl, sir,' Rhys said.

'Now, we're talking gastronomies. My kind of language.' Gil's bass voice entered the fray. 'Who would have guessed that combination would be on someone's guilty pleasure list? Straw Poll?'

Jess and Gil put their hands up. Catrin's and Rhys's stayed down. Everyone looked at Warlow for the casting vote. 'I am a fence sitter on this topic. I like Marmite, and I like peanut butter, but I have to say, I've never attempted the combination.'

'You haven't lived,' Jess said, adding a scathing look for good measure.

'It's the salty sweetness that floats the boat,' Gil agreed.

'Whatever the appeal, it's making Gina a highly useful tool in our box.'

'She'll love that, sir.' Rhys grinned his approval.

'You might want to phrase it a little more subtly,' Gil suggested.

'No need, sarge,' Rhys said. 'Very practical, is Gina. She's not scared of getting dirty and handling the odd tool.'

'Oh, dear.' Gil shook his head. 'I knew we were straying into very dangerous territory on the tool front the moment you used that idiom.' Gil threw Warlow an accusatory chin-down tilt of the head.

Rhys, seeing the head shakes from his colleagues, replayed his statement mentally and then flushed a fetching scarlet. 'I didn't mean it that way.'

'Of course you didn't,' Catrin said with a huge grin. 'That's what makes it all the funnier.'

'Never mind, Rhys,' Warlow said. 'DS Jones says you can stop at a fast-food emporium of your choice on the way to Cardiff for the postmortem.'

'Did I?' Gil looked flummoxed.

'You did. It's all confirmed. We need our resident ghoul firing on all cylinders while he sweet-talks Tiernon-of-the-undead in the morgue.'

'I'm sticking to polo mints.' Gil grimaced in anticipation.

'Bridgend has some good places, sarge.' Rhys was already planning.

'Let's go, then.' Gil stood and grabbed his coat. 'Want me to drive?'

'If it's the Audi, sarge, I'm happy to do it.'

'Funny that. Okay, you drive up, I'll drive back. Give you time to write up your essay on death-by-exposure after you get the details from the horse's mouth.'

They continued talking as they were leaving the room.

'Funny thinking of Tiernon as an equine, sarge.'

'Why not? He's always got a long bloody face. Even on his good days, he'd give Red Rum a run for his money.'

'Ha, good one.' A long beat followed as they drifted down the corridor.

Warlow said nothing, but he could almost hear the cogs and cables whirring and meshing in Rhys's brain. 'And, being a doctor, at least he's got a stable income.'

'Enough of this foalish talk. I do have some Hall and Oats for the car, though. Right, let's saddle up and get this wagon train moving. And you can do all the talking with Tiernon. I think I'm becoming a small filly.'

'You mean, a little hoarse, sarge?'

'Spot on, Rhys. *Arglwydd*, I knew you were the right man for this job despite what everyone else says.'

'Ha, good one.' A pause followed, and then, 'Everyone else? Even the Wolf—'

The door swung shut and with it came a cessation of banter. The three remaining members of the team simply exchanged glances and the odd shake of the head. Words, in instances such as this, were very overrated.

WARLOW WENT to the SIO office, aka cupboard, and made some calls. Gina had also arranged for a response vehicle to visit the address that Marc Dobbs was supposed to have visited on Friday afternoon. They should have got there by now.

While he waited, he logged onto the local database Catrin had set up to see that she had already inputted both addresses from Dobbs's last day of work. He'd punched in the afternoon address into "Go-ogle maps", as Gil liked to call it after one of his granddaughters, beginning to read, had renamed the search engine, when Jess put her head around the door.

'Just got off the phone with the addressee of Dobbs's morning call.' Jess came in and sat down.

'And?'

'And he did something to the outside lights above their porch, changed a sensor, and had finished by midday. She made him a cup of tea and he was chatty. She said there was nothing odd about the situation. He was polite and tidy and efficient. She'd never used him before, but he'd been recommended by an acquaintance.'

'I've pulled up the afternoon address. It's a cottage out in the sticks.' Warlow changed to street view and turned the screen for Jess to see.

'Oh, you can't even see the place.'

'No, it's down a drive. Uniforms are on the way. Should hear soon.' He glanced up, changing tack. 'How was the weekend?'

'Busy. I'm calling in to the clothing bank on the way back to Nevern. The car's full of stuff.'

'Ricky, okay?'

'He made an appearance. On crutches. So, he was even more useless than normal.'

Warlow snorted. 'Was it hard to say goodbye to the place?'

Jess inhaled deeply through her nostrils. 'Surprisingly not. Rick's partner has been there. She'll be moving in fully now that Molly and I are out of it. That locomotive, as Gil would say, has already pulled out of the station. Now I need to get Molly to go through the suitcase full of stuff that's hers and that'll be it.'

Warlow searched for any regret in Jess's face but saw none. 'I spoke to one of the land agents on the weekend. There are a couple of places he knows about that might be worth you looking at as a purchase. Both need a lot doing to them.'

Jess brightened at hearing that. 'Good, I am open to ideas.'

Warlow's phone buzzed, and he took the call, one eye on Jess to imply that it was relevant. He listened for three minutes and then ended the call.

'That was a Uniform visiting Dobbs' supposed last workplace on Friday. It's an empty cottage. It hasn't been occupied for several months. They're sending through some photos.'

More pings from his phone. He opened up the images that came through and shared them with Jess. A whitewashed building in need of more paint. Outbuildings with a collapsed roof and, parked at the rear away from the road, a Nissan van with Dobbs Electrical Services stencilled on the sides.

Jess handed Warlow his phone back. 'I'll get onto Povey right away,' she said. 'Should we get up there?'

'Povey won't want us anywhere near until she's done her voodoo. Let's wait and see.'

Jess got up. 'Then I'll chase up those phone records.'

CHAPTER SEVEN

AN ACCIDENT on the fifty-miles-an-hour stretch of the M4 near Port Talbot meant Gil and Rhys arrived at the post-mortem well after Tiernon had begun proceedings. But, for once, the grumpy Irishman reined in the vitriol.

'Maybe someone put a little happy juice in his nosebag,' Gil whispered to Rhys, who barely managed to retain a straight face. Luckily, the mask he wore helped in that regard.

Tiernon held court, using all the unnecessary jargon at his disposal in order to make absolutely sure his audience was aware that he knew a lot more than they did.

'External examination has been interesting. The findings in hypothermia can be minimal where environmental factors play a significant role. Often there is a non-traumatised body. The cause of death in such circumstances is related to mechanisms pertaining to thermogenesis maintenance and vasoconstriction. Death results from a combination of events such as ventricular fibrillation worsened by increased circulating catecholamines such as adrenaline and electrolyte imbalance.'

Another whispered aside from Gil to Rhys. 'I hope you're making notes. There's likely to be a quiz.'

'But, in this instance, other findings are significant.' He pointed to the corpse's legs. 'These, I would suggest, occurred before death. Both thighs and the genitals show some blistering from scalding. Boiling water, I suspect.'

Gil winced. Rhys made notes.

'There are also stab wounds in the legs, three in the right calf and one in the thigh on the left. These are not deep, less than one inch. Facial injuries show contusions around the eyes, the left with a subconjunctival haemorrhage. There is also significant bruising on the upper lip with a two-centimetre split and damage to the top teeth, one having been broken. I'd say he was struck several times around the head and mouth areas.'

'They worked him over,' Gil said.

Tiernon looked up at the sergeant. 'Much as I'd like to use those charming descriptive terms, I cannot. They would not be appropriate in the courts. But yes, he was hit more than once, boiling water poured over his lap and genitals, and a knife used to stab his extremities.'

The HOP then turned to the already opened chest. 'One fractured rib on the left side and bruising of the overlying muscles. Spleen, liver, and kidneys are intact. No other obvious internal injuries, though I will check the brain for contusions.'

'But none of the injuries you've seen so far were fatal?' Rhys asked.

'No. As mentioned, hypothermic postmortem findings are subtle. In this instance, aspirated synovial fluid from the knee joint showed clear evidence of blood staining, as well as erosions in the stomach lining. Both are consistent with metabolic trauma from hypothermia. However, the most significant finding is here.'

Tiernon pointed to the crook of the corpse's left elbow. 'He's been injected here. Intentionally, and with some difficulty, judging from the bruising. Unless, of course, he's had some blood taken recently?'

Rhys and Gil exchanged a glance, and Rhys said, 'We're not aware of that.'

'Something you ought to have checked before coming,

then.' His eyes, malevolently delighted at this minor opportunity to serve a critical ace, danced over to Gil's. 'The toxicology screen will give us more information if he was injected with anything. But the bruising around the antecubital fossa here is stark.'

'And there's no other evidence of self-injection?' Gil asked.

'No.'

'So, are you saying this was a one off?'

'I repeat. No other injection site is obvious in any of the typical areas – groin, toes, or arms – from my examination.'

Tiernon took the brain out, weighed and examined it. He reported nothing untoward.

By five-thirty, both officers were back in the car and heading home. Gil drove. Rhys stayed busy on his laptop. 'Any idea how to spell antecubital fossa, sarge?'

'Yes. E, L, B, O, W.'

'Nice one.'

Jess and Catrin left moments before Warlow took the call from Gil. Catrin was keen to meet with her partner Craig at the end of his shift. His grandfather was not well, and the result of a hospital visit was up for discussion.

'Right, all done,' Gil said down the line to Warlow. 'Rhys is writing everything up as we drive.'

'Good. Tell Rhys to save the slides for tomorrow. Sergeant Vetch says he'll be here bright and early, too.'

'Okay. You off now?'

'Soon. I have a couple of calls to make. No need for you two to come back to HQ. Drop Rhys off at his and you go home.'

'Will do.'

Warlow ended the call, opened one of the desk drawers and removed a manilla envelope. Inside was a copy of a handwritten letter sent to him by his deceased ex-wife,

Denise. He'd been meaning to deal with this properly ever since he'd received it, but the manic summer meant he'd always managed to put it on the back burner.

But, today, he'd allocated time.

The letter had been hand-delivered to him by Denise's partner, Martin Foyle, who she was living with. A letter she'd written whilst in her hospital bed just days before she died. He was drawn again to a paragraph he'd marked up. A section that kept gnawing at him like a rat in a cage.

My Dearest Evan, Alun, and Tom,

… What really weighs heavy on me is knowing I'll never meet my grandchildren in Australia. My greatest regret, Evan, is that I'll never hold Leo, smell his hair, whisper nonsenses, or share those precious moments. Please make sure our grandchild (it may be grandchildren when you read this) knows their grandmother loved them, even from afar. Tell them stories from when I was fun. Show them pictures of before I was possessed. Let them know that I would have given anything to be a part of their life.

There is one more thing that haunts me. After we split up, some of your lot came digging. They said they were investigating you. They told me their names, but I've forgotten who they were. They were looking for dirt, telling me that if I ever wanted to get even, they could provide evidence. I told them to bugger off. But what they were really after was something else. They wanted to know if you'd ever spoken about an old case. I didn't know what they were talking about. But I remember the name they used. Funny, because I can't remember a lot about what happened over the last five years, but I remember that name because it's a pretty name and one I'd always liked.

Fern. I remember having to look it up. The booze has a lot to answer for, including what it did to my brain. It probably means something to you, Evan, but it meant nothing to me. Now it's like a ghost lingering in my memory. I wish I could offer more clarity, but I don't have all the pieces. What I can say is that these men left me cold. I should have asked for badges. I should have asked for names. I told them nothing because I could remember nothing. Not that there was anything to remember. Evan Warlow, corrupt? So, when did hell freeze over? They didn't like it when I said that. I've lost the contact number they left. I threw it away as soon as they left. But I remember one of them had a Brummie accent. You know, peaky blinder type…

He'd tried very hard to remember a Fern, but for the life of him, he could not. And so, he'd rung Martin Foyle. He should have done it before all of this, to check on him. Martin had taken Denise's death a lot harder than Warlow had. Understandably so, given that the DCI's relationship with her soured many years before. Still, her epiphany in the short period of her final illness, facilitated by a forced separation from the booze that tainted both their lives, surprised him.

They exchanged pleasantries, but Warlow quickly got to the point of his call.

'I read the letter you gave me. The one you found in Denise's effects from when she was in hospital.'

'I'm sorry that I didn't get to you sooner, Evan. I was in no state to deal with her things. In all honesty, I'm still not great.'

'I'm sorry to hear that, Martin.'

'Yeah.' Martin breathed out the word long and hard. 'She was good for me. We were good together. We used to go away, but I don't have much spark in me now. I can't motivate myself to go somewhere alone.'

'Haven't you got a place in Spain? Bit of late sunshine might do you good.'

'Maybe,' Martin said, and Warlow sensed little in the way of conviction in his answer.

'Look, I'm ringing about her letter. Did she show it to you?'

'No. I had no idea there was a letter until I started going through her hospital things.'

'So you said. And she never mentioned a Fern to you?'

'Fern? No. Who is Fern?'

'That's just it. I have no idea. But she said someone had been to see her about a Fern in relation to me.'

'Right. No, it doesn't ring any bells with me.'

Warlow scrunched up his face. No one saw him do it, but it was the physical equivalent of counting to ten mentally. 'It was only a thought,' he said.

'Mind you, towards the end, she got her words a bit muddled.'

'What do you mean?'

'The booze. Definitely addled her a bit. She'd substitute words. The psychiatrist had a term for it. Uh, hang on. I have a letter somewhere.'

Martin went off, and Warlow heard the crackle of shuffled papers. 'Yeah, here it is. She suffered a bit from Wernicke's encephalopathy. The booze did that.'

'I didn't know.' Warlow was shocked.

'She didn't want anyone to know. But yeah, the psychiatrist had lots of big words… uh, here it is, "coordinated semantic paraphasia". It's when the target word is replaced by one that is related to the target but isn't quite the right one. Like wolf for dog, or sock for shoe. Wasn't very obvious in her but it was there if you looked for it.'

'I'm sorry.'

'Don't be. She hid it well. And it only got bad in the few months before… before she died.'

Warlow should have said something empathetic, but his mind was spinning. 'So, this word, Fern, it might mean something else. Something related to fern?'

'Yeah. It might.'

He continued speaking with Martin for a few more minutes, wished him all the best, and added a few encouraging words. Five minutes later, he was online go-ogling synonyms for the word fern. Bracken, sedge, brush, undergrowth, reed…

He stopped there, staring at the screen. Perhaps Denise really had meant Fern. Then again, she might have meant any of these other words.

Frustrated, he sat back and re-read the letter. The only absolutes he could take from what Denise had written were a man with a Midland's accent and the fact that this had occurred after they'd broken up. That had taken place shortly after Alun and Reba's wedding. A good five years before.

As for the Midland's accent, the one name that sprang immediately to mind, a name that easily fit the bill, was Kelvin Caldwell, a DI in the Dyfed Powys Force.

But KFC – Kelvin Fucking Caldwell to his enemies, which encompassed everyone Warlow knew because the sod had had no friends – was now dead. There'd be no answers there. That he, a corrupt officer with definite links to organised crime, had been digging for dirt came as no surprise. If indeed it had been him.

Warlow had evidence aplenty of KFC's dislike of him. Attempted murder would do for that. An attempt that would have succeeded had it not been for the homicidal intervention of the man they had been hunting together.

But now, Warlow pondered once again the motive behind KFC's desire to eliminate him. He'd assumed the man had been acting on instruction. A desire to remove a meddling thorn from the side of whatever schemes KFC and his gang overlords were into. But had there been a deeper reason?

Fern?

Talking to Martin Foyle had provided unsatisfactory answers and a raft of even more questions. Warlow turned back to the screen and tried once more to look for inspiration in the quagmire that was the World Wide Web.

CHAPTER EIGHT

DC Rhys Harries did not get back to the rented house he shared with Gina Mellings until almost seven-thirty. They were saving for a deposit on something of their own but, for now, this would do.

Traffic was busy coming out of Cardiff, and he'd needed to pop back to HQ to pick up his car. He was officially starving by the time he slid the key in the door. Gina was in their kitchen, a glass of wine in front of her, a table setting next to her ready for him.

Rhys bent to kiss her cheek, and they both spoke together, voicing the same sentence. 'How was it?'

That triggered a mutual laugh, but it was Gina who managed to get out, 'Your dinner is in the oven. Sunday left-overs,' before Rhys said anything else.

'Fantastic,' he replied and washed his hands.

'You first,' Gina said, sipping her wine. 'How was the postmortem?'

'Bad. I mean, not as bad as some I've been to, but he was tortured, there's no doubt about that.'

'Leah was telling the truth, then?'

'Didn't you think she was?' Rhys turned from the sink.

'It's just that it's so weird and random. Why would anyone kidnap someone like Marc Dobbs?'

'Nothing to suggest he's caught up in something illegal, then?'

Gina sighed and shook her head. 'It took most of the afternoon for Leah to come out of shock, but after that, I got a load of information. She's shown me their bank accounts. Given me a list of his friends. He's a soccer player, by the way. He didn't drink much, a hard worker since going out on his own as self-employed. All in all, squeaky clean.'

'The Wolf will be chuffed with that,' Rhys said, referencing Warlow with the term the team often used for him. 'Not the fact that he's squeaky clean, but that you've got all that stuff so quickly.'

But Gina's smile of gratitude for the encouraging words was fleeting.

'What?' Rhys asked.

'I don't know. I think it's her age. Leah is only a year or two older than I am. And all this after what happened to poor Dan Clark, I mean, I'm there to liaise and gather information. I'm not there for bereavement support, but I can't help thinking if it was you someone had taken, or shot, or…'

Dan Clark had been a uniformed officer shot dead near Telpyn Beach a few months before. Gina had been the FLO there, too.

'Whoa, horsey.' Rhys tossed the towel he was wiping his hands with onto the work surface and scooped Gina up in a hug. 'I'm here, in case you haven't noticed.'

She replied with her face buried in his broad chest, 'I know. But this one is so raw and senseless.'

She disengaged herself and strode over to remove Rhys's dinner from the oven. An aroma of roast vegetables and gravy filled the room. She put the plate down, and Rhys sat.

'Do you want to finish your food before you tell me about the postmortem?'

'No,' Rhys said, dismissing the question. 'But maybe you ought to top up your wine before I start. It's not an easy listen.'

WARLOW STAYED at his desk for another hour and a half and eventually spoke to Alison Povey, the crime scene investigative lead who had already set up at the cottage where they'd found Marc Dobbs's van.

'Unlocked,' she'd said when he'd asked. 'As opposed to the cottage, which we have not yet gained access to. We're waiting for keys. But we've found tyre prints at the side of the house, which suggests more than one vehicle has been here recently. That's about all I can tell you for now.'

Warlow thanked her and turned the light off in the SIO room when he left. Denise's letter had been replaced in the drawer.

When he finally got back to Ffau'r Blaidd, it was well after 10 pm, and he was surprised to see Molly's yellow VW Up parked outside, but no light on in the cottage.

He crept around to the back door and into the kitchen, where he ate a ham and cheese toastie with the help of a very attentive black Labrador sitting patiently at his side. A small pool of drool gathered on the floor under Cadi's chin.

Warlow fed her some crusts and then wiped dog dribble up with a kitchen towel before heading for bed in the garden room that he'd occupied since the Allanbys had moved in with him. It was warm and comfortable and only inconvenient in its distance from a loo. The garden had benefitted from a little extra nitrogen feed over the summer as a result.

As always at the beginning of a case, Warlow found it difficult to get to sleep. He knew that with progress, he would find it easier, knowing they were on track. But at this stage, with so many unknown factors, the woods for the trees' state of mind that came with it made for uneasy rest. Tonight, in amongst the images of a lost Marc Dobbs on the exposed slopes of the Brecon Beacons, were dreams of Australian beaches and wineries from his visit to his son. And as with all such unprocessed thoughts, each of these ideations got mingled up with all the others into a tenuous dreamscape that plagued Warlow through the night.

He got up at five-thirty, collected some notes he'd made, showered and changed, and was surprised to see Molly in the kitchen making coffee.

'Didn't you know it is mandatory for students to stay in bed until midday?' Warlow said.

'I always enjoy a cliché first thing in the morning,' Molly replied without taking her eyes off the espresso dripping from the machine into her cup.

'Isn't the Union Bar enough of a draw for you?'

'It is, but my mother insisted I come home and chuck out the few clothes I left in Manchester. And like the good and obedient daughter that I am, I complied. However, I have a 9 am lecture and need to go back to my digs because I forgot my notes.'

'Aren't you the lucky one.' Warlow grinned.

'I'm going to get away before Mum gets up. She was knackered last night.'

'Manchester is a long drive.'

'So is Swansea,' Molly objected.

Warlow responded with a sceptical glare, to which Molly responded with, 'It is when you have to get up early to avoid traffic.'

'And how is it, Uni?'

'So far, so brill. The course is fun. Student nights out are mad. But I miss Cadi.'

On hearing her name, the dog pricked her ears up and began a fresh tail-wagging session as Molly grabbed her in a hug.

'You know where she is if you need a fix.'

'I do. That's really why I came back, isn't it, girl?'

'Jess said she spoke to your dad. He's a bit crook, I hear.'

Molly guffawed. 'Crook? You're spending too much time talking to those Australians.'

'It's a good word and much better than cactus, which has terminal connotations.'

'Serves him right for pretending he's twenty-five, that's all I can say. And what are you doing up so early?' Molly took her cup over to the milk frother and made the espresso into a flat white.

'Couldn't sleep. Can you ask your mum to drop Cadi off at the sitter? It's too early for me to do that.'

'I'll ring her on my way to Swansea.'

Warlow drank a quick coffee, and grabbed an old, battered, leather doctor's bag he'd dragged out from a box room.

'Oooh, what you got in there, Evan?'

'Old stuff that I need to get rid of. Seeing you and Jess recycling got me thinking. I'll offload it on the way today.'

'How very green of you.'

'Just like my valley.'

That got him a blank look.

'Classic book by Richard Llewellyn. Classic film ruined by John Ford not knowing what a Welsh accent is and opting for Irish ones instead. Overly sentimental, but at least it was about Wales. You have to see it to understand.'

'I'll look it up.'

'The book is better. Do you do reading at university these days?'

'Hilarious.' Molly leaned against the sink, ankles crossed and lips pursed.

Warlow riffled Cadi's head and said, 'Be good,' and threw a pointed look at Molly when he said it as well before adding, 'I'm off.'

To his secret delight, Molly got up and gave him a quick hug goodbye, tempering it with, 'That's 'cos Cadi can't.'

Warlow was on the road at six-thirty, sitting in Starbucks St Clears by 7.15. Not one of his usual haunts, but he'd brought the bag in with him and found a quiet corner for his laptop.

In truth, he wasn't using the laptop, but had it open as a blind. Instead, he was going through the notebooks he'd brought with him in the doctor's bag. Notebooks which, by right, he should not have had, but which he'd used in almost all of his cases. These were not the official ones provided by the forces he'd worked for. Those were often used in evidence and were police property to be handed back when full.

These in front of him now were his personal notebooks. And they were full of all kinds of private jottings about cases, and the people involved. He hadn't wanted to explain them away to Jess at the cottage. But he needed to go through them. He needed to find a reference to a fern or something like a fern, and his best bet was to wade through these old books.

It would take some time.

So, he'd set aside forty-five minutes to do that this morning.

He put one down, having found nothing, and opened another. He checked the date on the inside cover. 1995. He'd been a young DC in the Met. Two years later, he'd been a sergeant. A move back to Wales and a DI job was yet to come.

He began thumbing through the pages, names, and references, bringing back recollections of the cases he'd been involved in and the men and women he'd worked with. All the while searching for a name or a reference that might click, oblivious to the people who came and went as he delved into the past.

CHAPTER NINE

AT 8.30 AM, Warlow walked into the Incident Room just as frustrated as he'd been when he left Ffau'r Blaidd that morning. The perusal of his notebooks in an attempt at finding a fern, or something equivalent that might trigger a memory, had failed, and failed miserably. It was like pondering the world's worst crossword clue.

He suppressed a sigh and looked around the room, struck by two conspicuous observations. The first, the presence of DS Vetch. The second, the absence of DS Catrin Richards.

Vetch had not come in a suit. In fact, he was in jeans and an overshirt as his role demanded. Rangy, fashionably unshaven, and carrying bugger-all fat on his frame, Warlow remembered first working with the plain-clothes officer in Pembroke Dock. The first time he'd met the man face to face had been to visit a desolate spot on an embankment where the charred remains of Kieron Thomas, a small-time drug dealer, had been found. The second time had been at Newcastle Emlyn Rugby Club where Vetch coached some kids' teams. You did not need a MENSA membership to understand that the reasons he was prepared to be involved in dealing with the Kieron Thomases of this world were all running around on those rugby pitches on a Sunday morning.

Warlow had a lot of time for Vetch, who worked out of Aberystwyth. A university town with rich pickings for dealers.

The team exchanged the usual banter until Catrin arrived ten minutes later, looking flustered. A state that Warlow was more than willing to forgive given her advanced state of pregnancy. Indeed, seeing her turn up for work these days was a relief in that her absence might have all kinds of connotations of the maternity suite variety. Yet, Warlow knew he was underestimating her and jumping to all sorts of unfounded conclusions by assuming her condition as the cause of her lateness. There remained the distinct possibility that Warlow was meowing up the incorrect shrub – one of Rhys's favourite mangled idioms.

The DCI raised an eyebrow in her direction, and she mouthed a quick apology as she took the proffered mug of tea from Rhys. An act as ritualistic as anything the Japanese could come up with, and without the need for Kimonos.

'Right. Rhys, the postmortem, if you please?'

Rhys pushed off the desk he was leaning on and began with a reassurance. 'No photos this time, honest.'

That got him some relieved nods.

'The most significant thing is the evidence of torture. The scalding, the beating, the superficial stabbings you've all seen, since Tiernon has forwarded his photographs already. But the less obvious finding was a puncture mark in the crook of an elbow.'

'A bite?' Jess asked.

'No, ma'am. Tiernon thinks it was caused by a needle.'

Warlow glanced at Jess. 'One thing Leah Dobbs said was that the kidnappers had threatened to dose him up with heroin, am I right?'

Jess nodded.

'We'll know once we get the toxicology screen, sir,' Rhys said.

'If he was injected with a narcotic, that might go some way to explain his wandering about on a mountainside.

Though what he was doing on that mountainside is anyone's guess,' Jess observed.

'There was also blood in the synovial fluid of the knee joint and also W erosions in the stomach, sir. Wischnewsky spots.' Rhys enunciated this carefully. Obviously, he'd been rehearsing. 'Dr Tiernon said they were consistent with hypothermic stress. No one knows why they appear, but they do.'

Warlow pondered for a beat. 'And there's nothing in Dobbs's background to suggest a link to drug dealing or drug use?'

'Nothing,' Jess answered. 'He has no arrest record, nothing on the national database. Clean as a whistle, in fact.'

'Povey got to the van last night, I see.' Gil nodded at the Gallery. 'Parked outside the address booked online by persons unknown. Dobbs thought he was going to sort out a faulty ring main.'

Warlow walked to the Gallery where an image of Dobbs's van had been posted up outside the empty cottage. 'The van door was unlocked.'

'Do you think someone was waiting for him, then, sir?' Catrin asked.

'Povey's been on the property. She says there is no sign of anyone having been inside for months. The owners have moved to France, hoping to sell the place once the market improves. But there were other tyre marks.'

'It's on several websites,' Catrin added. 'It would have been no secret that it's empty.'

'Sounds like he was ambushed,' Rhys said.

'By his kidnappers, if we accept Leah Dobbs's story,' Warlow muttered. 'And that brings this right back to the drugs angle. DS Vetch, any thoughts?'

Vetch didn't move from where he'd been standing, arms folded. There were hints of a Swansea accent still in his voice as he spoke. 'I have to admit, this has come as a bolt from the blue. As mentioned, Dobbs has not been on our radar at all.

What I have done is ask the team to run an ANPR check on known vehicles. See if there's been any odd activity.'

'Is that a technique you use, sarge?' Rhys asked.

'Vehicles that move in and out of the area to larger cities where there are known supply chains are always worth noting. All part of our T and C.'

'T and C, sarge?' Rhys asked.

'Tactical Intelligence Tasking and Coordination.' Vetch didn't expand on that. There was a time and a place for elaboration. 'You say that his wife and Dobbs kept telling the abductors they had the wrong bloke. Again, I'd suggest someone not local is involved in that case. Locals would get it right. We have had some encroachment. There are always new kids on the block who think they're going to muscle in. They'll buy drugs in Manchester or Birmingham, Derby or Leicester and drive across to target the students. Or, once, the comedy festival in Machynlleth. We've had a sniff or two of late.'

'Doesn't that upset the usual dealers, though?' Jess asked.

'It does. These are rogue dealers out to make a quick killing. Excuse the phrasing there. Best I can do, other than telling you for definite that Dobbs was not involved in anything our end.'

'That's worth knowing, though.'

'Pleasure,' Vetch said. His mouth twitched into a smile. It struck Warlow then that the sergeant smiled very little. He could not hold that against the man. Not in his line of work.

When they'd finished and Vetch had left to get back to Aberystwyth, Warlow rang the hospital to inquire about the other Dobbs. Emyr, the brother. The ward manager told him that he was much better, sitting up and eating breakfast.

Warlow was on the point of asking Gil if he'd like a trip to the hospital with him when Catrin knocked on the SIO room door. Warlow, tainted by Rhys's pregnancy observations, waited for her to ease herself in sideways.

She did not.

'I wanted to apologise about this morning, sir. Rough night.'

'Everything alright?' His eyes drifted involuntarily to her abdomen.

'Oh, yes, sir. That's fine. Craig says I can watch telly and eat my tea without a tray now. Balance my plate on the sprog. Craig's words, sir.'

'Not for long,' Warlow said.

'No.' Catrin's response was tinged with distraction.

'I know with Denise, sleeping became much more difficult towards the end—'

'It's not that, sir. Craig's grandad received some bad news yesterday. He was at the hospital. He'd been getting some pain in his side and his back and what he thought was a rash. An itchy rash.' She sighed. 'Anyway, he had a CT scan, and it's cancer. Pancreatic cancer.'

Warlow knew what that meant. Cancer never meant balloons and a bouncy castle. But pancreatic cancer was in a league all of its own when it came to shits and giggles.

'They say three months at best. He doesn't want treatment, at least not the kind that's going to make him feel worse than he does now, which is not too bad at all. Craig is very close with his grandfather. He lost his grandmother a couple of years ago after a stroke. It's Craig who couldn't sleep last night, sir.'

'I'm so sorry. Catrin. We can manage if—'

'No, sir. What is there to do at home? It'll be bad enough when I finish work. I'm not into crochet or knitting. I'd rather stay busy and so would Craig. It meant we talked last night, though, just the two of us. And sleep didn't come easily when we went to bed.'

'I'm sure.'

Catrin's laugh was mirthless when she let it out. 'Everything happens at once, doesn't it?'

'But he'll be able to see the baby, right?'

'I hope so. It's just—'

Warlow let her finish, but she didn't… or couldn't.

Instead, she let out a sigh big enough to inflate a zeppelin. 'Sorry. This is not a work-related problem. I apologise.'

'You know if there's anything we can do.' Warlow spoke for the team.

Catrin smiled. 'Thank you, sir. I may take you up on that.' Her chin came up. Business as usual. 'But, for now, I'm going to ask Gina to get hold of Marc Dobbs's work schedule for the last two months. See if there's any pattern.'

'In case he has been dipping his toe in murky waters, you mean?'

'Yes, sir. Scratching the surface is what we're all about, isn't it?'

'It is, indeed, sergeant. Good thinking.'

Catrin half turned away. 'Today is all about keeping busy.'

'Well, if you want to lose half an hour, ask Rhys about Wischnewsky spots. I'm sure there's a lot more he would have loved to tell us. He might even have photographs. Or, God forbid, draw you a diagram.'

'Remember the one he did to illustrate tapping fluid from an eye to measure the time of death?'

Warlow's eyes widened. 'Do I remember it? I still wake up screaming with the image in my head.'

'What got me was the colouring in.' Catrin giggled.

'Don't. All those red veins like a road map of Hades.'

'Thank you, sir.'

'For what? Suggesting an art lesson with Rhys?'

'For listening, sir. And not judging.'

'As the dreadlocked sage, Mr Bob Marley, once said: Before pointing fingers, make sure your hands are clean.'

'You a Bob Marley fan, sir?'

'I don't mind a little jammin my doughnuts now and again, so yes.'

Catrin hesitated, but then said, 'Gil told me a joke about Bob Marley last week, sir.'

'Sorry to hear that.'

Catrin ignored him and carried on. 'What did Bob Marley say when his wife ran off with the TV?'

'Pray, tell.'

'No woman, no Sky.'

Warlow shook his head. 'And I'm about to go on a road trip with him.'

CHAPTER TEN

Emyr Dobbs had not required blood re-warming for his hypothermia, as the nurse who took the officers to his bedside explained.

'Is that a thing that can be done?' Gil asked.

'Yes, we take blood out, warm it up, and pop it back in.'

'Like soup? *Mawredd*,' Gil said. 'Incredible.'

Blankets, hot drinks, and sleep had done the necessary for Dobbs. The fact that he'd gone to find his brother dressed appropriately in rain-proof clothing and several thermal layers had helped. Even so, the time he'd spent on the mountain had taken its toll, and the harsh glow of fluorescent lights overhead heightened the pallor of his skin as Warlow and Gil stood next to Dobbs's bed. The DCI took his phone out. 'Mind if we record this?'

Dobbs shrugged.

'We're sorry about your brother, Emyr,' Warlow said.

Dobbs nodded his gratitude.

'This will be difficult, but we need to find out as much as we can as soon as we can,' Gil explained. 'We'd like you to start with when your sister-in-law got in touch with you. Was that on the Friday or Saturday?'

'Friday. Friday night. I got the phone call and—'

'Were you at home?'

He nodded. 'I'd come off an early shift.'

'As a paramedic for the ambulance service, correct?' Gil asked.

'Yeah. I'm not sure how long after the kidnappers called her, but not long.'

Warlow studied Dobbs. He looked small in the hospital bed. Raw and vulnerable. 'What did you think?' he asked.

Dobbs hadn't shaved, and little streaks of peaty mud still clung to the side of his face under one ear. 'My brother was not much of a joker, but I thought they, Marc and Leah, might be having me on. That didn't last 'cos Leah …' He squeezed his eyes shut recalling the painful memory. 'I've never heard anyone cry like that, and I've been to accidents where people have died, lost limbs, been in real, horrible pain. But this … the noise Leah made … like an animal. Made that idea that they were messing about go away very quick. I said I'd go over. I dropped everything and drove down there.'

'From where?'

'Cross Inn. Up near Aberaeron.'

'Right,' Gil said. He had his notebook out and wrote the name down, even though it was on record. Gil preferred things in black and white.

'You have a partner?' Warlow asked.

'Not at the moment.' Emyr's rueful clamping of his lips together suggested another story. But Warlow did not delve.

'So, the call to you from Leah came at what time?'

'Before seven. It must have been before seven because the news came on the radio as I drove off. I got to Marc and Leah's at half seven.'

'How far?'

'Twenty miles, give or take. She was beside herself when I got there. She'd put a video on for Becs. Leah was in the kitchen. She couldn't keep still… hysterical-like but trying to keep it down because of Beca.'

'You and your brother were close, Emyr?'

'We looked out for one another. My dad died when I was eighteen. My mother's in a home. Early Alzheimer's.' A recalled memory made Emyr wince suddenly. 'It's Beca's birthday next week. Oh, shit.'

'You got to your brother's place, and Leah was in a state.' Warlow drew Dobbs back to the relevant.

'Hard to take in. Kidnapping, I mean… Jesus. I kept asking her if she thought it could be a joke. I even tried to convince her. Some of his mates are a bit wild. And there's this pranking thing on Tik-Tok. I said we should wait. Or I could go to the football club and ask around. But he wasn't answering his phone. And then, they rang.'

'The kidnappers?'

'Must have been around ten. An unknown number. That's when I heard the voice.'

'How would you describe it?'

Dobbs didn't hesitate. 'Deep. Not local. I can't tell you from where. But not British. African possibly.' He snorted. 'You've got to be careful what you say these days. But I'm telling you what I heard.'

'And they threatened Marc?'

'Yes. They said they'd hurt Marc if they didn't get what they were owed. I mean, Leah didn't let on about me. They didn't know I was listening when they told Leah not to tell anyone, not the police, not anyone, or Marc would get hurt or worse. Like I say, they said they only wanted what they were owed.'

Warlow narrowed his eyes, his gaze fixed on Dobbs's face. 'What do you think they meant?'

'I have no idea. My brother is an electrician.' Emyr coughed. 'Mind if I have a drink of water?'

He picked up a plastic beaker from his bedside table. It wavered in his hand, but he kept it close to his chest after drinking.

'Afterwards, after the call, what did you do?' Gil probed.

'I wanted to ring you lot. I even had my phone out, but Leah went berserk. I mean, she was terrified. When I asked if she knew anything about this, she flipped out. She made me promise not to tell you or anyone. Then she asked if I'd help her get money out of the bank.' Emyr huffed out some air. 'Friday night. Nothing open. My brother had a business account with maybe fifteen thousand. She showed me the statements, said she'd give that to the kidnappers because it was all they had.'

Dobbs shook his head. 'We went over and over it that night.'

'Did you go home?'

'No. I stayed. I stayed with Leah the whole time. I wasn't on shift until Monday afternoon, so the next day, I took Beca to her grandma's and told her Leah had the flu. Leah stayed home, wondering if they would ring. I tried to get money out for her, but I could only get £400. There was like a withdrawal limit. So, Leah wanted me to do it again on Sunday. Marc had some cash lying around too, no more than £1500, tops.'

'What about contact with the kidnappers?'

'They rang again, and Leah kept telling them they'd made a mistake. Over and over. By Sunday morning, we had two thousand quid. I'd been through all his stuff. Tools he had at home. I didn't find any drugs. Nothing like that.'

'And what about Sunday?' Gil said.

'Oh, God.' Emyr's head fell forward and began shaking back and forth. 'It was a nightmare. We got this call, early Sunday afternoon, from Marc. He sounded bad, said he'd been dumped, and they'd walked him across some wild place in the mountains before they gave him back his phone. He told us they'd made him wear a pillowcase over his head the whole time. When they took it off, one bloke was there with a balaclava on. He threw Marc's phone at him. Took him ages to find it. Then he rang Leah. I got a fix on his phone with Leah's app, and I said I'd find him. But it came up in the middle of nowhere. Christ knows how he even had a signal, but then you do sometimes, right? On the tops of mountains, even.' Emyr trembled as he spoke, seeking assurance from what he was telling them.

'Yeah, that happens,' Gil agreed.

'How did Marc sound when he phoned?' Warlow asked.

'Weird. Half pissed, almost. Sounded like they'd maybe drugged him. But I set off. The phone was showing at the bottom of the Fans. I know Llyn y Fan Fach. Been there a few times. I thought I could get to him before we lost the light. I borrowed some of Marc's clothes. Waterproofs and coats. The weather was foul, and the visibility rubbish. But I had the phone to guide me. When I got to where his phone should be, no Marc. I eventually found the sodding thing. I kept ringing it and ringing it, and I found it just lying on the grass.'

Dobbs took another sip of water and swallowed loudly, letting out a little gasp afterwards before continuing. 'The wind was fierce, and I was close to Llyn y Fan Fawr, the other lake. I kept calling for him. Calling his bloody name into the wind. I kept walking and looking. I have no idea how long I looked. Must have been hours. I was getting cold and wet. Eight by then and pitch black, and I knew I was in trouble. I had a torch and my phone, but even if I found him, it was going to be hard to get off the mountain. I kept looking, and then I saw him. Just lying there. Wearing only a bloody shirt and jeans at the side of the lake. He was freezing and soaking wet. It looked like he'd been in the water, no shoes or socks. I kept thinking, why the hell had he done that? Such a stupid thing to do. I called for help. I should have done it earlier. I should have… it took another hour for the rescue people to come. Then the helicopter. He was alive when I found him. I tried to keep him warm, I tried …'

The words finally dried up.

'You did well,' Warlow said.

But Dobbs shook his head once more. 'We should have called you at the start. I should have called the rescue people once Marc had rung us. If we'd done either of those things, he might still be here.'

'Thoughts like that will eat you up,' Gil said.

'I can't help it.'

'There is one other thing I need to ask you.' Warlow

lowered his voice. 'Leah and Marc. What about their relationship?'

Dobbs frowned. 'Relationship? Good. They had Beca, and she's fantastic.' He glanced at Warlow with haunted eyes. 'Marc had the brain. He was practical. Didn't drink much, played a bit of football, though he was getting on a bit. He thought the world of Leah and Becs. Why are you asking that?'

'Because I didn't know your brother, but I'm the one that is going to find out what happened to him. And you will hear things that are not easy to hear. Get used to that.'

'With the kidnappers, you mean?' Dobbs's expression became pained.

'Yes. They tortured him.'

The beaker in Dobbs's hand fell away to his left, spilling water onto the bedclothes, but the man ignored it and brought a hand up to move his fingers back and forth over his eyes and forehead.

'But I intend to make sure they pay for that,' Warlow continued.

The DCI thanked Dobbs for his time and explained they would want to talk to him again and take a formal statement. But the officers didn't linger. The man needed to be alone with his horror and grief. Ultimately, it would be only he who could deal with it.

CHAPTER ELEVEN

'HE'S A TOUGH KID,' Gil said as they drove away from the hospital.

'What would you have done?' Warlow drove slowly through the hospital grounds, pulling in to let an ambulance pass him. 'Assuming you were not a member of the Constabulary?'

'Are we talking existentially now? If we are, then if I wasn't doing this, I always fancied a job writing slogans. A sort of Mad Men thing. I'd be good at that. I've always had this idea for magic pile cream. You'd put it on the end of an applicator that you could mock-up as a wand and call the cream something catchy, like Expelliaranus.'

Warlow powered through the joke without passing Go. 'I was not talking existentially. I was referring to Dobbs.'

Gil tilted his head and looked up at an imaginary point on the horizon. 'Hard to say. People distrust the police, and if I was not one of them, I might too. I am one of them, and I wouldn't trust DS Slemen from CID further than I could throw the bugger. When it comes to filching Hobnobs, he's the bloody Pink Panther. But Dobbs has some training as a paramedic. I suppose I'd feel more capable than your average punter, if I was him, I mean.'

'Nothing average about the Black Mountains on a pitch-black night in a storm.'

'No,' Gil conceded. 'But then I'd be desperate, and I suppose I'd also do anything to save my brother.'

'He suspected that Marc had been drugged. That will be salt in the wound.'

'I did note that.'

'Best we wait until we know what it is before discussing it any further' Warlow drove on and pulled up at the T junction with the main road. He paused there, glancing left and right and. Even when a gap in the traffic opened up, he remained still, not moving.

'Left,' Gil said.

'Thank you. I'm not having a senior moment. But since we're out and about, fancy a quick trip to Ystrad Meurig?'

'Where Dobbs's van was found?'

'Yes. Povey has come up blank. But I need to see it.'

'Certainly. Happy to ride shotgun.'

'We'll take a right, then.'

Warlow took the A484 towards Bronwydd. The time was accelerating towards mid-morning, but at least with Gil in the car, there'd be no danger of any auscultatory assault from Rhys and rustling crisp packets.

'I meant to ask,' Warlow asked, 'how is it going with that video case you're chasing?'

The illegal and very unpleasant episode Warlow was referring to revolved around Royston Moyles, and the solicitor he shared an office with, John Napier. Both were victims of Roger Hunt, who died by his own hands via a pipe bomb. The whole sticky mess was the subject of a soon-to-be external enquiry by Essex Constabulary. Gil's involvement concerned images found on a thumb drive of Moyles. The files contained images – non-explicit or graphic, thank God – of some of the underage guests who had had the unfortunate experience of being part of the family who'd rented one of Moyles's properties. Gil had been asked by Superintendent Buchannan to assess the files. He'd been triggered by the image of a young boy who bore a striking resemblance to a child on their misper list from some years before.

'Still in the doldrums with that one. Until the inquiry runs its course, I've been asked to not put my "bloody enormous size elevens in there", and I quote.'

'A catchy phrase. One that I suspect I know whence it came.'

'Yes, and no prizes for guessing that one. Superintendent Goodey is worried that Mrs Napier is contemplating a civil action against the Dyfed Powys Force.'

'For what?'

'Negligence.'

'Good luck with that.' Warlow added a snort to the words. 'Hunt had survival skills to put Koala Hobb to shame.'

'By Koala Hobb you mean Bear Grylls?'

'Did I not say that?'

'Anyway, watch this space for the Sillitoe kid until the dust settles. Then I will see Mrs Napier myself and ask for access to his files. Add a little one-to-one charm.'

'Will you be using aftershave?'

'Probably.'

'Promise me you will not use the one that your grandchildren gave you last Christmas.'

'You mean the one that smells like a combination of chemical toilet and prawn cocktail?'

'That one.' Even thinking of it made Warlow's eyes water.

'Time Lord. They bought it because they liked the bottle. It even came in a little blue police box, though that might have doubled for a portable loo. It looked a bit like the Tardis. Unfortunately, it also smells like a two-word something that rhymes with Tardis.'

Warlow winced. 'Of course, you could take Rhys. She'd be eating out of his hand within minutes.'

Gil threw the DCI a sceptical glance, one eyebrow raised higher than the other. 'We both know there'd be no food left in that hand to feed anyone. But it's a thought. Double-charm offensive. Bonnie and Clyde. Or, as Rhys once famously said, Bonymaen Clive. Which is what he thought I'd said.'

Warlow let out a gentle chuckle. That sounded like a classic Rhys-ism.

'How about you? Any further with Denise's letter?' Gil asked.

Warlow's head shook slowly from side to side. 'Did I tell you that the letter's content is now most definitely cryptic? All jokes aside, Martin Foyles told me Denise had coordinated semantic paraphasia which made her prone to using words like, but not exactly the same as, the one she was trying to use. So, Fern could be anything.'

'Mrs Malaprop?'

'Not quite, but a close second.' Warlow drove on for a few seconds and then threw Gil a wary glance.

'What?' the sergeant asked.

'What indeed? I've just thrown you a word-play bone that would normally result in you picking up the baton and running with it like headless poultry, gathering puns and witticisms as you saunter by.'

'I have never sauntered, I'll have you know. Besides, it is no laughing matter. It's Denise we're talking about here, and though I was not acquainted with the woman, she was still your wife and I respect that, even if she was leading you up the garden path or even around the Mulberry Bush.'

'Couldn't resist, could you?'

'Nonsense. Wouldn't dream of it. Oh, and watch your speed, there's no need to rush.'

'Oh, God.'

'Have you tried Go-ogle. Say you're asking for a frond. Or I might see how many times I could squeeze fern in for the rest of the day. See if you notice.'

'I'd rather you didn't.'

'No, you're right. Nothing ferny about it. Should we fern ahead? See if Povey's still there?'

'Why not? The car's gone, but they might still be sniffing around.'

JESS SPENT an hour going through Marc Dobbs's phone records in the week leading up to his death. There were a lot of numbers, and she'd begun sifting out common contacts with the relatively uncommon. It took little time to separate out the personal from the business, too.

Leah Dobbs's number appeared most frequently and by a long chalk.

After that, she might delegate more of the work of cataloguing and tracing the numbers to a non-warranted member of the team drafted in for admin and donkey work. Jess could then go over the data and target the commonest numbers and speak to them directly. Or at least she or one of the team would. That side of it could be painstaking.

They would do the same for Leah's phone.

When Catrin came back into the Incident Room after taking another personal call, there was no hiding the troubled expression she wore, even though she did her best to.

'Craig again?'

Catrin nodded. 'He's been over at his mum and dad's place. Discussions about what they were going to do in terms of caring for his grandad when things got bad. Which they will. Of course, he's as stubborn as Craig is. In fact, that's where he gets it from. His grandad wants to stay in his own place.'

'That's natural, though.'

'I know it is. Except Craig's mum and dad live in Llangennech and his grandfather, Iorrie, is on his own in a place near Hendy. He has some chickens and two dogs. There's all that to think about, too.'

'Never easy, is it?'

'Sorry, ma'am.'

'No need to be. We can all pretend that there isn't any life outside this office, but as lies go, it's a stinker.'

'Craig wants to do what's best for him. It's all he talks about at the moment. And I feel so mean when I think to myself that there are other things to consider that may be even more… pressing.'

She didn't need to look down at her bump, but Jess did it pointedly. 'Exactly,' she said. 'How are you feeling?'

'Fine. A bit tired, but fine. How about you, ma'am? What is life like without Molly?'

Jess exhaled loudly. 'Different. That's about the best I can do for the moment.'

Catrin nodded, mouth turned up and lips shut. Her phone rang, and she glanced at the screen. 'DS Vetch, ma'am.'

'Good, I was wondering when he'd call.'

'Shall I take it to the SIO office? We could both listen, then.'

'Good idea. Go on, you lead the way.'

'Like an icebreaker, you mean, ma'am?'

'That thought never crossed my mind, Catrin.' Jess was behind the sergeant, so the latter did not see her smile. But it was an indulgent one. She remembered the jokes all too well.

THEY WERE STILL THERE. A couple of crime techs remained on site when Warlow and Gil arrived. The cottage stood down an unmetalled track three hundred yards off a road wide enough only for one vehicle. They were about sixteen miles southwest of Aberystwyth, having taken a right at Lampeter and headed towards Tregaron. Neither man had commented that the last time they were up in this neck of the woods, they'd been searching for Catrin Richards. This time, they kept going north, though, not east.

The cottage was, in effect, a detached bungalow, semantically transformed by estate agents into a charming cottage. Red-brick walls, slate roof, flat-roof extension. One of hundreds scattered over West Wales. They'd passed properties on their way here, the last one half a mile back. But this one, named *Tŷ Drysi* – Bramble House – stood alone and a little forlorn. Two of Povey's team were inside, and one of them gave the two officers a quick tour. A kitchen with an old-fashioned Aga, lino on the floor, scraggy curtains over the single-glazed windows. The other rooms were furnished with old but decent furniture. Two bedrooms, one still with rumpled bedding, walking frames piled into a corner next to a commode. On the dresser and the bureau were framed photos of times gone by shared with family. Weddings. Posed school photos; memories of a life that would have brought comfort but now seemed little more than sad totems.

'Let me guess. The owner has either passed or moved into a home.'

The tech, an older man, nodded. 'Got it in one. Relatives are in Spain and have power of attorney. They're the vendors.'

'Nothing here, is there?'

'We've sent photos to them, the people in Spain. They say it's as they left it.'

'Doesn't look like they've even moved the fern-iture,' Gil said, emphasising the first syllable and with a face as straight as Mother Teresa's hemline.

Warlow walked outside so that the DS didn't see his smile. The views across the countryside of Ceredigion were spectacular. But it would also have been a lonely place to live alone.

'Well?' Warlow called back to Gil.

'It shares certain features with other places where there's been drug involvement. I'm thinking especially of drop-off spots.'

'Agreed. Chosen because of where it is rather than what it is. So long as it was empty.' Warlow's phone rang. 'Ah, it's one of these group call thingies Catrin has set up. Jess and Dai Vetch want to talk to us.'

'Catrin's an expert on that fern.'

'Really?' Warlow winced.

'Kitchen?' Gil suggested.

'Good idea.' Warlow turned back and entered the cottage.

CHAPTER TWELVE

At about the same time as Warlow and Gil took the call, at Leah Dobbs's house, Gina Mellings opened the door to a man who looked as if he did not want to be there. She placed him in his early thirties and, despite the telltale signs of a receding hairline, he appeared presentable and physically fit, dressed in a fashionably tight suit, which, she concluded, he probably wore for weddings and funerals only. The black tie, with a hopelessly small knot over the white shirt, were give-aways. The suit's arms strained against the solid biceps beneath, and the thickness of his neck meant the shirt could not be done up.

The startled expression on his face at seeing Gina, in uniform, did not help.

'Oh, I wasn't expecting … uh, is Leah in?'

'She is. Who shall I say it is?'

'Nico … uh, Nico Bajek. I play football with Marc. I heard about what happened. One of the boys knows someone in the Mountain Rescue Team and…'

'Give me a minute.'

Leah was in the kitchen, sitting at the table with her fourth cup of coffee of the morning. The only thing she took as sustenance. 'Leah, someone called Nico is at the door. Says he's a friend of Marc's.'

'Nico?' She looked surprised.

'Isn't he a friend of Marc's?'

'He was. They play for the same football team. Nico's the captain. It's just that…' Leah hesitated.

'Just that what?'

'Nothing.' A look passed over Leah's face. One Gina couldn't quite decide might be panic or something else.

'I think he wants to pay his respects,' she said, not knowing quite why she felt the need to clarify.

Leah's turned-down mouth became even unhappier. Gina knew that grief was raw sometimes. Not everyone cleaned the oven and did the hoovering for distraction. Though she'd seen that enough times, too. Some people became zombies, their emotions frozen. The psychologists probably had a phrase for the damned thing. She should ask Rhys.

'Shall I tell him to go away?' Gina gently cajoled the paralysed Leah for an answer.

But Leah shook her head and stood up, smoothed her open hands over her face, and wiped backwards quickly twice. 'I must look a right state.'

'No one is going to care about that, Leah. So, I can let him in?'

'Yeah. Fine.'

'I'll bring him in here?'

Leah nodded and slipped into the bathroom.

She's going to put some lippy on, Gina mused on her way back to the door to show Nico in.

'How is she?' The question came out nervous and quick as he stepped over the threshold.

'About as you'd expect.'

He seemed to steel himself. 'The boys said I should come. Caercastell Football Club. Once we heard.'

'And you're the captain?'

He nodded, and Gina led the way inside.

'Cup of tea?'

'Ooh, yeah. Two sugars and milk, please.'

They were in the little kitchen now with its fold-down

table that worked as a breakfast bar and where Beca ate most of her meals with Leah. Where she did her colouring in, too. Nico didn't seem to know what to do. Gina pointed to a seat. No sooner had he taken it than Leah walked back in. Hair combed, no makeup as such, but a fresh coat of shimmery pink on her lips.

Nico stood up.

'Shit, Leah.'

Leah began an ugly cry, half a smile of acknowledgement fighting with the misery to make her mouth momentarily grotesque.

'What the hell happened?' Nico asked.

The telling of the story always helped. In Gina's opinion, anyway. And easier the more times Leah told it. But this was one of the first, and this version was full of jerky asides and a search for reasons where there would be none.

Gina left them to it and went into the living room where she had a laptop open and work to do. Apart from her role here as the FLO, she had other jobs in the Service. Today, she was collating questionnaires on some house-to-house enquiries following anti-social behaviour complaints about a family on a street in Ammanford. Most H2H was scutwork, but sometimes it revealed useful information. But that information needed to be extracted for it to be in a usable form. Questionnaires were useful in that they ensured uniformity, but also needed analysis.

Half an hour later, she heard chairs scraping in the kitchen, and she got up and went back to the hall. The kitchen door stood open. Nico and Leah were on their feet.

'Thanks for coming. I know it wasn't easy.'

Gina filed that one away. Leah suggesting to Nico that it couldn't have been easy. Surely, the opposite applied?

'I had to come. This is awkward, but you've got my number if there's anything …'

The smile on Leah's lips was small and grateful. She walked over and embraced the man. He stood there, not really knowing what to do with his hands until finally, he put one on her back, but gently and gingerly, as if she might break.

When they disengaged, his face had reddened.

'Thanks for coming, Nico,' Leah said. Her voice was once again tiny and on the verge of a cry.

He looked over her shoulder at Gina in the corridor and then was out of the door.

'Okay. Well, he was in a hurry,' Gina said.

Leah nodded and sighed. 'I didn't think he'd come.'

'He's the captain of Marc's football team. Why wouldn't he come?'

'Because ... because I used to go out with him before Marc. And worse, he and Marc were not exactly besties.'

Gina's eyebrows went up. 'Oh.'

Suddenly, the trepidation and nervousness Nico displayed became clear as day.

'Do you want to talk about that?'

Leah shook her head. 'It's been awkward. Even after four years. At football do's and that, it's… difficult.'

'I can imagine.'

'But he's a good bloke, Nico. His parents are Polish, but he's as Welsh as Brain's Bitter. I can't believe he actually came. Good of him, though, wasn't it?'

'It was indeed,' Gina said and felt some cogs mesh in her brain.

WARLOW HAD his phone up against a bowl that might once have contained fruit or nuts. Propped upright. Three images appeared. Dai Vetch shared the top half on a vertical split screen. Vetch on one side, Jess and Catrin – with the DS sitting and Jess behind – on the other. Warlow filled the bottom half of the screen.

'What have you got for us, Dai?' Warlow's voice cut through the silence.

The drugs office leaned forward. 'As mentioned, we track

some vehicles that are known to be associated with drug-related activity. One such, a black Merc, was flagged as coming over the bridge last Thursday. It headed west to Swansea. Then three hours later, we have it heading north and west via the A—'

Jess interjected. 'That would have taken it towards Ystrad Meurig?'

Vetch nodded. 'There are few cameras up that way. But it puts it in the vicinity at around Friday afternoon.'

'Where then?' Gil asked, and Warlow sensed his impatience.

Vetch continued. 'Then, it's flagged up as heading even further north towards Machynlleth. It does not appear in the town itself. In fact, it drops off the radar. But sightings narrow it down to about a three-mile radius. Half a dozen likely properties in that area matched the kidnapper's criteria.'

'Based on what?' Jess asked.

'Same criteria as the house they used to ambush Dobbs. Empty, isolated, not visited. It isn't difficult to find these houses. Places that have been up for sale for some time. Places on estate agents' lists online. The economy is in the toilet, interest rates are stratospheric. It isn't a buyer's market at the moment.'

'So, are you saying that gangs have a list of these places?' Gil asked.

'I am saying that. They'll pay locals to visit these spots and properties. Watch them for any activity.'

'*Iesu post.* Hard to believe, isn't it?' Gil said.

'Not when it comes to drugs and money,' Jess added.

'Much of a drug problem up that way?' Gil asked.

'Enough. It's not that far from Aberystwyth. And where there are students, there will be demand. But the good news, if you can call it that, is that we think we've found where they were holding Dobbs. It's an old farmhouse near Glaspwll, six miles south of Machynlleth.'

'Not exactly around the corner, then?' Gil's dry observation brought a few smiles.

Warlow heard the words as an echo of his own thoughts. Machynlleth was within their patch. Still within Powys, but on the border of Gwynedd and all points north. 'What have they found?'

'Uniforms found signs of recent occupation. It's listed as empty, but they've had a look through the kitchen windows. Someone has been there recently, judging by the debris. They're sorting out access from a land agent. Plus, we found a business card on the floor outside. It has Dobbs's name on it.'

'Deliberate?' Warlow asked.

'Could be he dropped it there as a breadcrumb,' Vetch said.

'What did you think?' Jess asked.

Vetch hesitated before answering. 'Right, well, there's the thing. I haven't been up. I'm due at Swansea court in two hours. No way I can make it up there today.'

'If Marc Dobbs's effects are there, it has to be the place,' Warlow muttered. 'But it would be useful to have a look. Gil and I are halfway there. It's another hour from here, isn't it?'

'About that,' Vetch said.

'Ah.' One word from Gil full of disappointment and warning. 'This afternoon, at four, I have the pleasure of a long-awaited discussion with my betters, pertaining to the explosion that killed John Napier.' Gil had been within a hundred yards of the blast. It said a lot about the man that he had not once mentioned to Warlow that it had been a narrow miss for him. Instead, he had only ever expressed regret that he had not got to the spot ten minutes earlier. 'No getting out of it.'

After a moment's silence, Jess said, 'Right, I'll come up to you in a job car, you come back in that, and DCI Warlow and I can go on together.'

Catrin, though looking a little uncomfortable, stayed quiet. No question of her going on a long trip like that into the wilderness. She needed to be near somewhere that could deliver babies.

'There's always Rhys,' Gil suggested.

But Jess disagreed. 'And that's the point. It's always Rhys, poor sod. No, I'll go. After all, I do not have a daughter to pander to for the moment.'

'All I'd say is that you ought to try to get there as soon as possible,' Vetch added. 'It's in the sticks, even though it's only a few miles from Machynlleth. The Uniforms had a job to find the spot. Plus, the forecast is awful. Another storm on the way. Can't remember if it's E or F, this one.'

'F for Foxtrot,' Gil muttered. Everyone knew that Foxtrot was a polite synonym for another word, beginning with F, but which had significantly fewer letters.

'Right, I'm on the way.' Jess pushed back but did not get up.

'I'll get the Uniforms to provide an accurate location, ma'am,' Vetch added.

'Let's meet in Pontrhydfendigaid. At least we can get a coffee or a lemonade,' Warlow suggested. 'And there are a couple of pubs.'

'Right, you'll have to text me that name. Sounds a right mouthful.' Jess leaned back.

'Went there once for *Cerdd Dant* competition,' Gil said.

'A what?'

'*Cerdd Dant*. Where you sing a song to an improvised tune over a given melody. Very traditional.' He registered Jess's sceptical glance. 'It's an acquired taste. To be honest, I prefer the funny English version of singing the words of one song to the tune of another. I once heard the Smiths' *Girlfriend in a Coma* sung to the tune of *Tiptoe Through the Tulips*. I have it on my Dessert Island Discs list.'

No one corrected the Dessert. Everyone knew he was being deliberately obtuse, which, Warlow concluded, would have been a great epitaph for Gil's gravestone.

CHAPTER THIRTEEN

EMYR DOBBS WAS ready for discharge. There were few perks left in being an NHS employee other than the pension. Even so, as a paramedic, he came across the A&E staff on almost a daily basis. That, and the circumstances of his admission, had elicited some sympathy and that rare thing these days, being treated as "one of their own". And so, that morning, a visit from Cudmore, an SAS doctor who always seemed on duty whenever Dobbs brought a patient in, was welcome. Specialist, associate specialist, and specialty doctors got grouped together under the SAS umbrella which, though nothing to do with the military, lent them a certain kudos, especially when it came to the ignorant. He'd come across a few who announced they were SAS doctors without the long-winded explanation about how they were not consultants or elite soldiers. Though some might argue that they did the job of the former, and sometimes a little better.

Cudmore, in scrubs and bareheaded, revealing a thinning patch of red hair, adopted an upbeat approach.

'Everything is back to normal. I wouldn't run a marathon for a week or two and a few days off work might be sensible, but otherwise, you are good to go.'

'Thanks.' Emyr had dressed and packed, aware of this

being the necessary hand off that every patient required. 'But there's no reason I can't work?'

'No. Except that you're going to be exhausted for a day or two.'

'Yeah. Being in here doesn't help.' Someone in the corridor had paraded up and down half the night, demanding to know where George was, whoever George might be. And the man in the bed opposite Emyr had a snore measurable on the Richter scale.

'We're all sorry about your brother,' Cudmore said with practised sincerity.

'Thanks.'

'Is it true he was kidnapped? That's the rumour?'

'The police have asked me not to talk about it.'

Cudmore nodded. Emyr's lack of denial, from the conspiratorial look on the SAS doctor's face, seemed as good an admission as a "Hell yeah".

'Christ,' Cudmore said, his voice dropping low. 'Anyway, take care of yourself. You know where we are.'

'Only too well.' Emyr allowed a little smile to twitch over his lips.

Cudmore left, and a nurse in scrubs appeared. 'Ready?'

'Yep.' Emyr grabbed his possessions. He'd dressed more or less in what he'd worn on the mountain, minus a few layers. They'd all dried out, but they carried a peaty aroma of a sweaty and desperate search about them.

'How are you getting home?'

'By ambulance.'

The nurse frowned.

'I'm cadging a lift with a crew heading back up my way.'

They walked along the corridor towards a lift. When it came, they had to stand back to let out a patient in a wheelchair.

The nurse accompanied him to the ground floor. She didn't talk about his brother, thank God. He'd had a lot of time to ponder what had happened. Those memories were also a major reason for his restless nights.

'Anyone at home with you?'

'No. But I'm going to stay with my sister-in-law. She needs my support.'

'You'll be support for each other,' the nurse said. The words sounded genuine, and she had a kind face.

'Yeah. We will.' The lift doors opened, and Emyr descended to the ground floor and walked away towards an exit and the earmarked area where ambulances parked. Just before he entered a reception area, he turned off towards a familiar door. One not on display to the public. The sign on the door read "staff toilet". Emyr entered and locked the door behind him. The toilets on the ward were far less private. There seemed to always be someone in the cubicle next door, and they were not lockable. In case someone collapsed in there and needed to be extracted.

For the first time since the rescuers had found him, Emyr had a chance to be truly alone.

He sat on the toilet seat fully clothed.

Sat and shook, sucking in huge gasps of air and letting them out in ratcheted huffs, well aware that this had to be delayed shock. A panicky sensation that had begun the moment the lift doors opened at the end of the ward and ballooned into something unstoppable.

His brother was dead.

Kidnapped and left on a mountainside.

Kidnapped by a gang demanding money or goods. Demanding what they claimed was theirs.

A horror show, alright. A murky, terrible, monstrous horror show with only rumour and half-truths to go on. As the smoke cleared, there would surely be a fire. But for now, all he could think about was his brother, on that mountainside, shedding his clothes as the wind howled and the rain poured and the freezing waters of the lake lapped against his skin.

———

With Jess no longer in the Incident Room, the most senior officer was DS Catrin Richards, who, at this moment, simmered with annoyance. Not because of being heavily pregnant and realising how it limited her function, nor with the fact that her junior colleague Rhys Harries had not yet recovered from the disappointment of having been passed over for the road trip with Warlow to Machynlleth. Though he was making a good fist of being the cause of her annoyance, since he'd mentioned the town five times in the last ten minutes.

'I mean, not that I know it well. But I've been there. To the comedy weekend and the Alternative Technology Centre. Went there with school. Worst trip I've ever been on because Iestyn Williams was sick on the bus before we'd got to Peniel. I can still smell—'

'Look,' Catrin said, keen to nip that little recollection in the bud. 'DI Allanby fancied a change. Maybe she wants to keep her mind occupied because her daughter has gone off to uni.'

'Empty nest syndrome.'

'Exactly. So, what are you up to next?'

'Background checks. Gina texted me to say that Marc Dobbs's football team captain called to give his condolences, and she thought there was something off about it.'

'Really?'

'Yeah. Weirdly, I know one bloke that plays on the team. A pretty good rugby player when he was in school, and I think we played for West Wales together in some trials. Worth a quick call, I thought.'

'Sounds like a plan.'

Rhys, though, did not pick up the phone. 'Fancy a cuppa, sarge? Only you look down in the dumps.'

Catrin put down her pen and looked at Rhys. And there it was. The source of her annoyance. That she couldn't get Iorrie Peters out of her mind, and it showed. She hadn't wanted to broadcast Craig's grandfather's situation, but annoyingly, her lack of sparkle gave her away. 'Okay, why not? A cup of tea and a chat might help.'

'Great. I see no reason not to open the Human Tissue For Transplant box, do you?'

'None at all. I could do with a baked goods pick-me-up.'

Over tea and custard creams, Catrin shared her problem. Rhys, who'd gone through a family illness of his own recently, was a good listener.

'You should do something for him,' he said. 'Go on holiday, or a theme park.'

'He's seventy-two not twelve.'

'Good point. And not much chance of them letting you on the Colossus at Thorpe Park.'

'Not unless they wanted to induce labour, no.'

'Still, it's for you and Craig as much as his grandad. You know, a shared experience.'

Catrin paused to watch Rhys dunk a digestive. Not with any hostility, but with pensive appreciation. What he said made sense, and the germ of an idea was sprouting in her head.

'Right,' Rhys said, consuming the remaining half of tea-dunked digestive in one, 'I am going to give this guy a bell.'

He turned to his screen and picked up the landline handpiece. Catrin saw him do it, and even heard some of the exchange, but none of it registered because the little seedling inside her head had already grown into quite a large and exuberant scheme. Her contemplation, not only audacious in its concept, would either make Craig's year, or get him on the blower to his psychiatrist of choice to get her sectioned.

Rhys put the phone down, and Catrin's mind re-entered the room.

'Well?' she asked.

'Bit of luck, sarge. Noah works with his dad in demolition and they're up in Newcastle Emlyn today, pulling down some old woollen mill storage barns.'

'Noah?'

'Yeah. Of course, his nickname is Arky. Said I'd pop up to

see him. I'd go tomorrow, but he thinks they won't bother coming down because of the weather warnings. That okay?'

'Oh, please. Feel free. I'm helping DI Allanby wade through these phone records.'

'Righty-ho.' Rhys grabbed his coat. 'Want anything? I'll be a couple of hours, but I can call back somewhere. I read about cravings that expectant mothers go through the other week on TikTok. You know, pickles and peanut butter, tuna, and condensed milk. One woman wanted to chew on sand soaked in honey.'

'Ugh. No, I'm fine. I brought a tub of bananas in a ketchup marinade.'

'Really?' Rhys's eyes shot open.

'No, not really. Now, if you want to make it out of the building alive, I suggest you leave immediately. I possess a very particular set of skills.'

'Hah, Tom Cruise. Great.'

'No, forget it. But if you pass a garage, I could murder a Starbar.'

In the doorway, Rhys shut one eye and pretended to sight down the barrel of a finger gun while he made a clicking noise with his tongue.

Catrin's count to ten took a lot longer than the same number of seconds. When he was gone, she eased up out of her chair, waited until the extra bit of ballast she carried centred, and took her phone out into the stairwell of secrets, where most private telephone discussions took place away from the inquisitive ears of secretaries, indexers, and people manning phones beavering away in the back of the room. There, she rang Craig.

'Right, I've been thinking about your grandad, and before you bite my head off, please hear me out. How about this for an idea?'

Five minutes later, she walked back into the Incident Room, feeling lighter, both on her feet and mentally, but with a tingling anticipation that had a smidgen of dread swirling around in it.

She sat down at her desk and leaned back in the chair, wondering what the hell had possessed her to suggest what she just had to Craig.

She supposed, if push came to shove, which as a woman nearing term was not a phrase you wanted to use lightly, she could always blame it all on Rhys.

CHAPTER FOURTEEN

NEWCASTLE EMLYN STRADDLED the counties of Carmarthenshire and Ceredigion. Tadrick Groundworks vans had parked along the A484 and an access way leading down into an industrial unit where the remains of the storage sheds were being demolished.

Rhys parked up and wandered in. Noah Tadrick met him wearing a Hi-Vis jacket and a hard hat. Nearby, a large yellow machine scooped debris into a waiting lorry. Rhys had to shout to be heard.

'Hey, Rhys,' Noah said, grinning.

'Any chance we could have a word somewhere quieter?'

Noah nodded towards a pub fifty yards away. 'There's always the Coopers for a quick lemonade.'

Rhys glanced at his watch. Not yet midday, but the pub would be open.

'Good idea.'

They sat inside. From the window, they could see the extended arm of an orange crane over the site.

'Long time no see,' Noah said. He was not as big as Rhys and had played in the backs during their short time on a team together.

'Football, then. What made you go over to the dark side?' Rhys asked.

Noah was quick to smile. Stocky and dark-haired, his features rugged from being out in all weathers. 'I don't get battered as often, that's for sure. Plus, soccer was always my game.'

Rhys didn't argue. Noah had been a nippy and swift centre with a low centre of gravity.

'You said this was about the soccer team?' Noah asked.

They had not yet released details of Marc Dobbs's death officially. That was going to happen in a few hours' time now that next of kin had been informed. 'Did you hear about that death on the Beacons on the weekend?'

'I got a text from some of the boys. Don't tell me that really was Dobbsy...'

'Marc Dobbs. Yes, it was.'

For several seconds, all Noah could do was blink his disbelief. 'It's true then? But… what the hell was he doing up there? That wasn't his thing. Not in a million years.'

'It's complicated,' Rhys said. 'I can't give you details, not yet. And some of these questions are going to sound very odd, but as a teammate, what can you tell me about him?'

'Dobbsy? Plays midfield for us. Good, too. Quiet bloke unless he's had a few pints. Just an ordinary bloke. Oh, shit, man. He has a kid.'

'I know. How's the team doing?'

'Okay. Mid-table this year. We're hoping to do better in the county cup… why are you asking that?'

'Do you do much as a team? Go out much?'

'Sometimes. Birthdays, you know. End of season party and stuff like that.'

Rhys did. Much the same kind of social arrangements applied with the rugby team he played for.

'When you do go out, is it Carmarthen?'

'Mainly. Unless we're already near Aberystwyth, then we might make a night of it.'

'Did Marc Dobbs ever indulge in anything other than beer?'

Once more, Noah gave a surprised laugh before answering. 'What kind of question is that?'

'A simple one. Did you ever see him do drugs?'

'Once or twice. I mean, we'd smoke a bit of weed, though he wasn't a smoker. A couple of the boys sometimes got hold of a bit of blow, but no… Marc didn't. Why?'

Rhys shook his head. 'So, he would sometimes partake, but not a lot?'

'Very rarely, and only then when we were all in. Like I say, some Mary Jane, that's all, like we all do.'

Rhys raised an eyebrow.

'Well, everyone except you, maybe.' Noah grinned. 'Sometimes, your job must stink.'

'Would you say there was much of a drug culture in the team?'

'No way. We all have a few pints, and that's it.'

Rhys picked up his orange juice and lemonade, took a healthy gulp, and set it back down. 'What about your captain?'

'Minty?'

Rhys frowned. 'I thought Nico Bajek was the captain?'

'He is. Sorry, we call him Minty. From way back in school. Polo mint. 'Cos his parents are Polish.'

Rhys nodded. He was used to this side of laddish culture. Many of his own rugby club teammates had obscure nicknames that sounded laughable to outsiders. Minty was positively benign compared to some.

'But he doesn't do drugs. Some roids for the gym boys, yeah, but nothing else. Nothing heavy.' Noah added quickly.

Nothing heavy clearly excluded anabolic steroids, but Rhys let it go. 'I didn't mean drugs. Someone said there'd been some bad blood between him and Marc.'

Noah's mouth dropped open. 'Uh, how the hell did you know about that?'

Rhys glanced down at his lanyard. The one that read Detective Constable.

'Okay, yeah, there was a thing. Nico had been seeing Leah

for a couple of years but then she and Marc started going out.'

'At the same time?'

'Only for a week or two. Then she broke it off with Nico. He didn't take it well. Kept pestering her for a while. I'm not sure if your lot was involved.'

'Restraining order?'

'More a quiet warning. Took a while, and it was shit for the team. They wouldn't talk to each other, changed in opposite corners. I thought one of them might leave, but they're both stubborn as shit. I wouldn't say they were pals, but it wasn't as frosty as it was.'

'Is Nico in a relationship now?'

'Don't think so. At least nothing steady.'

'He's been around to see Leah Dobbs.'

Noah nodded. 'Kind of thing he'd do. Representing the team and stuff. Loyalty is a big thing for him.'

'Did he ever threaten Marc?'

'At the beginning, yeah. There were one or two altercations at the start. Once in the changing room I heard about. But not for the last eighteen months.'

'The child, Beca, was she Nico's?'

'No. Leah had Beca before Nico or Marc. You need to ask her who the dad is.'

They chatted for a few more minutes, about sport in the main and then Rhys let Noah get back to work on the understanding that none of what they'd discussed should be talked about until there'd been an official announcement and even then, their discussion would be better kept under wraps.

Then he got into the car, found a garage, and bought a Starbar.

Three Starbars, in actual fact. One for Catrin, one for him, and one … for emergencies.

PUBS SEEMED to be the order of the day.

Gil and Warlow ended up in the Black Lion in Pontrhydfendigaid to await Jess's arrival. They ate some sandwiches and drank tea.

Jess arrived at a quarter to one, declined food, but had a quick drink to slake her thirst before handing over the keys of a job Focus to Gil. All three officers left together. Gil stood outside the pub and glanced up at an ominous sky. Rain had held off mostly, but it both looked and felt imminent.

'You two sure about going north?'

'There's a chance it'll miss us up here. It's more likely you'll get the brunt of it further south,' Warlow said.

'This is West Wales weather we're talking about here,' Gil replied. 'Lottery doesn't come into it.'

'Sooner, the better, I say.' Jess turned towards Warlow's Jeep.

'I doubt we'll be back for vespers. I suggest an early start tomorrow.'

'I'll pass that on.' Gil's phone notified him of a message. 'Povey. She says she's stuck at the side of a river. She may be up later, if not tomorrow morning.'

'Let's hope the Uniforms have secured the site.' Warlow marched off.

Jess gave Gil an old-fashioned look just as the rain began to fall. 'I hate people who are always right,' she said.

'Take care, Jess.' Gil hurried over to the Focus.

The drive north kept them east of Aberystwyth, on the A487. By the time they got to Talybont, the gentle rain had become an incessant downpour. They skirted the Dyfi River and it would have been a fantastic view had there been one. As it was, visibility in the rain and spray had deteriorated to a misty seventy-five yards through the windscreen. They turned off at an exit with no signs, other than a warning – the way was unsuitable for HGVs. The narrow lane, with cut hedges but few passing places ran east for two and a half miles. Warlow took it slowly, praying he wouldn't meet anything coming the other way. Water had already pooled into puddles where the road sank into a dip, and it looked as if the storm was determined to leave its mark.

'How far to… what was it called again?' Warlow asked as they negotiated yet another sharp bend. In these sorts of conditions, it was almost better to drive at night where you could at least see the lights of oncoming vehicles.

'Bryn Teg. Is that how you say it.'

'Bryn, yes, but the Teg is pronounced Tay with a g on the end.'

Jess repeated it, but this time as Warlow had pronounced it. 'Bryn Teg. Another mile,' Jess said, one eye on her phone. 'I need to phone this woman who has the key.' She dialled a number and explained that they were a mile away. The woman, a Sally Meade, said she'd meet them there.

Eventually, Warlow pulled into a drive that led up and back on itself to a farmhouse that looked, in this weather, very sorry for itself indeed.

'Bloody hell,' Warlow said. 'Half of the windows are boarded up.'

Only the lower floors had glass still in the windows and the front door, flecked with faded-blue paint, had a thick chain and a new padlock.

Almost immediately, a Land Rover pulled up behind them.

Blue and white crime-scene tape crisscrossed the front door, but there was none over the gateless entrance. Warlow reasoned that Vetch would have told the Uniforms of his impending visit, which would render sealing off said entrance irrelevant.

The DCI grabbed a waxed jacket and an umbrella from the back seat.

'Stay here until we get the door open, Jess.'

She offered up no objection with one troubled glance out of the window.

Warlow struggled into his coat in the driver's seat, cursing when one arm failed to find its target, and when he opened the door, rain teemed in, driven by an almost gale-force wind.

Cursing again, he exited, fumbled with the umbrella, and then abandoned it as the wind threatened to yank it from his hand. He crossed to the farmhouse door and waited until the Land Rover driver, better dressed in waterproof trousers, wellies, and hooded anorak, exited and ran, head down, across the yard to join him.

'Hello,' Warlow shouted.

'I'll just open the door, shall I?' she shouted back.

'Good idea.'

A key turned in the padlock and the chain slid out. The door needed a couple of pushes until it swung forward enough to let them in. Dripping, but at least out of the wind, Warlow and his new companion stood until Jess splashed her way in.

'My God, is this a monsoon?' Jess asked.

'They've named it Frida.' The driver slid off the hood. 'Sally Meade.' She held out a wet hand. Warlow shook it and introduced himself and Jess.

'You could have picked a better day,' Sally said.

'Unfortunately, in situations like this, time is against us,' Warlow explained.

The woman nodded. She had a lot of curly blonde hair under the hood. Younger than Warlow expected, early forties maybe. Her English accent showed that she was in this part of the world for a reason not related to birthplace. Romantic or business, he hazarded a guess.

'Do you want me to stay?'

'No, best you don't.' Warlow looked around the dark interior. 'If this turns out to be a crime scene, we need to limit contamination.'

'After the police called yesterday to ask about the key, I came back with another padlock, but I didn't come in. The old one was on the floor, cut. They took it away.'

'They would. Thanks for meeting us, Mrs Meade,' Jess said.

'No trouble. It's the most excitement we've had since … forever.'

'One question before you go. No doubt the uniformed officers asked if you'd seen anyone around here? Either recently or in the last few months.'

'I haven't. We head to Machynlleth to shop, and we wouldn't pass this. And there is not much traffic out here. Sometimes, we go weeks without even hearing anything. We're down the lane another three-quarters of a mile. *Sgubor Coch* Holiday Lets.'

'Red barn,' Jess said.

Warlow looked suitably impressed with her translation skills.

'But I'm still amazed to see you here. We've had two cancellations already for the weekend. This storm looks like a beauty. But if you need me, I'm there, or at the end of the phone.'

When she'd gone, Warlow turned back to see Jess already donning overshoes and nitrile gloves. Though it was not yet mid-afternoon, November's gloom, augmented by Frida's sodden skies, had claimed the day.

'Did you bring the flashlight? Mine's in the car.' Warlow looked hopeful.

'Two,' Jess replied.

That earned her a smile from the DCI. The kind that had I-didn't-doubt-that-for-a-moment written all over it.

CHAPTER FIFTEEN

RHYS GOT BACK to HQ to find Catrin looking flushed, but she greeted him with a cheery enough smile.

'You okay, sarge?' Rhys asked.

'Yes, why?'

'You seemed a bit down when I left.'

'Right, well, I'm sure I can make my mood descend again now that you're here.'

Rhys looked hurt.

'Sorry,' Catrin apologised. 'And yes, I am fine and feeling better. Thank you for asking. How did you get on?'

Rhys levered himself into a chair. 'Nothing much. Marc Dobbs did what every other team member did on a night out. Smoked a little dope, took the odd E perhaps, but he was no addict. Nor a supplier. At least according to my mate. But the thing between him and Nico wossisname, uh, Bajek, is real enough. And never really settled.'

'But not vendetta-worthy, surely?'

'How do you mean?'

Catrin arched her back with her hands behind her head and an expression suggesting a spasmodic discomfort in her lower back. An expression which almost immediately dissolved in exaggerated relief as bones and ligaments and all the associated accoutrements responded to the change of position. But the movement, which made her large abdomen protrude even more than it did ordinarily, made Rhys more than a little anxious.

'Don't worry, I'm not going to pop,' she said. 'By vendetta, I mean, do we think Nico Bajek is capable of kidnapping?'

'Bloody hell. I don't know the guy.'

'Then I suggest we do a bit of background on him, too. Plus, there is a firm that Marc did some work for on a semi-regular basis. Wiring and such. We ought to talk to them. Get their take.'

'Name?'

'Mitchell and Sons, roofers, and builders. Based in Cynwyl Elfed.'

'Oh, good. Not too far, then.'

The village was fifteen minutes from Carmarthen by car.

'They're working on a house in Johnstown, actually. Call in on your way home.'

'Good idea, sarge.'

'Meanwhile, I'll do some more digging on Nico.'

Rhys didn't turn back to his screen immediately. 'I was thinking about Craig's grandad on the way back. It was stupid to suggest a holiday. I mean, if he's unwell, he might not be up to that.'

Catrin beamed. 'Don't apologise, Rhys. On the contrary, it's a great idea. Maybe not the holiday, but the celebration thing. I've run it past Craig, and he thinks it's a good idea, too. He says he owes you a pint.'

'He already owes me several,' Rhys replied, relieved, and intrigued at the reception his suggestion was receiving. 'You having a bash, then?'

'Sort of.'

'Good. Right. So, where is this address in Johnstown?'

———

Warlow found the evidence that the Uniforms had seen through the window on the kitchen table. He touched nothing. A four-pint half-empty milk carton with its top unscrewed, sat next to discarded sandwich wrappers, and the inevitable remains of cut plastic ties scattered both on the table and on the floor next to a pulled-out chair.

He tried the light switch. Nothing eased the gloom of the dark room.

'Must have been cold and miserable without power,' Jess said.

The room, in fact the whole place, exuded an air of abandonment. At least the cottage where they now assumed Dobbs had been ambushed had evidence of recent occupancy. This place looked very unlived in. The chairs and the wooden table were utilitarian. Whatever soft furnishings once made this room habitable had long gone.

Warlow turned on the tap. No running water, either.

'They must've brought stuff with them to last here for a couple of days,' Jess said. 'Portable stuff.'

'Camping gear? I doubt they'd have planned for the long term. I bet they hoped to not even spend one night.'

'There's evidence here, though. For Povey.'

'Let's hope so.'

'What a miserable place to spend your last hours.' Jess kicked a dust bunny over the floor.

Warlow didn't argue.

Jess shone her torch over the strewn, cut zip ties. 'Something dark here. Could be blood.'

Warlow trained his own beam and knelt in the doorway to get a little closer. A plum-coloured smudge besmirched the flagstones not eight feet away.

'That would do for blood, definitely.'

The remainder of the ground floor held nothing of interest except for the back room, where a pile of old clothing and the contents of several black plastic bags had been thrown into a corner.

The officers stayed well away.

'I doubt these have anything to do with Dobbs.' Warlow looked at a spill of grey sheets. 'But you never know.'

Jess lit up the corners of the sorry-looking space and went back into the little hallway. 'It would do. As a place to hold someone, I mean.'

Warlow didn't need to voice his agreement. The house was isolated, not overlooked, and abandoned. They'd bargained on being undisturbed.

'We ought to look upstairs,' he said.

Jess stood back. 'After you.'

The stairs creaked, but they were intact. An unpleasant aroma reached Warlow's nose as he stepped onto the landing.

'I don't think they flushed,' he said.

The rooms, three in all, stood damp and empty, but the telltale disturbance of dirt, cobwebs, and leaves that had somehow got in suggested someone had been here lately.

'My guess is sleeping bags.' Warlow anticipated Jess's question as they looked at the swirled shapes in the dust on the floor.

'That would be my take, also,' Jess agreed. Neither of them entered the rooms. They stood on the thresholds instead, gathering what information they could whilst disturbing nothing. Both knew that any attempt they made at looking for evidence, other than the basics, fell well short of the detailed assessment Povey's team was capable of.

Outside, the rain, impossible as it might seem, had increased its drumroll on the boarded-up windows both in frequency and volume. The wind gusted and howled and rattled the roof slates.

Warlow and Jess exchanged glances, their expressions mirroring the desolate atmosphere that surrounded them. The storm outside seemed to echo the turmoil within their own minds as they grappled with the realisation that this was highly likely to be the place that Dobbs had been held.

'I don't suppose there's any option. I ought to check the bathroom,' Warlow said.

'I do hope they put the seat down.'

Grumbling to himself, Warlow took a deep breath and made his way towards the last door at the end of the landing. As he turned the tarnished doorknob, it creaked in protest – of course it bloody well did – to reveal a room with a stained enamel bath which he doubted had ever been cleaned, a sink, and a toilet that he peeked into with his breath held.

The air was heavy with a putrid stench – a pungent, ammoniacal mix of decay and dampness.

'Nothing,' Warlow mused, his voice barely audible over the raging storm. 'I wouldn't recommend using it, though. Definitely, no paper.' He turned back towards where Jess stood, but as he retreated from the foul-smelling room, a sudden thud reverberated throughout the house, echoing above the storm's cacophony. Jess threw Warlow a startled glance. Their torch beams danced madly across the walls and ceiling but no sign of any damage was evident.

'Sounded like it might have been at the back of the house,' Jess said in a whisper.

'There was a lean-to mudroom, wasn't there? I'll take a look.'

Warlow took two steps down when an unfamiliar noise made him freeze. The front door burst open, only to stagger and shudder as the flagstone floor snagged the water-swollen door's bottom rail. Two ominous thuds followed, until the door reluctantly yielded and scraped over the stone to fully open and reveal a hooded figure silhouetted against the gloomy daylight, dripping wet.

For a heartbeat, the world seemed suspended between reality and nightmare. Then, as the figure pushed back the hood, a familiar face emerged – Sally Meade's, the neighbour who'd let them in. Her eyes were wide with concern, rain-drops clinging to her tangled hair.

'DCI Warlow,' she gasped, breathless and soaked. 'We've just had a call from some neighbours. Three fallen trees this end, and the road back towards the Dyfi has flooded. It'll be flash flooding, I expect, but it's a nightmare out there. I thought you should know.'

Relief washed over Warlow, followed quickly by concern.

'Ah, right. What does that mean, exactly?'

'It means no way out for now.'

Jess appeared behind Warlow with a wrinkled nose as she too took in the news.

Sally grinned. 'You could stay here. Or you could come to us. As I say, we've had cancellations. There's a Shepherd's Hut all set up. It overlooks our smallholding. It's separate from the house. But they won't clear the trees until tomorrow. Not until after the storm, which will blow over by midnight according to the Met Office.'

Warlow caught Jess's eye. She shrugged. 'I don't fancy staying here much longer. I feel like one of the three little pigs.'

'No sign of the big bad wolf out there,' Sally said.

'That's because he's in here.' Jess gave her an enigmatic smile. 'I, for one, would be very grateful to accept your offer.'

'We have a generator if the power goes out, and there's a log fire. There's food, too. Louise, my partner, is a wonderful cook. She's stocked the freezer for emergencies. And of course, there is a complimentary bottle of wine, both red and white.'

'Is it Italian?' Jess asked.

'It is. Chianti. Louise is an Italophile.'

'You had me at fallen trees,' Warlow said. 'But the Chianti seals the deal. Let's get out of here.'

CHAPTER SIXTEEN

GIL GOT BACK to the Incident Room after half an hour of discussion with the powers that be. Not a bad internal enquiry as internal enquiries went. They'd wanted to know if he had any inkling that Roger Hunt planned to exterminate John Napier with an IED that afternoon on the Angle Peninsula.

He truthfully admitted that he hadn't. However, just knowing that Hunt was present in the small community was enough motivation for Gil to try to ensure Napier's safety—a task that ended in a disastrous failure.

Did he think that they, the Police Service, could have handled things better?

He'd thought about that a lot. Accelerating towards a stone cottage only to see its outbuildings reduced to rubble in front of your eyes tended to concentrate your mind. And thoughts of how, if he'd been just a few moments earlier, he would have ended up a part of that rubble, added grist to the mill.

Of course, things could have been different. Had the Force redoubled their efforts to find Hunt, a death might have been avoided. But then, history was full of what ifs. Misheard whispers, notes, and letters which, had they been delivered, might have altered how life turned out.

Dear Dr Fleming,

Please get rid of those Petrie dishes near the window as they are furring up and triggering our cleaners who have been instructed to bin them tomorrow morning unless dealt with today!

Hotel services, St Mary's Hospital.

But even before Hunt was in Pembrokeshire, he'd hidden out in an ROC bunker in the absolute middle of nowhere. No one had thought to look for him there. Inquiries were necessary, but wishful, or even magical thinking, got you nowhere.

No one was accusing Gil of anything, but fingers would be pointed. Unfortunately, the heads towards which those digits were aimed had yet to roll. And were unlikely to. Underneath all of this superficial whitewash was a deeper stain. The one where an officer had been put in real and present danger by some modernist agenda seeking to make the Force's public relations as cringingly media friendly as possible.

When Gil exited his car on the day that Napier had been blown to smithereens by a pipe bomb, half a dozen bolts, nails, and metal nuts needed to be removed from where they had embedded themselves in the grill, bonnet and, fortuitously, in the two inches of front-facing metal roof just above the windscreen of his car. Two inches lower and a three-quarter-inch slotted nut would have gone through the windscreen. In which case, Gil would've been severely injured or even killed. Cactus, as Warlow, after visiting Australia, liked to say.

They thanked Gil for his input. The Assistant Chief Constable even shook his hand. But then the DS escaped and headed back to work to find only Catrin manning the office – or rather, duetting the office, given her carrier state – with a few other people around but nowhere near the numbers expected. Marc Dobbs's death had been allocated a category B major investigation status. That meant they'd rope in twenty officers or more to the core team, plus support staff, once the SIO had decided on what needed to be done. The likely involvement of organised crime meant that Vetch and the drug squad team were peripherally involved already. But this afternoon, bodies were thin on the ground.

'Where the hell is everyone?' Gil asked.

'Frida,' Catrin said. 'Everyone's taken fright. Official weather warning from the Met office, and we're about to warn people not to travel unless they need to.'

'You're still here, I see.' Gil sat in a chair and its pneumatic cylinder hissed in protest.

'That is because my life partner is not yet off shift.'

'And where, pray tell, is Tintin?'

'Rhys has gone to meet someone who works a lot with Marc Dobbs. Background stuff.'

'Really?' Gil's voice dripped with doubt.

'Some builders.'

'Really?' Gil repeated. 'Unlike Rhys, I looked out of the window. Any builder with a synapse of sense will have packed up and gone home by now. Cement does not do well in this weather.'

Two minutes later, Rhys, his black anorak shedding water like a surfacing seal, appeared in the doorway. 'Decided against it, sarge,' he said and, noting Gil's presence, added, 'sorry… sergeants.' Adding a sibilance to the end of the plural for emphasis.

'A few drops of water hurt no one,' Gil said.

'This isn't just rain, Sarge, this is… Biblical.'

'Biblical, you say. You a student of the Scriptures, Rhys?'

'Sunday school from the age of four to twelve. After that, thank the Lord, rugby took over on a Sunday morning.'

'One religion for another, then,' Catrin observed.

'Ah, religion. The opiate of the masses, and the cause of more misery and death than any pandemic.' Gil delivered this with an over-egged smile.

'Aren't you a believer, sarge?' Rhys asked.

'Let's just say that I'm with the bloke who thinks that feeding the five thousand is less miracle, more an early example of the small plates movement whereby you're made to share food you would not normally order with those that would, get less of the stuff you actually like, and pay through the nose for the privilege.' He watched Rhys shed his wet coat. 'I can't believe that, a few hours ago, I was up in Ystrad Meurig with our DCI, and it wasn't a bad day at all.'

'How did it go up there?' Catrin asked.

'Not much to see. Empty property, no overlook. Would make my top ten West Wales cottage hijack spots. And only recently vacated by the look of it.'

'Easy to find online as a recent posting, then,' Catrin said. 'Plus, would not look suspicious or too abandoned when Dobbs showed up.'

Rhys took his anorak across to a coat rack. 'Wonder how they're getting on in Machynlleth.'

Gil huffed. 'One thing's for sure, the storm will be worse up there.'

'Anyone heard anything?' Rhys asked.

'Not yet.' Gil jiggled the mouse on his desk to get the screen alive, but then a fresh thought struck him. 'What's the name of the builder you were going to visit?'

'Mitchell and Sons,' Rhys replied.

Gil's face lit up. 'Right. No need for you to do anything. I know them. Did a job for one of my girls. I'll talk to them. I've made the buggers enough tea to float the … Ark.'

'You brought that back around nicely, sarge,' Rhys said with an admiring grin. 'Noah sweat.'

'I really hope Craig gets off soon,' Catrin muttered.

GINA OPENED the door to a man she did not know, but who bore a resemblance to the man whose photograph she saw in frames scattered around the Dobbs's house. The man stared back at her; a black duffel bag held in one hand.

'You must be Emyr?' Gina asked.

'I am. Where's Leah?'

'Inside. She said you'd be around. I'm DC Gina Mellings, the Family Liaison Officer for Leah and Beca.'

Emyr Dobbs shook her hand. His was cold.

'Come in, Mr Dobbs.'

'It's Emyr.'

'And I'm Gina.' She stood back.

He put his bag down on the hall floor.

'Leah has explained that I'm coming to stay for a while, yes?'

'She has. I'm sure she'll be glad of the company and support. She's in the living room with Beca.' Gina turned away but felt Emyr's hand on her arm. Not a forceful touch, but enough to make her pause.

'Sorry, I …' He took his hand away quickly. 'I spoke to someone this morning. An Inspector Watkins.'

'DCI Warlow, probably.'

'Yeah, that's him. He knows what he's doing, doesn't he? Or does he?'

Gina let out a little laugh. 'If it was me in your shoes, it's DCI Warlow I'd want to be in charge of my case.'

Emyr Dobbs held Gina's gaze. 'Only, it's my brother we're talking about. Might be just another case to your lot —'

Gina pulled him up on that.

'I can assure you, Emyr, there is no such thing as just another case to DCI Warlow and his team.'

'Anyway, I want to help. Whoever did this to Marc, I want them to pay for it. The bastards.'

'We're already doing everything we can.'

Emyr's face hardened. 'See, that sort of thing is just… we both realise you have to say that.'

'But it's true, that's why we say it.'

He glowered at her. 'Like I say, I want to help. I got some ideas of my own, but I want to be kept informed. I want to know that everything that can be done is being done.'

Gina sensed the anger in his words. They were still there as he carried on venting. 'It's bad enough knowing that we might … if we'd contacted you a lot earlier …'

This was where the anger was coming from, Gina realised. A lorry load of guilt.

'I promise once there is something I can share with you, I will.'

'Please,' Emyr said.

'I'll do my best.'

'And Leah, how is she? Any visitors?'

'Lots of police, of course. Her mother… Oh, and Nico Bajek.'

'What was he doing here?'

Gina had no qualms sharing this information, since Leah would undoubtedly tell him.

'Do you know him?'

Emyr nodded. 'Vaguely. He's bad news.'

'How?'

'He's a bloody pest, for starters. Made life difficult for Marc when he and Leah got together. He lost work because of it.'

'He was very well-behaved when he was here,' Gina added.

'Yeah, but always had a soft spot for Leah, he did. Probably still does.' Emyr cocked his head. 'You don't think that he could be involved? I wouldn't put it past him.'

Gina decided to pursue this line. 'You obviously know Mr Bajek. Did you ever see him being violent towards your brother?'

'Once or twice, yeah. Mainly words. A couple of pushes and waved handbags in a pub. He took the breakup with Leah very hard. What about the kidnappers? Found anything out about them?'

'Not yet. But some leads to follow up.'

'I want to know.'

'You'll need to run that past the DCI.'

The door to the kitchen opened to reveal Beca, her enormous eyes taking in the interaction between the officer and her uncle. On seeing Emyr, she broke into a broad grin and ran towards him, arms around his waist, in a hug. He bent at the hip and scooped her up. Leah stood in the doorway, and a hug was repeated this time between the adults.

Gina took a step back and walked into the living room to the accompaniment of Leah's gentle sobs as she took solace in the arms of her brother-in-law.

In her notebook, Gina wrote Nico Bajek's name down once again and this time, underlined it.

CHAPTER SEVENTEEN

They'd called the Shepherd's Hut *Cwt Y Bugail*, which, Warlow assured Jess, was a literal translation.

'Coot Uh Bee-ga-eel.' He laid it out phonetically for her as they followed Sally Meade's car up a stoned track that ran around the perimeter of the main stone-built longhouse to the little standalone, dark building that was going to be their shelter. It had a small flagstone patio in front that led to wooden steps up to a door. The walls and curved roof were clad in black corrugated tin, with a black steel chimney stack protruding from the top. It stood behind the stone farmhouse and its nearby outbuildings, partially sheltered by a stone wall at the back.

Warlow reckoned there was perhaps only fifteen minutes of daylight left on this November day as he pulled up and he and Jess ran to the door, which Sally had opened.

Inside, any semblance of an actual hut evaporated. The walls were plastered and painted a tasteful cream colour. At one end of the hut sat a bed, next to a sofa behind a little breakfast bar and two stools. The kitchen had a sink and a hob and on the other end, Sally threw open a door next to a wood-burning stove. It opened out into a fully equipped and modern bathroom.

'Wow,' Warlow said.

'Very nice,' Jess agreed.

Sally had a plastic bag dangling from one arm. 'There's some beer and wine in the fridge under the microwave. I've got some homemade lasagne, and some frozen veg and other bits and pieces in here.'

'This is very good of you. I'll make sure we get payment sorted out.'

Sally looked momentarily affronted. 'We wouldn't hear of it. It's here, you're here. Frida is most definitely here. We are just down the hill, though once you're in, I doubt you'll want to venture out in this. But you know where we are. The fire will take five minutes to light and if we lose power, the genny kicks in.'

'Great. And not a bad signal up here, either.' Warlow glanced at the four bars on his phone.

'Okay.' Sally threw up her hood again. 'Oh, bedclothes are under the bed for making up the sofa. Need anything just ring me. Number is in the visitor's book. I'll see you in the morning.'

She opened the door. The wind started up a banshee howl and a fresh spatter of rain hammered in.

Jess closed the door quickly and stood at the window to watch her leave. 'Hard to contemplate, but I believe it's getting worse.'

Warlow grunted and punched some numbers on his phone. 'I'd better let Buchannan know we haven't been washed away.'

'Good idea. I'll make some tea.'

Warlow got through to a relieved Superintendent Buchannan and explained their predicament. When he'd finished, he took off his coat, soaked from even the run from the car to the hut.

'What did he say?'

'Nothing. Glad we were okay, that's all. I've also texted Gil. They're all still at work. We could sort a video catch up once tea is on the go.'

'Yep, I'm all for that.'

With tea made, Warlow set his phone to lean against the sugar canister on the breakfast-cum-dining bar – there was no table as such – and, at five fifteen, made the call to Gil.

'We wondered if you'd been washed into a ditch somewhere,' Gil said by way of a greeting.

'Unfortunately for you, we have not.'

Catrin squinted at the screen on her end. She took centre stage, Gil at her side, and Rhys hovering behind above the two of them. 'What do you think, sir? Is the farmhouse where they kept Dobbs?'

'Highly likely. Zip ties, blood stains. Something unpleasant has been going on there. But we need Povey to sweep the place,' Warlow said. 'Any progress at your end?'

Rhys went first and gave them all a rundown of his visit to Marc Dobbs's teammate and the fact that it had come up blank, other than the information about Nico.

'And he is a different animal,' Catrin said. 'Unlike Marc Dobbs, Nico Bajek does have a bit of form. A couple of drunk and disorderlies for which he got a slapped wrist. Speeding fines and one fine for affray. Interestingly, all those offences occurred after the breakup with Leah, if Gina's timeline is correct.'

'It will be,' Warlow said.

'But the most interesting thing is that he is also on DS Vetch's radar. A couple of years ago, he was arrested for possession and intent to supply IPED.'

'I still prefer anabolic steroids,' Gil said.

'Yes, well, Image and Performance-Enhancing Drugs sounds a lot more inclusive.'

Gil shook his head. 'Even the addicts are becoming woke.'

'Was he charged?' Jess asked.

'No. He convinced the CPS that they were all for his own use. I haven't seen him, but Gina says he's a big lad.'

'But it does put him in the frame as someone who knows suppliers,' Jess pointed out.

'Exactly, ma'am.'

'So, he didn't like Marc Dobbs and has drug connections. Are those enough for us to make him a POI?'

'A person of interest, definitely, sir,' Rhys said.

'I'm not sure when we'll get away from here tomorrow. What's on your actions list?' Warlow was determined not to let Frida have it all her own way.

'We need to make certain Dobbs was the innocent victim everyone claims he was. A warrant to search his house would be my next move,' Gil said.

'Gina said that Leah Dobbs has given her permission verbally for us to search the house. We won't need a warrant,' Catrin said.

'Okay. But we need that consent witnessed again before it's begun,' Jess warned her.

'Does he own any other premises? A business lock-up, anything like that?' Warlow asked.

'Gina has asked that question, sir, and the answer from Leah Dobbs was no. He was a one-man band. His van was his office.'

'And we have that as evidence, correct?'

'It's been moved to the pound, sir. Povey has it in her clutches.'

'Then I agree, a search of Dobbs's house first.'

'And I'm about to talk to a builder who used Dobbs a lot. I know Eifion Mitchell, and I trust his take on things.' Gil slid his glasses down from the top of his head to his nose and looked at his phone. 'I have his number somewhere.'

'What's it like up there, sir? The storm, I mean?' Rhys asked.

'Not good. The worst is yet to come, and it's heading your way. I would suggest you all get home as soon as you can. Tomorrow is another day.'

'What about you, sir?'

'Now then…' Jess picked Warlow's phone up and did a quick three-sixty scan of the hut.

'That looks amazing,' Catrin said.

'Not bad as a shelter from the storm, ma'am,' Rhys agreed.

'And there's a log fire, I see.' Gil nodded his approval.

'Gina's always wanted to stay in a Shepherd's Hut after seeing that programme about the sheep farming family.'

'The one where there were umpteen kids?' Gil asked.

'Yes. I'm sure she was a shepherdess.'

'Probably a bit of rabbit in there, too,' Gil muttered. 'From the rate at which children were produced.'

'Gina thinks it's romantic. But all sheep do is poo.' Rhys grimaced.

Into the lull that followed this statement, Gil was the first to respond. 'A Shepherd's Hut does not necessarily come with sheep, Rhys.'

'I know that, sarge. But what I'm saying is that being a shepherd, or a shepherdess, isn't that glam, is it? All that sheep dung. And have you seen their backsides? Talk about a mess. Those dagnets hanging from their tails.'

'Dagnets?' Jess asked.

'Yes. You know, ma'am, the bit of poop that hangs off the fur on a sheep's rear end. Or hangs off anything come to think of it.'

'*Argwlydd mawr*, I'd rather not think of it,' Gil murmured with a distasteful shake of the head.

'It's a word we used in school, and there were a lot of farmers in the school I went to.' Rhys's defensive explanation was strident.

'It's always an education talking to you, Rhys,' Gil said, a broad grin across his face. 'I take it that shepherding is not on your bucket list, then.'

'Defo not, sarge.'

'Thank God we've cleared that one up, then,' Gil added. 'Which is more than can be said about sheep dagnets.'

'But at least you're safe, ma'am,' Catrin said.

'We are. Where it was not safe was the abandoned farm-house. I'm not sure the place will survive a storm like this.'

'Our intention is to get away as soon as we can,' Warlow

said. 'It'll take a good couple of hours to get back to Carmarthen. Let's see if we can get DS Vetch along to an early afternoon briefing, once Frida blows over. There's a lot to do. But for now, get home safely. And that is an order.'

He rang off and finished his tea.

'Right, I'd better talk to Molly, too. She can be a right worry wart.' Jess picked her own phone up.

'Fine, I'll get the fire going. No telly, I see. But I do have my iPad. If push comes to shove, we'll have to watch a film. But first things first. I need to phone the Dawes to let them know I'm stuck here.'

'So that they can break the news to Cadi.'

'Indeed. She is going to have a sleepover.'

CHAPTER EIGHTEEN

GIL MADE the call to Eifion Mitchell as he drove home. There were several points along the A40 where the road dipped perilously close to the valley floor, where the river, when it overflowed its banks, was happy to reclaim its floodplain. There had not been enough rain for that to happen yet, but it would be heavier up in the hills and that had to flow somewhere. Often, the highest water happened hours after the rain stopped. Either way, Gil was taking no chances. The road was open for now, and he could talk to Mitchell as easily on the phone as he could face to face, though the latter always yielded better results when it came to perpetrators, in his opinion.

Leaning in close, maintaining eye contact, even smiling, or not, at the right time, were vital parts of the interrogator's armament. But Eifion Mitchell was not a suspect here. None of that applied. Instead, Gil opted for that tried and tested opener, an insult.

'Eifion, it's Gil Jones. I hear that three of the buildings you and your lot built last year have collapsed because of the bad weather.'

On the other side of the phone, Mitchell paused for all of two seconds before coming back with, 'It would take more than a breeze like this to blow over one of our builds. Now, if you leaned against one, that's another story.'

Gil eased out a deep chortle. 'How are you, Eifion? Busy?'

'Can't complain. Hopeless this time of year, of course. Not enough daylight hours and at the whim of the weather. Hard to keep the boys at work.'

Mitchell employed a dozen people on various projects, and it was difficult to be on the road for more than a couple of days without seeing one of his vans heading somewhere to and from work.

'How are the girls?' Mitchell had done work for both of Gil's daughters.

'Well, thanks.'

'Keeping you in check, are they?'

'They keep producing even more girls, so I've given up the fight.'

'Good to see you being in touch with your feminine side.'

'The nail varnish gives the Uniforms something to talk about. Though never out loud these days. God forbid. Let them think it's a lifestyle choice, and a chosen identity, not me falling asleep in the chair with my seven-year-old granddaughter decorating the ends of my fingers the colours of the South African flag.'

'What can I do you for, Gil?'

'You probably heard on the news about Marc Dobbs?'

'Christ, an hour ago, it came on in the van as I was driving home. Bloody hell, he was with us a week ago on a job up in Peniel. Hard to believe.'

Gil heard genuine shock and distress in Mitchell's voice.

'What the hell was he doing up in the Beacons in November?'

'That's an excellent question and part of the reason I'm ringing you. We didn't know him. Or rather, he wasn't known to us, as most law-abiding citizens are not. What was he like?'

'I've got no complaints. He was a good kid. Hard working. Knew his stuff.'

'How long have you used him?'

'He's one of two or three sparks I'm happy to work with. Depending on availability. But he never messed us about. Turned up, did the job when we asked. But my relationship with him was always as a contractor. Why are you asking? The news said he got lost up there.'

'He did. But it's the reason he got lost we're looking into. Is there anyone on your crew that knew him better than you did?'

'I can ask my foreman. He was supervising the build when Marc came and did the first wiring fix. He'd have been on site with Marc. Let me call him.'

'Better still, give me his number and then you tell him I'll call him.'

'Right you are.'

Five minutes later, as Gil approached Nantgaredig, he got a text notification. He pulled into the car park of a pub in Pontargothi and dialled the number with a thumbs up attached. The man who answered was called Ashley, sounded a lot younger than Eifion Mitchell, but equally shocked about Marc Dobbs. Yes, he'd known Marc for a few years, and yes, he was a good worker, always willing to put in the extra hours to get things finished.

Gil understood how important this was for builders who depended on various trades to finish before they could move on to the next stages.

Gil composed his next questions carefully. 'And you'd noticed nothing strange about him when he worked with you last?'

'Other than he was a Liverpool supporter, no.'

Gil smiled. Sport. Nothing that was more inclusive or divisive when you got a bunch of men together.

'No odd behaviour. Did he look well?'

'Yeah. Marc got on with it. Bit of banter when we had a cup of tea or a sandwich. That's when I'd see him mainly. Sparks are always crawling about in small spaces for hours on end.'

'This is a tough question, so I would appreciate your

discretion. Was there any suggestion that Marc might be involved in anything drug related?'

'Drugs? Christ, no. He played a bit of soccer, had a kid, but that's all I know about him. None of the boys ever mentioned anything to do with drugs when it came to Marc. Why? Is there—'

'No, there isn't.' Gil shut off the tap before it could start running. 'And that's the point. I have to ask these questions. You don't need to worry about them. And I would be grateful if, for now, all this stays between the two of us.'

'Of course,' Ashley said. 'Why was he up there, on the mountain, I mean? Any idea?'

'We're looking into lots of angles at the moment.'

'I'm sure you are.'

'Indeed. That's why they pay us the big bucks.'

Ashley laughed. 'My partner's brother is a copper in Swansea. I know how much he gets paid. He doesn't do it for the money.'

'Must be love, then,' Gil said.

'Yeah,' Ashley agreed. 'Must be.'

THEY DRANK two cups of tea, and ten minutes after Warlow lit the fire, *Cwt Y Bugail* had warmed up enough for both officers to have shed their coats and jackets. Darkness had fallen, or rather, the afternoon gloom had descended into inky blackness. Frida rattled and shook the building as her breath screamed outside.

'My God, I hope this thing is anchored down,' Jess said.

Warlow was busy on his iPad, finding out anything he could about the property they'd visited that afternoon, *Bryn Teg*. After a good half hour, he sighed and put the iPad down.

'It's been unoccupied for three years.'

'That's a shame. Why does that happen?'

'Who knows,' Warlow said. 'Families die out. Or the children of farmers move away. The land is rented out to other farmers, but the buildings remain neglected and decay. It's a common story. Anyway, there's nothing here that helps us. What time is it?'

'Nearly seven. Hungry?' Jess walked over to the defrosting food.

'A bit. How about a drink first?'

'Thought you'd never ask. The white is nice and cold in the fridge.'

'And I saw a Bluetooth speaker over near the bed, there. Let me see if I can find us some music.'

Warlow grabbed the little speaker. The same make that he'd bought Jess for Christmas last year.

Glasses clinked as she removed a couple from a cupboard above the little sink. It drew Warlow's attention. She reached up, stretching on tiptoes. It tightened the muscles in her legs and tightened the fabric of her trousers around her backside at the same time. Warlow looked away quickly, hoping she hadn't noticed his glance.

'This reminds me of a holiday I once went on with a boyfriend. I was nineteen. He had a car, and he knew someone with a caravan. We went to the Wirral, and it rained for a week. I remember it because I froze in a bloody mini skirt that I was too proud of to not wear.' She shook her head.

Warlow let out a little laugh and tried not to think of Jess in a mini skirt at nineteen.

He got the Bluetooth to work and found a Young Gun Silver Fox playlist that he knew Jess liked.

She grinned. 'It's like being on holiday. Except for the howling wind.'

'So, it is like being on holiday. But in West Wales.'

She held out a glass. He got up off the sofa and joined her where she was leaning against the breakfast bar.

'Well, isn't this nice, Mr Warlow. Cheers.'

Warlow was aware of several things simultaneously. That they were in this situation because of their work, not of their own volition. That he was her boss. That she was standing very close. That she smelled wonderful, as always. And that she had the most remarkable grey-blue eyes. Two of those facts weighed heavily upon him. The other two were observations that he had made to himself many times before. Observations that were difficult to ignore.

But now, in the moment, her proximity made what happened next an inevitability. At least he told himself that. *Midnight in Richmond* played over the speaker, with just the right amount of poignant longing in the lyrics. Warlow noted how the wine left Jess's lips moist when she took the glass away.

He tilted his head forward to kiss her while a part of him, the instant he did it, screamed out that he was a stupid, reckless, old, bloody fool. That voice was loud enough to make him pull back two seconds after he did it, because she didn't respond.

Surprise registered in her eyes, and the voice in his head screamed louder.

There, happy now? You've ruined it, you stupid bloody idi—

But that thought was guillotined off when Jess moved her own head forward and slid her free hand round the back of his head and the nape of his neck to pull him towards her.

This time, the kiss was much longer and something so fresh, so unlike anything that had happened to him for such a long, long time, that he didn't know how to stop it. When it did, all he could do was stand there and blink.

The urge to apologise was strong, so he began to speak—

'Don't,' Jess said. 'Just say nothing.'

Outside, a fresh gust howled a new deep note around the chimney stack. Jess laughed. 'You certainly pick your moments, DCI Warlow.'

'I can't tell if the gods are with me or against me,' he muttered nervously.

'Let's find out, shall we?'

She put her wineglass down, and this time put both arms around him to kiss him again.

CHAPTER NINETEEN

AND A GOOD KISS it turned out to be. A long kiss. A hungry kiss.

Another gust rattled the hut.

Jess glanced up at the roof. 'I have to hand it to you, Evan.' She laughed. 'Dramatic doesn't come anywhere near.'

He didn't reply immediately. Instead, he searched her eyes, so close now, and stayed deadly serious. 'I can still go somewhere else. If I'm reading this wrong.'

She jerked back; the smile tinged with confusion. 'What are you talking about?'

'I'm your superior officer and your landlord. I mean, these days this could be construed as … I don't exactly know what, but …' He ran out of words. And for an instant, wondered at that, too, because they were words he was bombarded with daily just by switching on the news. Appropriate consent, toxic masculinity, sexual predation. They were a foreign language to him, but suddenly he felt the need to open the dictionary.

'Bloody hell, man. I'm not a wide-eyed innocent desperate for a part, and you are not a media mogul.' She tilted her head. 'Is that it, though? Is that why you've waited all this time?'

'That… and the other thing.'

'The HIV.' She nodded as his words confirmed what she'd realised. 'And haven't I bent over backwards to show you how much that should not be a reason for you hiding away?'

She had. Right from the outset. But all he could do now was mutter ineffectually, 'You have.'

Jess shook her head. 'God, I'd like to see the shattered pieces of the mould that made you.'

'I am grateful for that. For you making me chat with Mark Naismith. He was a revelation.'

In the summer, Jess had manufactured a meeting between Warlow, who'd contracted the virus from a malicious addict, and Naismith, who'd received it from contaminated blood as part of his treatment for haemophilia. A man who had embraced his treatment and was determined to live a normal life—balancing a job, raising kids, and coming to terms with it all.

She laughed again in reply. A full-throated affair. 'And even after that revelation, you've waited until a storm throws us together in a Shepherd's Hut before letting me know that you even find me attractive.'

'Christ. Attractive. That's an understatement if ever there was one.'

'Is that right?'

'It is.'

She leant back and picked up the wineglass. Even that movement sent Warlow's pulse soaring. The fire had warmed the room up, but it was as nothing to the heat building inside him.

Jess took another swallow and contemplated him. 'Okay, so now we know where we stand. You are an idiot, and I should have realised that the answer to my question of why you've waited would be simply Evan Warlow through and through. But we're here now, and, by some miracle, you've let the genie out of the bottle.'

'Have I?'

'Oh, there is no going back. And I get three wishes. The first one is that this storm does not blow the hut down. The second is that there is hot water.' She turned away. 'I'm going to shower, and I am taking my wine with me. Because I am not nineteen anymore, I prefer being nice and clean in bed.'

Warlow stood and watched her walk to the door at the far end of the hut, wondering if she went through it, this whole thing would dissolve like some fantastic dream.

'You didn't tell me the third wish,' he said.

'Oh, you'll find out soon enough, DCI Warlow.'

'I, uh … I don't … a condom,' he said.

'This is where I tell you not to worry because I do? Well, I don't. And I still don't want you to worry.'

He objected.

'No buts. We both know what the experts say. Let's listen to them for once, shall we?'

With that, she closed the bathroom door.

Five minutes later, she emerged, wearing nothing but a fluffy white towel that ended five inches above her knees. And so Warlow got to see what she looked like in a mini skirt which, had he been asked, was high on his wish list, too.

Then he was showering and looking down at himself and wishing he'd done a bit more in the gym and not been so fond of Molly's pasta bake by finishing what was left at the end of each meal. When he came out, with his own towel wrapped around his waist, Young Gun Silver Fox was playing *Love Guarantee*, which was wonderfully bloody ironic had it not been so grindingly close to the bone. Jess had discarded the towel and was in the bed, her shoulders bare but everything else covered.

'It's been a while,' Warlow said.

Jess let her eyes drift down to the odd folds in the towel. 'I can see that.'

He laughed at that. It lasted until the moment that Jess threw off the covers. Then it all became a lot more serious.

'Are we doing this, or what?' she said, her voice huskier than usual.

'We are,' Warlow said and got into bed next to her, put

first a trembling hand, and then his lips, on her smooth, astonishing skin.

There wasn't much talking after that. Only when she whispered what her third wish was. And Warlow was happy to comply because, strangely enough, her wish was not a hundred miles from his and, energetically and with a little manoeuvring, they found a way to make each other's wishes come true.

AT ABOUT THE SAME TIME, in the house they were paying a mortgage on, Catrin Richards and Craig Peters sat in front of the telly. Catrin was lying on the sofa, feet up on Craig's lap with a twenty-episode drama playing. Not that it mattered because Craig and Catrin weren't really watching. They were talking, as they had been for hours, about the idea that had begun with Rhys's throwaway remark.

That had blossomed into a plan from which they were, as a couple, still trying to tease the knots out of.

'Well,' Craig said. 'All I can say is that my grandad will be really chuffed.'

'He will.' Catrin squeezed Craig's hand. 'Are you worried that we might upset people?'

'I'm not worried about my crowd. They're all wracking their brains about how to make these next few weeks mean something for him. It's like having a clock ticking in your brain. What about your lot?'

'It won't change anything, will it? They know our situation. And we might as well do this while we can.' She looked down at her pregnant belly.

'Okay, then. I'll make some calls.' But he didn't move from the sofa. 'What about work?'

'Oh, they'll be no problem. I need to pick the right moment, that's all.'

'How's it going with the case?'

'We're going to go over Dobbs's property tomorrow.'

'You expecting to find anything?'

'Who knows? It's a weird case.'

'It's never straightforward where drugs are involved, right?'

'No.'

'Right, let me get a pen and paper and we can start a list.' Craig eased Catrin's legs off his own.

'Craig's list,' Catrin quipped.

'Hilarious,' Craig said as he walked away.

'Oh, and while you're up there, any chance of a hot chocolate?'

'With a fish finger in it?'

'Did you and Rhys read the same pregnancy joke book?' she flared.

'No,' Craig said, heading for the kitchen. 'But he did text me to tell me about the banana and ketchup.'

The only missile Catrin had near was a cushion. She launched it, but it missed Craig by a mile. 'Wait 'til I'm back to my fighting weight. That would have been dead on target.'

'Yeah, right,' Craig said as the kettle's element began to rumble.

LATER, though Frida showed no sign of abating, Warlow and Jess were ravenous. Almost as hungry as a fighter after training. Only, their bout lasted two rounds; the first quick and urgent, round two a slower, exploratory affair that still ended in a knockout. Now they used homemade bread to mop up their lasagne sauce. 'We need the carbs.' Jess had excused the dirty little habit with a conspiratorial wrinkling of her nose.

She wore only his shirt, a light-blue button down, showing off her olive skin. The heat from the wood burner meant she was quite comfortable half-dressed like that. Warlow didn't mind, and his eyes strayed to the smooth skin of her legs in between mouthfuls of food. If she caught him doing it, she didn't seem to mind. He'd run out to the car for a fresh shirt for the morning, which he'd learned, from old, to make sure he carried in the Jeep, along with an old rugby shirt he stored in case he got soaked walking Cadi. That was what he wore now.

'Always nice to dress for dinner,' Jess commented.

The red proved to be Chianti Classico. Made from Sangiovese as all Chiantis were. This one was velvety and smelt of cherries and leather with a touch of mint at the end.

'If it's Sally that stocked the cellar, she knows her stuff,' Warlow said as he topped up their glasses.

'Delish,' Jess said, her face flushed from the wine and the heat and good sex.

'So now, I need to ask you a few questions,' Warlow said.

'Am I a suspect?' Jess asked.

'You are, since the crime of going to bed with me has been committed.'

'Is it a crime?'

'Almost. I mean, look at you. You and Molly look like sisters. Whereas I'm ten years older than you, could do with losing a few pounds, and have HIV.'

'Have HIV with no perceptible titre, did you not listen to Naismith?'

'That aside. Indulge me. I mean, I'm not exactly fighting women off with a stick.'

'Well, you need to be in a position where someone can attack you to fight them off with any kind of weapon. And you have, instead, adopted a remain-in-retreat mode.'

'That's not an answer, though.'

Jess put down her red wine and crossed her legs. Warlow strained to not let his eyes stray down to her knees and just about managed it. 'Well, there is circumstance. I mean, we're here, there is no telly, and there is a storm raging. As Rhys says, the situation has a certain romantic charm. It's warm and dry. We're alive. So, why not?'

'Okay. And I am not complaining. Not for one minute.' He nodded at that. Though it wasn't the answer that he was hoping for, it was still an answer.

Jess played with the stem of her glass. 'Those are all pretty good reasons, I think. And I admit it's been some time since I had any physical contact of any kind. It's been a good two years of fasting.'

Warlow knew all about that, too. He and Denise gave up trying to be nice to each other long before they divorced.

Jess had not finished, though. 'But that's not the whole truth, Evan. When I was in Manchester, at the party with my girlfriends, a lot of them felt empowered. They still looked good, even without cosmetic help. All a certain age. They could easily find a man, or woman, more often than not younger than they were. Sometimes, a lot younger. But what does that all mean? They all want to be twenty-four again. Recapture what it felt like when they were at their peak.'

Warlow frowned. Funny thing that, and mystifying for a man. He had no desire to be in his early twenties again. No money. Higher than average risk of violence. Not really any idea of where his life had been going. But he kept quiet. Maybe it was different for girls, The drama of sexual pursuit maybe. The going out, the interactions. Fun, yes, but bloody exhausting the older you got.

'Ricky broke my heart,' Jess went on. 'And just proving to myself that I could be attractive to someone else, someone younger, seemed an empty gesture. Thirty-year-old men are not looking for mid-forty's women. At least not for reasons other than the obvious. Plus, Molly would call me all sorts of names. I don't blame my girlfriends. We're in a time when the narrative that's fed to us insists your own happiness and self-worth trumps all. I had no idea what I'd been looking for until I began to work with you.'

'This isn't just because you feel sorry for me?'

'Oh, my God. I see I am going to have to spell it out.' She took a breath and leaned forward. She had nothing on under the shirt, but Warlow somehow, under huge duress, managed to maintain eye contact. 'I'm damaged goods, and so are you. We have that in common.'

'I'm sure I'm not blameless—'

'No, don't do that. Don't skew it so that it's justified. Not Denise, not the HIV. No one deserves that.'

Warlow thought about objecting, but the light in Jess's eyes told him he'd lose that argument. But it was he who spoke next. 'Perhaps you're right. But you can't help wondering when all these things happen if you're meant to be alone.'

Jess flinched, and her eyes became moist. When she spoke next, it was in a whisper. 'Don't say that. You're a one off, Evan. I've been around lots of coppers. Good and bad, but I've never come across anyone as stubborn and straight and honourable as you. I didn't think I'd want to start this dance again, but then you came along. You say you think you were meant to be alone. The real question is, do you want to be?'

Warlow didn't answer immediately because these were questions he'd been afraid to face. So, he said what came into his mind without analysis. 'For the first time since I came back to work, or even since Denise and I broke up, I don't believe I want to be.'

Jess reached forward and grabbed his hand. 'Good. Because neither do I.'

CHAPTER TWENTY

WARLOW WOKE UP TO SILENCE. Daylight had not yet broken, but Frida had moved on and left the world battered and wet in her wake. When he opened his eyes, the hut was in darkness and, despite banking up the fire last night, only the merest red glow in the fireplace remained.

'Morning,' Jess said. She moved her hand over his chest.

'Morning. Sleep, okay?'

'Very well. Better than I have in a long time.'

'Must have been the storm,' Warlow said.

'You can believe that if you want to. My money's on the sex and the wine.'

'Yeah, well, there is that, too. I suppose I'd better get up and see if I can resuscitate the fire.'

'Good idea. And put the kettle on. Did Sally leave anything for breakfast?'

'Instant porridge, some bacon, and eggs.'

Jess wriggled up close to him. 'Brilliant. I'm coming back to this hotel,' she whispered.

'Yeah. It's been the best stay-away I can remember.' Warlow stroked her hair.

'Have you thought about what happens next?' she asked after a few beats of silence.

'Yes. Well, I'd ask you to move in with me, but I realise you already have.'

Jess pressed a finger against one of his ribs, and he twisted away. 'Who said romance was dead?'

'I haven't given it much thought. Back to work when we can, I suppose.'

'Good plan. And then I may have to have a tough conversation with Molly.'

'About what?'

'About you not having to sleep in the garden office anymore.'

'Want me to do it?'

'No. It could go either way. But I'll work myself up to it.'

Warlow slid out of bed and walked over to the wood burner to see what he could do.

When it was light, Emyr Dobbs got a lift from his brother's house in a response vehicle to the parking area at the bottom of the hill up to Llyn y Fan Fach. Gina set it up, and she was already at the house when he left.

His was the only car in the dirt pull-off next to the track that acted as a kind of car park, a few yards away from the bubbling, frothing stream of the Sawdde River, swollen by Frida's excesses. Emyr checked his car to make sure it started, then stood and waved the response vehicle off. They were in for a busy day thanks to the storm. Lines were down, and there'd been reports of local flooding in several places. By rights, he should be at work helping too.

But not today.

No one would blame him for not working today.

Once the police car had driven off, Emyr stood and looked up at the steep track leading up parallel to the stream, past the little hatchery and on to the lake that lay at the base of the bowl formed by the high escarpments of the Fans beyond. Without thinking, he ascended the track again, just as he had done three nights ago. If there was a purpose to this, he could not find one, other than that he somehow needed to do it.

He needed to look again at the place where his brother had wandered off into. He kept climbing, the day after the storm brighter and no rain in the forecast. But a chill northerly had replaced Frida's gales, and it carried a sharper, bitter edge to it.

When he reached the lake, it was still early, and the storm had kept walkers away. Alone, he stood on the water's edge watching rivulets crash down the face of the escarpment.

He sucked in the air and looked across towards the spot over the open moor where Marc had spent his last moments alive. Little more than a mile away, but very different in the pitch blackness of the night, with no lights around to act as beacons.

So close, but on that night, a different world.

'Oh, Marc,' he said to the wind. 'I'm sorry. I'm so sorry.'

And then he turned back and began the much quicker descent to his car.

HALF A DOZEN OFFICERS accompanied Rhys and Gil to Leah Dobbs's house. Gina opened the door. Behind, Leah looked past the FLO towards Gil and the Uniforms and CID officers behind him.

'Just to confirm, Leah, you are happy for us to conduct a search?' Gil asked.

'What are you looking for?' Now that it was happening, she sounded a little panicked.

'We need to see if there is anything that might give us some help in finding out what exactly happened.'

'Like what?'

'We don't always know until we find it. Chances are we will find nothing. But unless we look, we'll never know.'

She studied Gil with haunted eyes, desperately in need of

sleep or understanding in equal measure. But then she nodded. 'Okay, go ahead.'

Gil went first. 'We'll leave the living room until last. It's best you stay in there until we finish. We might need to take some things away, but we'll make sure you know what they are and that you get them back.'

'What things?'

'Computer equipment. Anything to do with the business.' Gil said all this in as reasonable and measured a way as he could.

Leah went back into the living room. 'Where's the child?' Gil asked Gina.

'With her grandmother.'

'And the brother?'

'Gone to fetch his car. He'll be back, but not for a while.'

Gil turned to the officers behind him. 'Okay, let's get it done.'

The Uniforms trooped in. Leah stood by the living room doorway, her eyes bloodshot as she greeted them all with a wan smile and a flicker of suspicion in her gaze.

Gil and Rhys took the stairs and went into Beca's bedroom, a space filled with innocence. A menagerie of teddy bears and stuffed animals, a rack of story books, in Welsh and English, a rainbow stencil on the wall and too many unicorns in various guises to count. Centre piece was a photograph of a smiling child, blissfully unaware of the tragedy that had befallen her.

'Hard to believe that her world is crumbling around her,' Rhys muttered.

The room's walls whispered stories of bedtime tales and hushed lullabies. Gil traced his fingers over the toys, a lump forming in his throat, memories of his own granddaughters threatening to overwhelm him. He watched as Rhys looked under toy boxes and opened and shut all the books.

'I'll take the master bedroom,' Gil said after a while.

But he found little relief in there. A wardrobe full of Leah's clothes, a smaller one for Marc's. A dresser and mirror that looked older, as if it had come from a grandmother's house. Photographs on the bedside table next to a lamp, snapshots of the Dobbs's love story. Gil picked up a framed photo. Marc and Leah, radiating happiness.

'The perfect family,' Gil muttered, a bitter taste lingering in his mouth. But then he got to work. He asked one of the female officers to look at Leah's wardrobe and the drawers that contained her clothing. He'd reassured Leah on that score. Gil had daughters of his own.

Gil wandered down to the little room the Dobbs used as Marc's office. Invoices and bills were stuck up on a corkboard – the mundane remnants of a life cut short. Another officer was going through the paperwork in here. He'd already placed a laptop and an iPad in a box, along with a sheaf of papers for further examination.

An hour in, Gil asked Gina to take Leah into the kitchen while officers searched the living room. Gil stood on the threshold watching two Uniforms upturn the cushions when a shout from outside drew his attention.

Gina appeared in the hallway. 'You probably need to see this, sarge,' she said in a low voice. 'It's Charvis. He's outside, going through the shed.'

Charvis, a uniformed officer, stood by the little shiplap-clad rectangular building, his expression grave. 'There's something in here, sarge.' He stood aside and pointed to a shelf where tins of paint and a canister of weedkiller stood. An arc of white powder sat in an area that looked like it had once held a curved receptacle but which now stood empty.

Rhys joined Gil. 'Probably weedkiller, sarge. Or slug killer.'

'Can't use that kind of thing these days. It's illegal.' Gil peered closely at the powder. 'Someone brought an EDIT kit, I hope?'

'I'll check.' Rhys disappeared. Evidential Drug Identification Kits were standard on most house searches, though in this instance they had not been looking for drugs particularly. He hoped someone had been thorough. They had.

The officer who came with the little handheld plastic box opened it up quickly and had been trained in its use.

'How long?' Gil asked.

'Ten minutes, sarge,' Charvis said. 'Steve will run the usual panel. Opiates, MDMA, amphetamines, cocaine, ketamine, and M-Cat.'

'Okay,' Gil said. 'I'm with Rhys. It's probably weedkiller. I'll go back and finish up in the lounge.'

The panel took seven minutes. This time, Charvis didn't shout. He came and fetched Gil.

'It's not weedkiller, sarge,' he said.

Gil followed him to the shed. Another uniformed officer held up the little plastic vial he'd put some of the powder into and shaken up next to the colour chart. 'This tests for PCP and ketamine. From the colour, more purple than blue I think, I'd say ketamine.'

'*Arglwydd,* that's all we need. Right, get some more samples and photographs and we'd better look in all these cans and bottles.' He glanced over at the main house. 'Rhys, get Gina. I'm going to have to have another little talk with Leah. But first, I must discuss these findings with our leader.'

'Are they still in Machynlleth, sarge?'

Gil glanced at his watch. Almost eleven. 'Let's hope not. Once you've fetched Gina, have a chat with Dai Vetch. Let's find out what the market for ketamine is like in this neck of the woods.'

CHAPTER TWENTY-ONE

Warlow and Jess had a lot to thank Sally Meade and her partner, Louise, for. Not only the Shepherd's Hut but also the fact that they'd marshalled the surrounding farmers to help clear the road and have a tractor standing by for when the Jeep negotiated a significant stand of pooled water on one of the many dips in the lane. A pool deep enough to make a bow wave but not come over the bonnet.

Once Warlow cleared the hazard, he'd stopped the Jeep and got out of the vehicle to shout his thanks one last time across the twenty yards of water. Sally, standing next to her Land Rover, waved an acknowledgement.

'Come back and see us!' she yelled.

'We may well do that,' Warlow replied with a glance back at Jess, grinning in the passenger seat. Warlow understood where this smile came from since they'd already talked about coming back in the summer, when the weather would be better. Rent the same *Cwt Y Bugail* and do some walks.

'You old romantic, you,' Jess had said to that.

'Less of the old, thanks,' Warlow objected. 'I am a man known to shed a tear at least twice in the watching of *It's a Wonderful Life*. Five times is my record.'

Once they got out onto the A road, traffic was sparse. It

looked as if motorists were still heeding the advice to travel only if necessary.

By midday, they made Cross Inn, about halfway to HQ, when Gil's call came through.

'Still in one piece?' he asked.

'We are. Thanks for asking,' Warlow replied.

'How was your night in the Shepherd's Hut?'

Several responses occurred immediately to Warlow. Some of them were even half decent. But he and Jess had agreed to spare one another's blushes for now and simply carry on as if nothing had happened. The fact that she was his lodger helped. Effectively, it was business as normal. Except that, for Warlow, it would be as far from normal as Mars was from Neptune. But in a good way.

A very good way.

He finally answered Gil's question with a nebulous, 'As comfortable as you might expect under the circumstances.'

Jess, next to him, simply stared with a one-eyebrow-raised expression and mouthed, 'As comfortable as you might expect?'

Warlow mouthed back, 'Shut up.'

'Not blown to smithereens, then?' Gil went on in sublime oblivion.

Jess let out a squeal, which she quickly camouflaged as a cough.

'Oh, dear,' Gil continued. 'Hope you haven't caught anything, ma'am.'

'I'm fine,' Jess said in a tight voice, barely managing to restrain the laugh that threatened.

Warlow shook his head and put an end to the innuendo. 'We're halfway back. Cross Inn.'

'That's good. That's also where Marc Dobbs's brother lives. But he's still at Leah's place, so Gina tells us.'

Warlow picked up on the edge to Gil's voice. 'Why? Anything happened?'

'You could say that. The search of Dobbs's property yielded a suspicious substance in the shed. Looked like it's spilled from something. Anyway, it turned out to be ketamine.'

'What?' Jess's voice had returned to normal. Or as normal as a high-pitched incredulity would allow.

'We've repeated the test twice, and it is definite.'

'In the shed, you say?' Warlow asked.

'The house is clean otherwise, though we are sending a dog team in there now to look for any more surprises.'

'Bloody hell, Gil. I can't leave you lot alone for two minutes. Next steps?'

'Good question. Hence this call. Should we get Leah Dobbs in for questioning?'

Warlow threw Jess a glance. She nodded in reply.

'I think that would be a good idea,' Warlow agreed. 'A chat down at HQ under caution with a solicitor present, don't you think?'

'I'll speak with Gina.'

The sound of raised voices in the background reached Warlow's ears. 'Where are you, Gil? Nant Rugby Club?'

'I wish. Still at the Dobbs's property. I don't know what that noise is. Hang on.' The muffled sound of movement followed, and then Gil again. 'Speak of the devil. It's Dobbs's brother, arriving back after fetching his car. Sounds like he isn't too pleased at the police tape around the garden and the shed. Let me find out what's happening. We'll see you at HQ.'

Once the call finished, Jess said, 'I, for one, did not see that coming.'

'No. Text Catrin and ask her to run Leah Dobbs through the system.'

Jess's fingers danced over the phone's touch screen.

Two seconds later, she received a reply.

'Catrin says she's on it.'

'No surprises there.'

They arrived at HQ at 1.15 pm, but delayed exiting while they sat in the Jeep for a minute.

'Here we are, then,' Warlow said. 'Back to reality.'

'Same old, same old.'

'Yeah. But not. Do we just carry on as normal?'

'We can pass notes under the desk if you like.' Jess had one eyebrow quirked.

'You know what I mean.'

'I do. I suggest we say nothing and carry on, regardless. Besides, there is Molly. She needs to be the top of the list.'

'Agreed. Right, you go first. I'll follow on.'

'Or we could walk in together like normal people.'

'Right, yes, of course. Normal people.'

THE MUCH NEEDED catch up took place with the usual sustenance of tea and goodies from the HTFT box. Dai Vetch had made it from Aberystwyth, and it was he who kicked things off.

'The car that we were tracing has gone off the radar. In a lock-up somewhere is my guess. Last seen heading to Swansea. SWP is on to that. They're checking CCTV. But I have a couple of names for you.'

Vetch walked to the Gallery and pinned up two mugshots.

'Faisal and Liban Daher. Brothers aged twenty-two and nineteen. Both from Leeds. And yes, it's a cliché with names like this, but this is what we find. These kids are dog soldiers in organised crime. Faisal Daher has previous convictions for possession of a bladed article and possessions of cannabis with intent and theft.'

'Are they illegal?' Catrin asked.

'No. They're both here from Somalia and had refugee status on entry in 2011. But they both ended up in the care system. Very messy. It's not a good story.'

Warlow looked at the two young, unsmiling faces.

'When you say soldiers, what do you mean?' Rhys asked.

'They're not drug masterminds. They've probably been offered some money to do a job. Along with the offer of money, and usually not much money, there's coercion, threats of violence. So, they are sent in as sales reps, mules, or to collect money or goods.'

'They're in the system?' Jess asked.

'Faisal is. So far, his brother has no sheet. But they've been stopped and searched together, so we know they're paired up. But the point I'm making is that there'll be someone behind them. This is classic county lines enforcement. Carrying in and out.'

'Carrying?'

'We have intercepted messages to known users which we suspect come from these two. The messages coincide with their presence in Ceredigion. Texts advertising their wares. "The best of both – the white stuff." That's heroin and cocaine. They were stopped once, a month ago, but no drugs were found in the vehicle. My guess is they were plugging.'

'Plugging?' Rhys asked.

'Hiding drugs internally. The clue is often rubber gloves and lubricant.'

Rhys's face was a picture.

'How does this tie in with finding ketamine in the Dobbs's property?'

Vetch blew out air. 'That's a different question. Maybe Dobbs could get his hands on that directly. We're in a rural area. Ketamine is used mainly by vets.'

'One more question,' Gil said. 'Nico Bajek. Any chance he might be involved in all of this?'

Vetch tilted his head. 'IPED misuse doesn't always go hand in hand with the things the Daher brothers were sales reps for. IPED suppliers are a bit more specialised. Often users themselves. But I'd never say never.'

'Can you hang on while we have a chat with Leah Dobbs?' Warlow asked.

'Yeah. Happy to.'

———

LEAH DOBBS LOOKED frail and anxious, sitting opposite Jess and Gil. The duty solicitor was a woman, too. Young, but already disenchanted by the system, judging by the hard look on her face. All very well maintaining a professional lack of emotion, but Suan Brown was in a class of her own.

Jess was being gentle with the widow Dobbs. 'These questions may seem harsh, Leah, but we have to do our job.'

'I want to understand why all this happened to Marc.'

'Good.' Jess smiled. 'We all want that.'

'Did Marc ever go to Swansea, Leah?' Gil asked.

'No. I mean, we'd been to Swansea. There's a winter fair thing at Christmas. A funfair and that. But, no… we wouldn't go to Swansea normally. Too far.'

'And not on business?' Gil persisted.

'No. Marc worked local.'

'Did you ever go into the shed, Leah?'

'The shed?' Her brow wrinkled. 'Well, yeah, to get a hammer or a nail to hang up a picture. But Marc kept paint and brushes and that in there. Plus, some tools. I wanted us to get a bigger shed so I could have an outside freezer …'

'Okay,' Jess said. 'Did Marc ever take drugs to your knowledge?'

This time, Leah's eyes looked like they may pop out. 'What? Why did you ask that?'

Gil leaned forward. "When we checked the shed, we found a small amount of powder. It wasn't much, but when we tested it, it turned out to be a controlled substance."

'What kind of controlled substance?'

'Ketamine.'

'Ketamine?' Leah's voice had risen. 'I don't do drugs.'

Gil nodded. 'It's okay, Leah. No one is suggesting you do. We're talking about Marc—'

'Marc didn't take drugs, either. If he did, I would know.' She spoke with authority.

Gil slid over photographs of the Daher brothers. 'Have you ever seen these men before?'

Distraught, Leah looked at the faces and then back up at

Gil. 'No. Who are they? Are these the men that kidnapped Marc?'

'Let me ask you again. You have never seen these men before?'

'No. Never.'

'Does the name Faisal Daher mean anything to you?'

'No. What kind of name is that?'

Jess ignored the implied and casual racism in that question. 'Marc isn't Beca's dad. Is that right, Leah?'

'Oh God, what is this?'

Suan Brown sent Jess a scathing look. 'I presume this is relevant. You can see what effect it's having.'

Jess didn't bother answering that. 'Leah?'

Leah had pulled herself in, hunched over now, as if she was trying to make herself small enough to fall through a crack. Any crack. 'No.'

'Who is the father, Leah?'

Leah's gaze snapped up. Anger and bitterness now flushing her pallor a dusky brick colour. 'Why are you asking since you obviously already know?'

'We're aware of who is on the birth certificate,' Jess said.

'Are you also aware that Kyle Greer is a total waste of space?'

'We know he's a drug addict and petitioned to get access to Beca three years ago.'

Leah's laugh was derisive. 'They denied access. And there is a court order banning him from coming anywhere near. I have no clue where he is.'

Jess glanced down. 'Last known address is in Swansea.'

'Good. Far enough away.'

'He has made no contact with you since the court case?'

'Nothing. Not even a birthday card. Not one word. And that's the way it should be. He only took us to court because he thought he'd get money if he could have access to Beca. Money to shoot into his fucking arm, or his toes, or his groin. I made a big mistake when I was younger. I admit it. But out of that came Beca. And Marc was … he didn't mind. He was

Beca's dad …' She broke down this time, shuddering quiet sobs, face buried in her tissue-laden hands.

But she paused long enough to add one last thing. She looked up, engaging both Gil and Jess in deliberate stares. 'I hate drugs. I don't go anywhere near them. And if I knew Marc had been involved, I'd have walked out. This, everything that you've told me makes no sense. No sense at all.'

She buried her head again.

Suan Brown, unsmiling, looked calmly across at Jess. 'Get what you want? Because I think my client has had enough, even if you two haven't.'

'Can I get you a cup of tea, Leah?' Gil ignored the solicitor.

Leah shook her head. 'I just want to go home,' she wailed.

CHAPTER TWENTY-TWO

Warlow, Vetch, and Catrin viewed the screens in the observation room. Catrin sat, Warlow and Vetch stood.

'She seems genuine.' Vetch had his arms folded.

'We've all heard that before,' Catrin said.

'Ever come across the partner, Leah's ex?' Warlow turned to Vetch.

'Oh, yes. Kyle Greer is everything bad an addict could be, only worse. Liar, thief, ruiner of his own life and others. I know the family up in Borth. He's estranged from them. Kyle's drug habit turned into a grenade that tore the family apart.'

'I suppose the question is, could Kyle have had a hand in what happened to Marc Dobbs?' Warlow threw it out there and watched Vetch tilt his head at an angle.

'Gut reaction is not. The last time I saw Kyle, he weighed eight stones, and if I blew too hard, he'd fall over. And apart from his physical decline, mentally, his day revolves around his methadone dose.'

'But there is a geographic link,' Catrin pointed out. 'He's in Swansea, and the Dahers were last seen there.'

Vetch nodded. 'But that also could simply be because Swansea has a much bigger drug problem. Plus, it's at the end of the train line to London.'

'The *Twin Town* connection?'

'Life imitating art,' Vetch observed. 'That film should be compulsory viewing for anyone thinking of working in this part of the world.'

Warlow let out a snort of air. The film, a snapshot of the grittier side of Swansea from the turn of the century, had lots of fans even now.

'Genuinely sounds like she hates drugs and what it did to her,' he said.

'I'll have a word with the SWP boys. I can pop across and see Kyle if it helps,' Vetch said.

Warlow nodded. 'Can I leave that with you, then?'

'You can.'

'Meanwhile, let's get Leah back home to her kid. We have nothing to hold her for.'

Vetch left. Catrin turned to Warlow. 'What was the Shepherd's Hut like, sir?'

'Any port in a storm,' Warlow said.

'It looked amazing. I haven't had a chance to talk to DI Allanby about it yet. I bet it was cosy.'

'There was an Atlantic storm blowing outside. Need I remind you? We are only glad that we weren't in a glamping tent.' He didn't like where this was going and so altered course. 'And how are you? Is this your last week?'

'It'll be thirty-seven weeks next week, sir. I said I'd work until then.'

'Are you coping?'

'I am, sir. And this keeps my mind off things.'

'Oh well, you won't need to worry about drug dealers after next week.'

'No, sir. But I was meaning to run something past you. Something I need to do before I finally take my leave.'

Warlow waited. Catrin Richards had never struck him as someone who harboured much in the way of doubt. Not about herself or the job she did. Seeing her hesitant intrigued him.

'Go on, I'm all ears.'

'Well, it has to do with Craig's grandfather.'

GINA HAD OFFERED to drive Leah to and from HQ. When they arrived home, Emyr Dobbs was waiting. He hardly gave them time to get in through the door.

'What did they want, Leah?'

'They asked about the ketamine. They wanted to know if Marc was taking drugs?'

'What?'

'I told them Marc didn't take drugs. He hated drugs. And they asked me about Kyle.'

'Your ex?'

They were in the kitchen. Gina stood at the sink, Leah sat at the table, Emyr near the window, his anger showing through in the way he paced.

'Marc would rather cut off his bloody arm than—'

'I told them that,' Leah muttered.

'Why did they want to know about Kyle? You haven't seen him in how long?'

'Years,' Leah said. 'But there was a link with two men, the Dyers… no, more foreign—'

'Dahers,' Gina corrected her.

'Who the hell are they? Have they got something to do with what happened to Marc?'

'They wouldn't say. They asked if I knew who they were, that's all, ' Leah protested.

Emyr sent Gina a dagger glare. 'Is this who took my brother?'

'I have no idea, Emyr. They are names that have come up as part of the investigation.' Gina spoke calmly, sensing the atmosphere in the room close to combustion point. At least when it came to Emyr.

'And ketamine? It's bloody lethal. I've picked people up after ketamine overdoses. It's not pretty. I'd have known if Marc was doing anything like that. So would Leah.'

'I'm sure,' Gina said reasonably. 'But we didn't imagine finding it on that shelf.'

'But who else had access to that shed?' Emyr asked. 'Wait, didn't you say Nico Bajek came here?'

'He did,' Leah said.

'And did you watch him? The whole time he was here. Could he have gone around the side of the house?'

'Whoa,' Gina said. But Emyr's words had made her pause. She'd let Nico in and seen him out. But as soon as he'd gone through the door, she'd forgotten about him. The house was semi-detached and there was a way into the garden at the side of the property. In similar houses on the estate, people had put a door in. The Dobbs had not. But it was conjecture, nothing else. 'You can't go around accusing people, Emyr.'

'Why the hell not? Your lot does. First, it's my brother, now it's Leah. Why the hell can't I have a go? Everyone knows Nico is a bloody roid-head. I wouldn't put anything past him. He hated Marc. You do know that, right?'

'We were aware there'd been some tension. Leah explained that.'

'Yeah, well, tension is one word for it.' Emyr's smile echoed the mocking light in his eyes. 'I don't suppose you've taken him in for questioning, have you?'

Gina didn't answer that one.

'No, it's easier to pick on a defenceless woman who's lost her husband.'

'Emyr, please.' Leah drummed up a smile. 'Gina's been fantastic.'

Gina responded, 'It's okay. You're both angry. But this is a process. Asking questions is painful, as are sometimes the answers. But we have to do it.'

Emyr looked ready to continue slinging mud, but the hurt, pleading expression on Leah's face stopped him in his tracks.

'I'm going to go back to work tomorrow,' he said. 'We're short staffed as it is. It's a struggle to get anyone to cover shifts. But I'll come back here after my shift.'

'You don't have to,' Leah said.

'Oh, really? From what I'm seeing, I think I do.'

'Thank you.' Leah's voice was even smaller than usual.

'Want me to pick up Beca from school?'

'Would you? I'll give them a ring and say you'll be at the gates.'

'You know that's never a problem,' Emyr said.

THE AFTERNOON FIZZLED out for Warlow after Leah Dobbs left. Things were in train, but the damned thing was yet to arrive at the station. Povey had made it up to the Machynlleth farmhouse and her team was hard at it. Rhys was trying to chivvy the HOP along for anything else they'd found out. Jess and he returned to Ffau'r Blaidd ten minutes apart, after he had visited the Dawes, Cadi's sitters.

Jess was in the kitchen when he walked in and immediately got down on her haunches to make a fuss of the dog. When she'd done that, she walked over to Warlow and made a fuss over him in much the same way, arms around his neck and a hug.

'Glad to see your priorities are right,' he murmured.

'The number of times I've wanted to do this since we moved in. And all that time we've danced around each other like …'

'Dancers?' Warlow said.

'Idiots,' Jess said.

'What do you fancy eating?'

'There's fresh salmon in the freezer. I can put a topping on that and have it with some couscous.'

'Brilliant. And there'll be some skin left over for you, madam.' Warlow reached out to the dog, who responded with extra wiggles.

'But first, I need to talk to my daughter. That could take a while.' Jess dropped her chin.

'Oh, are you broaching the subject tonight?'

'No time like the present.'

Warlow changed and gave Cadi a chew which doubled as a tooth cleaning exercise. Twenty minutes after arriving at the cottage, Jess emerged from the bedroom, still in her work clothes, looking a little flushed, and with her phone held out towards him. 'Molly,' she said.

'She wants to speak to me?' Warlow was genuinely taken aback.

Jess pushed the phone six inches further towards him.

'Molly?' Warlow asked, accepting the handset.

'And about bloody time, if you ask me.'

'I … um …'

'Lost for words, DCI Warlow? That's unlike you.'

Warlow saw the delighted expression of wide-eyed schadenfreude on Jess's face.

'Your mother has spoken to you, then, has she? Told you everything?'

'Oh, she has. Not everything. I mean, there are some things an eighteen-year-old doesn't want to think about when it comes to her ageing mother.'

Warlow laughed.

'But as for the romantic Shepherd's Hut episode,' Molly continued, 'I am fully briefed on that front, and, I have to say, impressed.'

'I'd like to say that there was some planning involved, but …'

'Sounds like someone else was doing the planning.'

'You believe in fate?'

'I believe that you two have wasted enough time.'

Wise words from an eighteen-year-old. But out of the mouths of babes, thought Warlow. He felt emboldened enough by this tacit approval to ask, 'Am I to take it you are okay with all this?'

'You are. Mum likes to think she's coated in Teflon, but she isn't. What Dad did … it really got to her. And when it was just me and her in Cold Blow, there were moments when I wondered if we'd have to give it all up and run somewhere else. But when we moved in with you, she changed.'

'That's the Cadi effect. We both know that.'

Molly laughed. 'Not to be underestimated. But she cheered up. More frustrated, but sunnier. And that's a volatile combo. Plus, you saved her life twice. Once from the cold and once from fire.'

Warlow considered objecting, or at least making a vague *Game of Thrones*, Ice and Fire type joke of it. But nitrogen poisoning and being trapped in a burning lock-up had not been funny when they happened, and nor were they now.

'And,' Molly added theatrically, 'I hear you will no longer be sleeping out in the garden office.'

'Bloody hell, you women.'

'You mean us girls, don't you?'

'Of course, I do. I'd forgotten that I'm the only Y chromosome in the cottage.'

'When I am home next, I expect a celebration.'

'You shall have it,' Warlow said.

'And thanks.'

'For what?'

'For making Mum happy. I can tell. That's all you, DCI Warlow.'

Warlow felt touched. 'Thank you, too, Molly. For being you. Jess was worried.'

'And so she should be. I'm a very sensitive character.'

That deserved a chortle before he said, 'You're eighteen.'

'Thanks for reminding me. And that student bar will not get lit up by my personality on its own. Bye, Evan.'

He stood afterwards, phone in hand, and saw Jess come out of the living room into the kitchen.

'Well?' she asked.

'That'll be Molly, then.'

'Indeed. Lucky for us, you're definitely on her Christmas card list.' Jess smiled and took back the phone.

CHAPTER TWENTY-THREE

Two days after the storm, things were getting back to normal. Power had been restored to those who had lost it. Roads cleared of debris. Wales settled back to await the next climatic assault.

The coffee shop on North Parade in Aberystwyth was a ten-minute walk from Bronglais Hospital. Nico Bajek was not a big coffee drinker. He found out a long time ago that he did not need the stimulation. When he tried it, his pulse sped up so much he thought he'd have a heart attack.

Tea did the job for him. And then only once or twice a day.

Mostly, he stuck to water.

The café had seats inside and out. Except, no one used the outside seating this time of year other than the odd nicotine addict. North Parade had shops, but many that had suffered during the pandemic never reopened. What remained were the charity shops, the banks, and a Tesco Express.

The text Nico received the night before came from an unknown number, but the message had been clear enough. And he knew the name belonged to a supplier.

Hospital guy has a load of Juice. Interested/ 10.45, Domachi's tomorrow morning.

And then there'd been an actual photo.

He'd been in situations like this before. A theft or a consignment would become available and would need to be shifted pdq. He only trusted what he could see for himself, and the texter's name was enough.

He'd come and bought a tea and found a seat while the café filled up with old biddies and mothers with unwieldy prams. But mostly, they took one look at him with his harsh haircut and upper-body shape and steered clear.

Nico whiled away the time, playing with his phone and trying not to let Leah Dobbs get inside his head. Or Leah Thomson as he had known her before she'd hitched her wagon to that waste of space, Greer. She'd been a mess when he first took her out. The kid had been just a few months old, and she'd left that twat Kyle in the dust. He'd tried to get to her more than once, but Nico made sure Greer understood the score. What the hell was she doing with Kyle in the first place? He would never understand. But then, he kind of did. It was a bad boy thing. There was a time when Kyle had been in a band, before the heroin got to him, took over, and turned the idiot into a zombie.

For a while, Nico even thought that Leah might have been the one. But they'd argued. A lot. And Nico didn't mind because he'd grown up in a household where arguing was a way of life. And he had his faults. Too possessive, she said. Too jealous. And then, like some clean-cut nightmare, Marc Dobbs appeared on the scene. In the pub, after games, flirting with her.

Nico tried warning the bastard off, but Marc was no pushover. Nico still remembered the painful night that Leah broke up with him and told him that yes, it was Marc she was seeing. That she was sorry. That she still liked him but didn't love him. If it hadn't been for the club, Nico would probably have done something serious to Marc Dobbs there and then, but he had not. He'd tried to be a man about it.

And now Marc was fucking dead, and the cops were sniffing around, and that was never a good thing. Lots of his mates were on the Juice. Gym users, rugby boys, soccer players. And Nico had a good thing going with the business. Some good PT clients. Steady part-time work for his dad, who knew his son's heart was in the gym, God bless him. And helping out with the Juicers was part of all that.

When the door opened and the man in the photograph he'd been sent walked in, Nico didn't move. He kept sitting while the man, whose name he only had as Leighton, bought a coffee and a cookie the size of a plate. Something, judging from the shape of him, he did far too often. Leighton didn't come across as a Juicer or someone who'd been within a hundred yards of a gym since Year Ten at school.

While he waited for his coffee at the end of a counter, Nico watched Leighton scope the café and his eyes drift over, and then back to the corner he was sitting in.

Still Nico did not move.

Eventually, the coffee came, and Leighton took it to a little counter where he spooned in some sugar and replaced the cap. Only then did he wander over to where Nico was sitting.

'You D?' Leighton asked.

'You Leighton?'

Leighton nodded.

'Juice?' Nico asked.

Leighton frowned. 'What?'

'Juice?' Nico repeated. 'I got a text about Juice.'

'This is coffee,' Leighton said. 'Your text said that you had some boxed Lego Spiderman—'

'Spiderman? Are you ten, or what?'

Leighton's face hardened. 'This is a scam, right? I should have known.' He turned away.

Nico put a hand on his arm. 'Wow, what about the Juice?'

'I don't know what you're talking about. This is a mistake.'

'I got your photo.' Nico showed Leighton the image.

Leighton shook his head. 'I got yours, too.' He swung his head around to scope out who else was in the café. But only the mummies and the shoppers occupied the seats. 'Either someone is winding us up or there are serious crossed wires here.'

'I've come up from bloody Cardigan.'

But Leighton was walking away, head down, and out through the door.

'Bastard,' Nico said, loud enough to draw stares from the tables nearby.

BREAKTHROUGH WOULD PROBABLY BE TOO strong a word for it, but the updated report from Tiernon made for a discussion point worth a quick gathering around the boards just before lunch.

'Rhys, you're our man in the morgue. What do you make of this?' Though there was, of course, a teasing element to the morgue reference, Rhys's genuine interest meant that he would have done his homework. And delegation, as a tool, remained an underused commodity in Warlow's book.

'Heroin and fentanyl? Going for gold was Dobbs,' Jess commented as Rhys handed out the report he'd printed off. They could all have read it in their emails, but this way, they'd all be on the same page for sure. It had been funny the first time Rhys had done it this way and made the identical "same page" joke.

Wisely, Warlow refrained from reiterating it now.

'Peri-venous haematoma?' Gil asked. 'Let's start with that one, Rhys.'

'Right. I spoke to the lab tech. Dr Tiernon was not available.'

'Polishing his instruments, no doubt,' Gil muttered.

No one commented.

'So, remember, there was a big bruise on the inside of Dobb's elbow. The report says that the injection went through the vein. In one side and out the other. Made it bleed.'

'Done by someone inexperienced?' Catrin asked.

'Or if Dobbs was struggling. It would also mean that the

injection was less effective and painful due to whatever it was getting into the tissue around the vein.'

'By whatever it was, you mean the heroin or fentanyl?' Jess asked.

'Heroin, ma'am. The tech said that once they saw fentanyl on the full tox screen, Tiernon revisited the body. The skin in particular. If you turn to halfway down the report, he found two small areas on the chest with traces of an acrylic adhesive. They're still waiting to see if they can work out which kind. But the adhesives and their distribution are consistent with the adhesive used in transdermal patches.'

'Patches?' Gil asked.

'Yes, sarge. We've all heard about fentanyl and how people are supposed to have overdosed from it just by being exposed to the drug, inhaling it even on opening the boot of a car. None of that is true. It has to be taken, injected, or swallowed. Or, as in cases of severe and prolonged pain, given as a slow-release transdermal patch.'

'So, Dobbs was given fentanyl through these patches? Why?'

'It would have made him very likely compliant if the heroin they tried injecting into him failed.'

'Missed the vein. Or went through it. Hence the perivenous haematoma,' Gil muttered.

'Fentanyl patches.' Catrin shook her head. 'I knew about them, but …'

'I know a lot more now, sarge,' Rhys said.

'Oh, no. Not a bloody Ted talk?' Gil winced.

'Fentanyl patches come in two forms. There's the kind where there is a reservoir of drug like in a bubble in the plaster that sticks to the skin. There is also the type where the drug is in a matrix, mixed in as part of the adhesive.'

'Obviously, there's a market for these, too?' Warlow asked.

Rhys nodded. 'Fentanyl is way more powerful than morphine or heroin. We all know that. These patches come in strengths from twelve micrograms up to a hundred micrograms per hour delivery. But used patches have significant residual drug. They can be heated to extract what's left. Some users even try swallowing them.'

'Oh, God,' Catrin groaned.

'But the implication here, in the postmortem report, is that an adhesive patch of some kind was attached.'

'What kind of level was in the blood?' Warlow asked.

'Twenty-nine-point-seven nanogram per ml, sir. That's high.'

'High enough to kill him?'

'Enough to contribute to his death is all Dr Tiernon will say. There's heroin in there, too, plus, there's the environmental factors, sir. The exposure. If we asked him, I think Tiernon would say something like a lethal cocktail.'

Gil looked grim. 'So, they dose the poor bugger up with heroin or try to. But he fights them. Then they stick on fentanyl patches until he's zonked, and then leave him on the side of a bloody mountain completely out of it. What the hell is wrong with these buggers?'

'Perhaps they wanted to make an example. Leave a message for tougher people,' Jess said. 'We saw that a lot in gang killings in Manchester.'

'Organised crime gangs here? It's sickening,' Catrin said.

'One thing's for sure …' Warlow glanced down at the sheet Rhys had printed off. 'There is no escaping the drug angle here. It's in everything we come across. Ketamine, heroin, and now fentanyl.'

'What are you thinking?' Gil asked.

'I'm thinking we need to find these Daher brothers,' Jess answered Gil's question before Warlow could.

'Swansea,' Warlow muttered.

'Greer?' Gil asked.

'It had crossed my mind.'

'Rhys and I could go down there with Dai Vetch.'

'It's a reasonable line of enquiry,' Warlow agreed. 'In the meantime, I want a look at Marc Dobbs's phone records again.'

'I've got those, sir,' Catrin said.

'And there is Nico B,' Jess said. 'Let's not forget him. I suggest a shufti at his phone records might be in order, too.'

'Right.' Warlow rubbed his hands together. 'This is the point at which the swimming pool slides open, and a spaceship takes off. Actions speak louder than words.'

'I knew a Tracy Island once. Lovely girl,' Gil said. 'She was friends with Barry Arif and Mr and Mrs Pelago's son, Archie.'

Everyone groaned except Rhys, who said, 'Pelago is an unusual surname, sarge.'

After a very long beat, Gil said, 'I can see it's going to be a long drive to Swansea.'

CHAPTER TWENTY-FOUR

'Before everyone disappears—' Catrin stood up. '—I have an announcement to make.'

'It's twins, isn't it?' Rhys said. 'I knew it.'

'*It*,' Catrin said, emphasising the one-syllable word, 'is singular. And not twins, thank you, Rhys.'

'My God, man, you're obsessed,' Gil said.

'Stranger things, sarge. Rosemary's—'

A glance that could cut a perfect circle in glass from Warlow ended Rhys's little verbal meanderings.

'Who's Rosemary?' Catrin asked.

'Rhys's cousin,' Gil, on the same wavelength as his DCI, slid in with a saving tackle.

Catrin shrugged. 'As I was saying, and apologies for this being a bolt out of the blue, but Craig's grandfather has had some terrible news. He's terminal. We're not sure how long he has, but it isn't much. Weeks they say.' She paused to suck in some air through her nostrils. 'Anyway, Craig and me, we've been talking about doing something nice for him. Rhys suggested a holiday, but I'm in no state to travel. We decided on the next best thing. I realise it's mad short notice, but a week Friday at 5.30, we're getting married.'

'Bloody hell,' Gil said, but in a Cheshire Cat grin kind of way.

'Oh, Catrin,' Jess said. 'I thought—'

'That we were going to wait until next year, and we probably will have a big bash then. This will be a small affair. Us, and the families, and you lot if you're willing to come. I said to Craig that I'd need to ask you lot, otherwise my name would be mud. I mean, it's stupid short notice, and if none of you can make it, I'd—'

'Lounge suits or tuxedos?' Warlow asked.

Catrin blinked at the question. 'Anything, so long as it's tidy, sir. I realise you all might be busy—'

'You try and keep us away,' Jess said. 'A new posh frock, yes.' A fist pump followed.

'And of course, Rhys, Gina is invited and the Lady Anwen, Gil.'

'Have you told Gina yet?' Rhys asked.

'No … this is fresh off the press now that Craig has sorted it with the registry office. Of course, the main event will be in the pub afterwards. I suspect there will be singing. My lot are terrible for singing but Craig's grandad definitely will …' She teared up.

'Oh, no,' Jess warned her. 'No tears. You'll start me off. Come here.'

The women embraced.

'Right, I'd better get on the blower with Lady A for her to cancel all engagements and to see if she thinks I'll still get into my navy suit.'

Warlow narrowed his eyes.

'Needs taking in,' Gil explained and earned a sceptical exchange of looks between Warlow and Rhys by way of response. But both officers refrained from commenting.

'Gina will be stoked,' Rhys said. 'She loves weddings.'

'Perhaps you can treat this as a run through, then, Rhys.' Warlow opted for exaggerated nonchalance.

'No need, sir. She already has a wedding book. She writes down everything she likes and all the bits she doesn't whenever we go to one. What kind of toilets and how many. That's often top of the list. Time between the cocktails and the speeches. Live band or DJ, I mean, I never knew it could be so complicated.'

'Says he who thinks having a baby was like shelling peas,' Catrin said.

'I never said that sarge,' Rhys objected.

'You might as well have.'

Rhys put his finger in his mouth and moved it sideways quickly so that it made a loud popping noise on emerging.

Gil side-eyed him. 'You are asking for trouble.'

Rhys shrugged. 'It's a fantastic thing to do for Craig's grandad, though.'

'Oh, he'll be chuffed,' Catrin agreed. 'Craig's telling him this evening. We've run it past his parents, and they both broke down. Said it's the nicest thing anyone could think of to do.'

'Right, stop it now, or you'll definitely start me off.' Jess was smiling as she said this.

'And we don't want presents or anything like that. As I say, we'll have a big party next year when we renew our vows. By then, there'll be someone to carry up the aisle.'

'No, Craig will be fine,' Rhys said. 'I'll make sure he doesn't drink too much.'

'That is not even funny, Rhys.'

But the DC's grin belied Catrin's warning.

Jess's mobile chirped a notification, and she excused herself to take the call.

'It isn't a long ceremony in the registry office, is it?' Rhys was stating this as a fact.

'No. Depends on the registrar, though. Some of them like to make it a bit special. Others are as dry as talc.'

'Nice,' Gil said. 'Remember talc? Used to volcano it on under the old jockeys.'

'Something to do with horse racing, sarge? Help them slide around in the saddle.'

'Nothing to do with horse racing, Rhys. But sliding around in the saddle might still apply. Not the done thing anymore, powdering the pomegranates. And after thirty years of it, they tell us it's a cancer risk. *Diwedd y byd.*'

'I'm not sure if there is hard evidence on that,' Catrin said. 'It's more a use as little as possible type thing.'

Jess appeared in the doorway after a visit to the stairwell of secrets, looking very perplexed.

'Whatever it is we had planned – I don't mean a week Friday – I mean today, needs to go back into the to-do pile. That was a sergeant from CID. Uniforms called to a person asleep in a lay-by outside Cardigan. Non rousable. The paramedics pronounced him dead at the scene. They've ID'd him as Leighton Sullivan, twenty-nine years old, an Applications Support tech for the Health Board.'

'RTA?' Rhys asked.

'No suggestion of a collision of any kind. But the paramedics noticed he had two fentanyl patches attached to the skin of his neck.'

'Oh, *merde*,' Gil said. 'Looks like our trip to Swansea is going to be shelved.'

'Agreed. I think we need to get up to Cardigan.' Warlow reached for his coat.

THE LAY-BY WAS A LONG ONE, a good hundred yards off the A487 outside Cardigan on the Aberporth road in open countryside, the entrance about fifty yards after a solitary house close to the road. Uniforms had closed it off. The car, a silver Audi A5, had pulled in and was facing west. Povey's team were already there, but the body had not yet been moved.

Warlow sent Rhys and Gil to talk to the Uniforms and to double-check that they'd already interviewed the owners of the property.

Halfway down the length of the lay-by, a screen had been set up around the Audi. Povey watched them arrive.

'Didn't expect to see you two here. What's the attraction?'

'The attraction is fentanyl.' Warlow explained the post-mortem results that had come back on Marc Dobbs.

'Well, there is no doubt that fentanyl is in play here. Want a sneak peek?'

Povey led them to the car and around the screens. Leighton Sullivan sat in the driver's seat, slumped over.

'Uniforms opened the door when they found him. It wasn't locked.'

'Who called it in?'

'Van driver who's stopped for a pee.'

'Is there a toilet?' Jess looked around, bemused.

'This is used mostly by van drivers. Bushes will do. Anyway, after the pee, the van driver saw that the shape in the Audi was not moving. He investigated and noticed this. Then he called it in.'

'What time?'

'1.47 pm.'

Warlow walked around to the open driver's side door. 'Formal identification to follow, of course, but we've retrieved a wallet with Mr Sullivan's driver's licence and Hospital ID.'

Sullivan had fallen to the side and forward, his shoulder almost touching the steering wheel, his head down, exposing the side of his neck. Two innocuous looking opaque inch square patches were clearly visible. Both had black typed letters spelling the word Fentderm visible with a number.

'They're 100 mg. About the strongest available,' Povey said.

'Two of them?'

'Yes. That's a hefty dose.'

'Enough to kill him?'

'That you'll need to ask the HOP. But I doubt he'd be sticking two patches on to treat his headache.'

'These are prescription drugs, though, right?' Jess asked.

'They are. You can't mock these up in your kitchen.'

Gil and Rhys were hurrying towards them. 'Anything?' Warlow asked.

'The couple in the house are elderly. It's a busy road.

They pay no heed to any comings and goings in the lay-by.' Gil shook his head.

Warlow nodded. He'd expected nothing less.

'What's happening here, sir?' Rhys asked.

Povey answered, 'Awaiting the HOP. Then we'll move the body.'

'He's wearing a Health Board ID. We know he worked at the hospital in Aberystwyth, is that correct?'

'I've checked with Catrin, sir,' Rhys said. 'He worked in Glangwili, too. Maybe they shared systems.'

'Looks like he was coming from Aberystwyth from the way the car is parked, so you two get up there and talk to someone in his department. Find out what you can. CID have already visited his next of kin, have they?'

'Yes.' Jess had been busy on the drive up liaising with CID. 'For now, they're treating the death as suspicious. Not ruling out an OD, nor that it could be deliberate.'

'It happens,' Warlow muttered. 'But you all know my feelings about coincidences. That's two deaths associated with fentanyl in a short space of time. And Marc Dobbs was no bloody suicide. Let's get CID to chase this one up. I want to know where Sullivan was coming from, what he'd been doing, and where he was going. And we'd better tell Dai Vetch. He needs to be kept in the loop on this.'

'I've spoken to him already, sir. He's kindly gone to Swansea to see Greer on our behalf.'

'Okay, we can tick that off, then.' He looked up at the sky. The day was blustery but dry. Blue patches kept appearing between the high clouds. 'Rhys, do you have some walking boots with you?'

'Always, sir. I've learned my lesson.'

Not so long ago, whilst attempting to follow a suspect in one of the many forests on the patch, Rhys, because of inappropriate footwear, had fallen, exposed his position, and triggered the suspect in the process, as well as twisting his ankle badly.

'Right. You come with me. Since the weather is good, I

want to go up to where they found Marc Dobbs. Not all the way across to the lake perhaps, but in the vicinity. The logistics of it are still bothering me. Unless you want to come, Jess?'

'No, had my share of the wilds for this week up in Machynlleth. Gil and I will chase up Sullivan's address. See what we can find there.'

'Good idea. It's not too far from here, ma'am,' Gil said.

They left Povey to it. Warlow saw no point in hanging on for the pathologist. There'd be a postmortem and a full report. Instead, with Rhys riding shotgun, he pointed the Jeep back south and east towards the Black Mountains and the unforgiving landscape that had witnessed death so many times in its long and ancient history.

CHAPTER TWENTY-FIVE

Sullivan rented a property in Carmarthen. CID had dealt with getting in touch with relatives: two sets of separated parents in Gloucestershire and an estranged brother.

The first-floor flat was in a semi-detached property on Mervyn Terrace that had cars parked half on and half off the pavement. There were no double yellow lines, but a sensible approach from occupants who realised that on-road parking would block the road.

Gil put the job Ford halfway along the street. Catrin had done an online search and found out that the flat had been rented for about three years with no change of occupant. She'd also rung the Property Management company – conveniently located in town – and an anxious-looking girl, who appeared young enough to be a school-leaver, hovered at the door dressed in a puffer jacket.

There were two keys on the keyring. One for the front door and one for the door at the top of the stairs leading up from the hallway. A second door guarded the entrance to the downstairs flat. It turned the hallway into an ugly boxed in space with scuffed walls, sticky vinyl flooring, and a bundle of unwanted correspondence piled up in one corner. Several pairs of galoshes of varying sizes were lined up against the wall. It looked like the downstairs occupants had a couple of kids.

Gil led the way up to Sullivan's flat after thanking and effectively dismissing the management company office worker who'd delivered the key with the promise that he would return it. The girl, a contender for miserable office worker of the year, shrugged and left without speaking.

Inside the flat, there was one bedroom, one bathroom, and a living room divided by a half wall, which functioned as a hatchway into the kitchen.

The living room had all the usual gadgetry Gil expected to find in similar, single-male occupant accommodation. An LG TV, twice as big as it needed to be, sat in the corner, facing a solitary gaming chair. On the side table on both sides of the chair, controllers and remotes, some with wires running into a variety of boxes under the TV, lay where they had been left. Behind the TV was a modem, its Wi-Fi logo glowing in front of a blue LED. The curtains were drawn, filtering out the daylight, but thin enough to allow a degree of visibility.

'Right,' Jess said, snapping on her nitrile gloves. 'I'll do the kitchen and bathroom; you do the living room and bedroom.'

The usual you'll-know-it-when-you-find-it approach to searches was tempered this time by both officers looking for some evidence of drug usage. They'd bring in sniffer dogs, but at this stage, any evidence would be of value.

A few retro video games allied to an old Nintendo box and kept apart from the main black boxes were the only physical evidence of gameplay. But Gil knew you did not need to buy the physical manifestation of any games these days. Most serious players simply downloaded and logged on. The nerds back at HQ would comb through all of that.

But, on the cabinet on the rear wall, he found some files which, judging by their dry-as-dust content with headings like "Network Data Operations and Duplication Strategies" and "ICT Infrastructure Development Plan Audit" showed that Sullivan must have taken some of his work home with him.

The bedroom was sparse. The wardrobe could roughly be divided into work clothes: several pairs of flexi-waist Farah's in various shades and shirts from M&S, and leisure: Farah jeans and Matalan shirts and layers. His bedside reading comprised Brandon Sanderson, Pratchett, and hard sci-fi from authors like Andy Weir and Neal Stephenson. The one surprising element was a second bookshelf containing no books. Instead, there were boxed figures: Marvel, DC, and Lego interpretations of the same. So, Leighton was a collector, too. His laundry basket was full, bedsheets, used but clean. All in all, a single-male bachelor residence. Here again, Gil found no evidence of any drug taking. No telltale powder in the bathroom, no stub ends in an ashtray. No odd-looking glass tubing or matches.

When he re-entered the living room, Jess stood there, eyebrows raised. 'Anything?'

'Bugger all,' Gil said. 'Lives alone. No sign of anyone sharing. More importantly, no sign of any suspicious substances.'

'Agreed. If he was a drug taker, he took them somewhere else.'

'I'll check to see if he has a locker or some such at his work.'

Jess mumbled a confirmatory, 'Mmm,' that sounded doubtful. 'I could double-check the kitchen drawers.'

'You do that, ma'am. I'll give his supervisor a ring if I can find one.'

Gil stood in the living room and rang Catrin, who, with access to a PC, soon came up with a couple of names. At the second attempt, he got through to a Digital Services team supervisor. Gil explained who he was, and that he was ringing regarding one of her colleagues.

'Leighton, yes, course I know him. Has anything happened? He was coming here this afternoon after a morning in Bronglais.'

'You're in Glangwili, in Carmarthen, now?'

'Yes.'

'Does Leighton have an office there?'

She laughed. 'He has a desk in an office.'

'Okay. Will you be there for the next couple of hours?'

'I will.'

He ended the call and joined Jess in the kitchen. 'Anything?'

'No,' Jess said. 'Though he only has one set of matching cutlery in among half a dozen sets of knives, forks, and spoons.'

'A collector, then,' Gil said. 'I played rugby with a man who collected a spoon from every away game club for ten seasons. No idea why.'

'I'm surprised you lot didn't give him a nickname.'

'We did, but we forgot what it was because the ladle fell off.'

Jess let out a resigned sigh. 'I should have known better.'

'I've arranged to meet with one of Sullivan's supervisors at Glangwili, ma'am. I can drop you off at HQ and get along there.'

'I suppose we might as well. There's nothing much to see here. But, as DCI Warlow always says, finding nothing is sometimes just as important as finding something.'

'Amen to that. Lucky we have Catrin at HQ to do the donkey work.'

'We are going to miss that woman,' Jess said.

Gil didn't argue. 'Any thoughts about a replacement while she's off, ma'am?'

'No, not yet. Any ideas?'

'Well above my pay grade.'

'Probably mine too. I expect Evan will have some thoughts.'

'No doubt he will. Question is, do we have another sergeant or let Rhys act up? He's good.'

'At acting up, you mean?'

Gil grinned. 'I left the door open for you there, ma'am.'

'He's still a bit green, although he is up for his exams.'

'He's competent as a DC, no doubt about that. Keen too. He's taking the written exam in March.'

'Well, it won't be up to us.'

'So long as it isn't up to Superintendent Goodey,' Gil said with feeling. 'Who knows who or what we'd get.'

'I'll speak to Evan to make sure he puts an oar in.'

The Digital Services team supervisor turned out to be an Irish woman who pronounced her name Neave but spelled it with an amh, the Gaeilge way.

'You have me worried, sergeant,' Niamh Monaghan said. They sat in a prefab set of buildings to the north and east of the main hospital block, beyond the car parks.

'This is part of a very serious investigation, and I am not at liberty to give you any details.'

'Oh, dear.'

'Mr Sullivan has been involved in a serious incident.'

Niamh's eyes widened in alarm. 'That doesn't sound good.' She took a moment to catch her breath. Mid-thirties, pale-skinned, auburn hair. She had a heart-shaped face and small features, which at the moment were frozen in horror. 'But… I spoke to him this morning when he was in Aberystwyth.'

'At what time?'

'Half ten. He said he'd be leaving at eleven to get here around lunchtime. We had an information governance and data protection committee meeting at two.'

Gil glanced at his watch. Three pm was rapidly approaching. 'So, as far as you were aware, Leighton was on his way here from Aber?'

Niamh nodded. 'But he didn't turn up.'

'What did he do here, exactly?'

'What we all do. We're the point of contact for equipment and networks.'

'Is that what he did? Go out and fix computers?'

Niamh let out a thin laugh. 'No. Not anymore. He'd been with us for a good five years. His role now was more one of managing information governance and services.'

'What does that mean, exactly?' Gil was already struggling with the terminology.

'Okay. We, that is, Digital Services, look after all aspects of information and communication technology. Hardware and software, systems like reporting services, health records, health analytics, you name it. But Leighton's role had veered towards governance, making sure that data was protected properly, monitoring access, and that kind of thing.'

'Can I ask if that involved any pharmaceutical links?'

'That's an odd question.'

'Nevertheless.'

Niamh shrugged. 'Only in terms of how pharmacy links in with all the other complex systems.'

'But he would have no physical link to the pharmacy as such?'

'No, of course not.' Niamh looked genuinely puzzled.

'And you said he had a desk? How about a locker?'

'No lockers. None of us have lockers. You come to work and hang your coat up, log on, and get on with it.'

'What about his desk?'

'It's a shared desk. Next door…'

Niamh took Gil into the room next door. Four PCs on two long tables in pale wood. One other person, a man, sat in the room.

'Kerry, can you give us a minute?'

Kerry, frizzy of hair and about the same age as the miserable management company girl from earlier, got up and left.

Gil sat at the desk Niamh pointed to. An unlocked drawer beneath slid out. It contained some thumb drives, papers, the odd pen, and some brochures. Gil asked for some Sellotape, shut the drawer, and taped it up. 'We'll need to look at this more closely. In the meantime, I'd ask that no one uses this desk or the PC.'

Niamh said, 'Okay.'

They went back into her office. Gil was apologetic. 'I'm sorry about all the secrecy, but this is a delicate situation.'

'Can't you tell me anything?'

'I can tell you that Leighton is not coming back to work, Niamh. You should prepare yourself for the worst.'

She went very pale in the blink of a long-lashed eye. 'Oh, my God. He isn't…'

'Until otherwise informed, I would ask that you keep all of this to yourself.'

'I …' The saliva she tried to swallow got stuck in her throat, and she needed two attempts at getting it down her pharynx. 'Yes, of course. Oh, God, poor Leighton.'

'Someone will be along to look at the desk and the PC. We may need to remove it. But in the meantime, it's out of bounds.'

'I'll unplug it and put a notice up.'

'I'd appreciate that. Talk to me about Leighton? What kind of bloke was he?'

'He knew his stuff. Of course, what he wanted to do was to be designing games. But then, that's what a lot of programmers want to do. I think he might have been a little frustrated. He was quiet. A bit of a gamer.'

'Partner?'

'No, not that I knew of.'

'Interests?'

'Gaming, I'd say. But you'd need to talk to some of the others.'

'We will.'

Gil thanked her and left not much the wiser when it came to Leighton Sullivan. If there truly was a link between him and Marc Dobbs, it was, as yet, proving to be a very elusive one.

CHAPTER TWENTY-SIX

WHILE JESS and Gil searched Sullivan's flat, Warlow and Rhys stood at the edge of the lake at Llyn y Fan Fach. Though it had turned out to be a better day than when Storm Frida unleashed its wrath, it was still November. And they were now well and truly in the Beacons, the Black Mountains of lore.

Ahead, to the south and surrounding them in a one-hundred-and-eighty-degree arc, loomed the gigantic horseshoe that made up the escarpment of *Bannau Sir Gar*. A collection of Fans or peaks that made this spot a natural amphitheatre carved out by an ice-age glacier. Behind them stood the bothy, a small stone hut as a shelter for walkers caught out by the fickle weather. It sat at the top of the path they'd taken from the car park below along a steep gravel track, doubling as a service road. To their right, the westernmost edge of the horseshoe led to a steep ridge walk up to *Waun Llefrith* – milky moor – and then on to the prominent ridge of *Bannau Sir Gar* and around over towards the second lake, Llyn y Fan Fawr. Where Marc Dobbs and his brother were found.

In fact, they now stood on almost the same spot Emyr Dobbs had stood the day he collected his car and had climbed, like the two officers had, to revisit this place. On the way up, Warlow and Rhys passed only a handful of people coming back down, but with the afternoon now passing, no one else had ventured out with the amount of daylight that was left in the day. Like Emyr Dobbs, though, both men stared about, captured by the majestic awe this place always evoked.

'Reckon they drove him up here, sir?' Rhys broke the silence. 'Marc Dobbs's kidnappers?'

'More than likely,' Warlow said. 'Otherwise, how the hell would he get up here?'

Rhys ran with this train of thought. 'So, they drove up, chucked him out with his phone, drove off, and left him to his fate.'

'Half cut from drugs,' Warlow added, anger cracking his voice. 'I can't come up with any other explanation.' He glanced at his watch. Two hours of daylight left, if they were lucky. Above, the clouds were high enough, but to the west, a darker front looked to be moving in. Ominous, heavy grey nimbostratus made the prospect of more rain a sure bet.

Though he could never be certain, Warlow concluded that Dobbs, in his disorientated state, would have looked around and seen what he was now seeing. He would not have wanted to climb up. More than likely, he would head along the path of least resistance. And, if not south, then east, over the moorland, towards the second lake. Warlow pointed in that direction.

'Let's see how hard the walking is.'

'My map takes us right under the base of the escarpments, sir.'

'I know, but there is a way across the moor. I've walked it with Cadi. It's flatter.'

And it was. A mile and a half over a soggy path dotted with puddles and those massive hills, their constant companion, on their right.

'I know they call these *Bannau Sir Gar*,' Rhys said. 'But they have other names, too, sir, don't they?'

Warlow glanced across. 'The plateau on the ridge of *Picws*

Du, black peak, leads on to *Fan Foel*, bald peak, and then *Fan Brycheiniog*.'

'*Brycheiniog*. That's the old word for Breconshire? Brecknock?'

'It's older than that,' Warlow said. 'It's Brychan's Kingdom. Fifth century. Maybe an adaptation of Broccan because he was probably Irish originally.'

'Came over on the ferry, then, did he, sir?'

'Or a faery,' Warlow quipped. 'You know what they say about these lakes.'

On their left, the distant Cambrian Hills rolled dark and mysterious, and in between, miles of open moorland peppered with treacherous shake holes and outcrops of rock. They crossed a stream several times over stone slabs, avoiding the trail at the very base of the mountains to a path that led north again to the second lake. There, Warlow called a halt and turned to Rhys.

'Impressions?'

'Not easy, sir. Worse in the dark. But doable.'

'He'd use his phone torch, perhaps. But that would only light up a few feet ahead. He'd get soaked just from walking, wouldn't he?'

Rhys looked at his damp boots. 'Definitely, sir. The weather was atrocious that night.' He looked up again at the surrounding emptiness. 'Difficult to imagine being up here alone in the dark. Not that there is anywhere that's good to die, but this … it must have been awful. No light anywhere. Nothing but the wind and the rain.'

'Indeed.' Warlow jumped over a large peaty puddle. 'By day, there's solitude, big sky, and tranquillity. At night, desolation, impenetrable darkness, and howling winds.'

A fresh gust from the west reminded both men of the danger of tarrying. 'Right, come on,' Warlow said. 'Back to the car. The only way we'll know the truth is by talking to the Dahers. Let's hope Vetch has some news for us on that.'

VESPERS.

Rhys made tea; Gil broke out the Human Tissue For Transplant box. But they were the only positives of the afternoon. Warlow gave them the rundown of the Beacons terrain and where he suspected Marc Dobbs had got lost.

'I still don't understand why the kidnappers went to all that trouble,' Jess said. 'I mean, why take him halfway up a mountain? Why not a street corner?'

'It would guarantee them time to get away,' Warlow said. 'There is a farm on the road leading to where people park up there. Rhys and I called in on our way back. The farmer denies seeing anything unusual that day. But then, I suspect he ignores most of everything that goes on. He was more concerned about making sure people with dogs kept them leashed because of roaming sheep.'

'Nothing much to report on Sullivan's property, either,' Gil said. He explained his and Jess's impression of a bachelor loner. 'Computer games and a collection of action figures were all we could find. We'll need to wait and see what Povey's team turns up.'

'No sign of anything drug related, I take it?' Warlow asked.

'Nothing,' Gil confirmed.

Vetch had similar disappointing news. 'I tracked Greer down to his squat. He was compliant and denied any knowledge of the Dahers.'

'You believe him?' Gil asked.

'No, but then I don't disbelieve him either. The guy barely knows what day it is. One thing is for certain: he isn't capable of kidnapping or extortion. That's not to say he might be in cahoots with someone, but I doubt it. I mentioned his daughter, and his reaction was … interesting might be the right word. He did a double take. As if he'd forgotten all about the fact that he even had one. When I reminded him, though, he became animated, calling his ex all kinds of names.'

'So, even though he strikes you as incapable, he still has a lot of animus towards her?' Warlow asked.

'He does.'

'Is it possible he paid someone else to do it?' Jess asked.

'Paid might not be the right word. Traded, possibly. Drugs are the currency. I'm not ruling anything out, but I think it's unlikely.'

Warlow let out a prolonged sigh. 'And still nothing on the Dahers' likely whereabouts?'

'They're still keeping a very low profile,' was all Vetch had to say on the matter. 'Makes me think they've been alerted to the mess they caused.'

'There is one thought I've had, sir,' Rhys said. 'The fentanyl patches. They're medical. Povey told us they had the drug logo stamped on them.' He glanced down at his notebook. 'Fentderm. Is there any way we could trace that?'

Vetch had an answer of sorts. 'I've seen patches like that, too. One of the commoner brands. Made by Seine Poulenc. Unfortunately, the packaging has a batch number, but the patch itself does not. But I can dig into the database to check for any reported thefts of Fentderm anywhere else in the country.'

'Nothing local?' Warlow asked.

'Nothing that springs to mind. As I say, I'll make some calls as well, but pharmacy or hospital break-ins and the like are immediately flagged up.'

'Of course, there is the faint possibility that these things are unrelated,' Catrin said.

'There is. But that would be my last choice on the options menu,' Warlow said. 'In the meantime, we need to allocate some time and resource to Sullivan. Gil, did you say one of his supervisors told you he left work in Aberystwyth to attend a meeting in Carmarthen?'

'She spoke to him before he left. And we have the time for that call, which was around half ten. Said he'd leave before eleven.'

'There's CCTV in the hospital. Let's get a confirmation of that and then see if we can trace his movements until he was found in that lay-by. What time did the call come in?'

Once again, Rhys consulted his notebook. 'Quarter to two, sir.'

'There are three-and-a-bit hours unaccounted for.' Warlow reached for the bit of stubble he always seemed to miss on shaving, found it, and rubbed it. 'It's what, forty-five minutes from the hospital in Aber to the lay-by?'

'Something like that,' Gil confirmed.

'Okay, say he left at eleven. He would not have got to the lay-by until eleven forty-five. Let's say midday. I doubt he had the patches on while driving. So, lay-by, patches, and…'

'Robert is your sister's brother, sir,' Rhys muttered.

'CID are accessing the hospital system as we speak, sir,' Catrin said.

'I see no point in anyone traipsing up to Cardiff for the postmortem. No signs of violence at the scene. It isn't Tiernon, it's Sengupta. If she finds something, she'll let us know. But the toxicology report won't be immediate. Rhys, can I leave you to liaise?'

'Certainly, sir.' Rhys nodded with an alarmingly enthusiastic smile.

'I hate drugs-related cases,' Gil said. 'Brings out the worst in people.'

Warlow hung on until they got a call from the CCTV coordinator. CID had gone through tapes. She'd found the relevant bit for Sullivan and sent it over. The team clustered around Catrin's desk to watch as, at 10.39, Sullivan walked out to his car and got in. He did so quickly, like someone in a hurry.'

'He's keen to get going,' Gil said.

'But his meeting in Carmarthen wasn't until much later,' Warlow said.

'So, you think he might have been going somewhere in between?' Jess added. More a statement than a question.

Warlow stood back. 'A timeline. Let's let the CCTV coordinator do her thing. Hopefully, by tomorrow we'll find some answers.'

'Let's hope we don't have any more bodies,' Gil muttered.

CHAPTER TWENTY-SEVEN

Ffau'r Blaidd had, almost overnight, become a very different kind of place for Warlow. All the small things that he'd been wanting to do, but never had a mandate until the visit to Machynlleth and a Shepherd's Hut, now seemed to happen spontaneously. If he made a cup of tea and included Jess without asking, she smiled and thanked him with a kiss on the cheek, or a squeeze of his arm.

He enjoyed her touch.

They watched TV together, her feet up on his lap, on the sofa. And he was still getting used to having a living, breathing human being in the bed with him while he slept. Waking up to feel a sleek smooth arm or leg draped over his body in the small hours in the morning left him surprised. Partly because of its strangeness and partly because it had been so long since that intimate physical contact. Now that it was back, he was shocked to find how much he'd missed that.

And even though laughter had been a feature of the Allanbys' presence since they moved in, now, he felt free to poke fun at himself and occasionally at Jess, though her foibles were few, but in a different way.

The wonderful thing about it was that she would laugh along, too.

Over coffee, next morning, Jess threw out a suggestion.

'This thing of Denise's, this Fern. Want me to mention it to Molly?'

'Why?'

'Because she is another brain to use, plus she thinks differently from you and me. She uses word clouds for essay ideas. In fact, she has an app that churns out synonyms and antonyms and links that we might not think of.'

Warlow was poised to object, but what little thought he'd given Denise's puzzle since the start of the Dobbs's case had yielded nothing helpful. Fresh, young input would do no harm.

'Fine. Run it past her. Let's see what she comes up with.'

They left for work in separate cars.

'In case Gwyn the farmer is watching?' Jess teased. But it made some sense because the job would undoubtedly require further field visits in separate vehicles. Plus, there was no point adding fuel to the already roaring gossip fire.

'Has someone actually said something?' Warlow asked in response to Jess throwing out this little remark.

'They've been whispering ever since Molly and I moved in.'

'Not to my face, they haven't.'

'No surprise there. Most people in HQ are terrified of you.'

'Me? What did I do?'

'Not suffer fools in any shape or form, let alone gladly.'

'That won't fit on a T-shirt, unfortunately.'

'Doesn't need to. Runs through you like Blackpool through a stick of rock.' She smiled sweetly, left a bright red rosebud of lipstick on his cheek, and drove off with a cheerful wave.

'Cadi, *fach*,' Warlow said as he let her into the back of the Jeep. 'What have I let myself in for?' The dog wagged her tail and tilted her head. Warlow smiled. 'Yeah, I know. Outnumbered now by the X chromosomes. Lucky bugger that I am.'

Povey's report on Sullivan's car was sparse. No evidence of any violence. Fingerprints of the dead man only. They were going to attack his Carmarthen flat that morning.

Warlow played the waiting game badly.

Which meant the team played that game too and knew better than to disturb him. He spent most of the morning writing up reports, knowing that this was dead time until something came up. The ship was becalmed, awaiting a fresh wind of change to kick-start progress.

Around eleven, Rhys stuck his head around the SIO office door.

'Prelim report on Sullivan from the HOP, sir. I've just come off the phone.'

'Good. Elevenses are called for. Let Gil break out the baked goods as well.'

But Rhys's report from Sengupta contained nothing much of use. 'They've done postmortem urine tests, and that's positive for fentanyl, sir. Nothing else.'

Once again, they were forced to wait for a full toxicology report.

Half an hour later, Warlow sat in Sion Buchannan's office. It did not take long to explain to Sion what they did and didn't know.

'Usual story. Awaiting forensics.'

'But fentanyl?' Buchannan, long in both limb and tooth, sat in his office because standing made the place look like something from Alice in Wonderland after she'd drunk from that bottle.

'Based on what we've seen so far, I'm convinced that these cases are linked.'

'Fentanyl?' Buchannan repeated the word and made it sound like something under his shoe. Warlow got the impression he was hoping he'd misheard.

'Not just fentanyl, but fentanyl patches and overdosing, if Sengupta confirms it, and I'm willing to bet she will. But it's a spread-out investigation.'

'CID are helping?'

'They are.'

'Dobbs's widow? Is she involved?'

'Not ruling it out. I'm going to catch up today. Sullivan's death bowled us a googly.'

'I dislike the idea of fentanyl flooding the patch.' Buchannan baulked at what he'd said. 'No pun intended.' He adopted a stern look.

'Join the club. But the fact is it's here.'

Buchannan nodded pensively. 'If you need any help, just shout.'

GINA TOOK Rhys's call out in the garden for the sake of privacy.

Sometimes, his calls were private. Other times, they were all business. Usually, they were a combination of the two.

'The Wolf asked me to give you a ring,' Rhys explained. 'He says he's going to call round in the next day or two to speak with Leah directly. Bring her up to speed on what progress we're making.'

'What progress are you making?'

'Yeah, well, that's the point. Not much.'

Gina sighed. 'She's going to ask me. I can tell. And Emyr, Marc's brother, is here because he's on a late shift. He's worse than she is.'

'Okay, well, I don't suppose it will do any harm to tell her that we're still trying to find the Dahers. She was asked at the interview if she knew them, so that will come as no surprise. And we've been in contact with her ex, uh … Greer. DS Vetch paid him a visit and we don't think he's directly involved.'

Gina paused a few feet away from the shed that had contained the incriminating ketamine. 'By directly involved, you mean you don't think he was one of the kidnappers?'

'Vetch says he's incapable. What we don't know yet is if there's any link between him and the Dahers.'

'That's where you're concentrating efforts?'

'Yes, though it might be wise to tell her about Sullivan because that will be on the news today.'

'Tell her what, exactly?'

'I talked to DI Allanby about that. It's all a bit messy, but the postmortem has confirmed that he had fentanyl in his system, and the DCI doesn't like coincidences.'

'Okay. Should I try to find out if there's any link between her and Sullivan?'

'No harm in trying. DI Allanby also thinks she ought to be aware that Marc Dobbs had fentanyl in his blood.'

'Oh, God. That will not go down well.'

'How is she?'

'Still ragged. The little girl is a cutie. She's gone off to school and then to her grandmother. She brings her back after tea.'

'Right, talking of tea. What are we doing for tonight?'

'You mean supper?'

'I mean food.'

Gina laughed. 'Pasta? I made double the amount of ragu the other week and didn't tell you, because you'd have eaten the lot.'

'Wow, that was epic. We're out of Parmesan, though. I can call in for some on the way home.'

'Great, I'll make a list of other stuff we need. I'll be home after six tonight.'

'Okay. I'll get the pasta on and find some Iglesias on Spotify.'

'Nah, Lizzo'll be fine.'

WHEN GINA GOT BACK into the house, both Emyr and Leah Dobbs were sitting over cups of tea.

'DCI Warlow says he'll be calling to see you,' Gina said.

'When?'

'That I can't say. But he wanted me to tell you about

something that's happened in the investigation and wanted you to hear it first from us before you heard it on the news. A man was found yesterday in a lay-by. We suspect he died from a fentanyl overdose.'

'Fentanyl?' Emyr Dobbs frowned.

'I don't know what fentanyl really is?' Leah said.

'It's an opioid. Like morphine or heroin. Only much stronger,' Emyr explained.

Gina sat on the chair opposite the two Dobbs. 'The reason I mention this other case is that we think there may be a link. The toxicology report on Marc showed that he had some drugs in his system.'

'Ketamine?' Leah asked, her lip already wobbling.

'No. Fentanyl,' Gina said.

'What?' Emyr spat out the word.

'The current thinking is that it's possible the kidnappers used it to subdue Marc.'

'Oh, my God.' Leah's words were whispers of horror.

Gina waited. She had to ask them directly. 'I have to ask you this. Does the name Leighton Sullivan mean anything to you? Either of you?'

'Sullivan?' Emyr repeated the name. 'Means nothing to me.'

'No. Nor me…' Leah muttered incoherently.

'Is that the name of the guy they found dead?' Emyr asked.

Gina nodded.

'You think he knew Marc?'

Gina reached over the table and took Leah's fluttering hand. 'We don't know, Leah. Investigations like this are always complex. Finding someone else dead and using fentanyl … it's not what we expected.'

'What about the people you were looking for? The Dohers?' Emyr asked.

'Dahers,' Gina corrected him. 'We're still looking.'

'I don't understand,' Leah said. 'What has this Sullivan got to do with what happened to Marc?'

'That's a very good question, Leah. And I don't have any answers. But you should definitely ask DCI Warlow when he comes to see you.'

Leah, a lost expression on her face, looked up at Gina. 'Last week, we were talking about how old Becs had to be before we took her to Disneyland.' She sniffed and smiled at the recollection. 'That's all we were worried about. Wondering how old she'd need to be to enjoy it properly.' The whole of the lower part of her face trembled as she spoke. 'Drug addicts don't talk about Disneyland, do they?'

She posed the question and waited for Gina to answer. But the FLO couldn't find anything to say.

Emyr watched the exchange, a strange look on his face. 'That's the trouble, though, right? You can't tell, can you? Maybe not a user, but perhaps he was looking to pay for the trip by buying and selling. As a bit of import export.'

'What?' Leah said, horrified.

'The more I hear about this, the more I'm wondering if Marc was tied up with something bad.'

'How can you say that about your own brother?'

Emyr's chair scraped across the floor as he stood up in one abrupt movement. He turned to the door and thumped his fist against it. Then he yanked the door open and strode out. They heard his footsteps on the stairs.

Leah watched him go, her expression distorted in misery. 'You don't think Marc was a drug dealer, do you, Gina?'

'I'm paid to wait until I have all the evidence, Leah.' It was a cop-out answer, and it rankled. But it was what Leah needed to hear.

'Your tea's gone cold,' Gina said, glancing at the cup, still three-quarters full. 'If in doubt, make another one. That's what we're trained to do. That okay?'

Leah's head was down, but she nodded in reply. Gina let go of her hand and turned to the sink to fill the kettle, blinking rapidly to stop her own tears from running down her face.

CHAPTER TWENTY-EIGHT

At HQ, Catrin was the next to flag up some results. Jess texted Warlow:

Phone records for Marc Dobbs.

The team stood clustered around the boards when Warlow, his eyes scratchy from staring at his monitor screen for too long, emerged from the SIO room. Everyone looked happy to be standing, and if his own twinging back was anything to go by, welcoming the opportunity to remove bum from seat for a while.

Catrin held court with a sheaf of printed out A4 sheets in her hand.

'Another negative, I'm afraid. Spent the last two hours with Gil re-checking numbers Dobbs used. They're all either work related, something to do with football, or Leah.'

Jess, arms folded over her chest, spoke for everyone when she said, 'I suppose it's to be expected. I mean, if he was ducking and diving, he'd use a burner.'

'We've not come across one, I suppose?' Warlow, ever hopeful, dangled the carrot. In response, he got head shakes all around.

'We've even checked his bank records for any dubious purchases in garages, online, nothing that suggests he might have bought a mobile,' Gil said.

'You're forgetting cash,' Jess pointed out.

'If he did, we are whistling into the wind,' Rhys said.

Gil cocked an eyebrow. 'Ah, whistling. A declining art. My dad used to whistle all the time.'

'Old songs, sarge?'

'No, he just liked to drink boiling water.'

Catrin suppressed the giggle that threatened, but her sigh emerged through a half smile.

'What about the ketamine?' Warlow asked.

This time, Gil answered. 'DS Vetch has been nosing around but hasn't come up with any credible links between known suppliers and Dobbs. Not yet anyway.'

A crease of discomfort flashed over Catrin's face, and she put a hand into the small of her back. Rhys caught it and swung a chair out from under his desk towards her. 'Do you want to sit, sarge?'

Catrin, never one to show any signs of weakness, sent him one of her signature half-lidded looks. An expression that usually presaged a disparaging comment. But this time, she said, 'Don't mind if I do, Constable Harries. All this weight training is no fun for the lumbar vertebrae.'

When a frustrated Warlow drifted back to the SIO office, he found a new email waiting for him. The heading read:

Compilation CCTV for Sullivan after leaving hospital.

The message read:

zip file in secure Dropbox labelled cell_surveillance.

Warlow immediately forwarded it to Rhys and then added a follow up text:

Set this up on your machine.

Five minutes later, the team once again stood, this time clustered around Rhys's desk monitor. All except Catrin, who remained seated and was orchestrating the showing. Rhys stood behind everyone else, tall enough to have an unobstructed view.

'Okay, so that's him walking to his car in the hospital car

park at 10.39. He drives out and is next picked up on Queen Street where he parks.'

'Does he pay?'

'No, it's free parking for an hour. Then he's seen walking along North Road and, I'm following the written timeline, he goes to a coffee shop. Uh, Domachi's.'

The scene jumped to a camera inside the shop. They all watched as Sullivan went to the counter and ordered a coffee and a large cookie. He looked around and then walked across to a table where another man was sitting. They began talking, faces serious.

Of course, there was no sound. But that didn't matter because everyone watching had held their breath.

'Is that—' Rhys began.

'Nico Bajek. Yes, it is.' Catrin brought up a photograph. She'd frozen the CCTV image. There was no doubt that the images were one and the same person.

'Keep running the tape,' Warlow said.

They observed as the conversation ended. Watched as Sullivan looked around and became obviously anxious and shrugged off Nico Bajek's restraining arm before leaving in a hurry. The tape ran on, Catrin scanning the text and commenting, 'We have Sullivan going back to his car and then nothing until the body-cam footage of the Uniforms approaching him in the lay-by.'

'Well, well,' Gil muttered. 'The plop thickens as my daughter once famously said.'

'Obviously, runs in the family,' Catrin murmured.

'She said that when she was part of an all-girl singing group run by the Chapel. Called themselves the Cisterns of Mercy.' Gil's grin was a cheesy one.

'Molly said they have vegetarian loos at uni.' Jess kept her face straight.

'Really, ma'am?' Rhys asked.

'Yes, they use treated beetroot and lettuce leaves instead of paper.'

'Wow,' Rhys said.

Then Jess put him out of his misery. 'And that's just the tip of the iceberg.'

Warlow could only shake his head. 'Et tu. DI Allanby?'

'If you can't beat them…'

'Should we get Nico in for questioning, sir?' Rhys said.

'I thought you'd never ask,' Warlow muttered.

NICO CAME TOOLED up with a solicitor. Someone Warlow and the team had not seen before from a firm with offices in Cardiff and Swansea. The guy had a winter tan and gelled hair.

Gil and Jess had the honours. Gil, like Baloo the bear; big and friendly. The only thing missing was a prickly pear.

Gil cautioned him, and Nico announced his presence, as did the solicitor.

'Jeremy Roebuck,' the solicitor said.

'Thanks for coming in, Mr Bajek,' Jess began. 'Just a couple of general questions before we start. You are a part-time personal trainer, is that correct?'

'Yeah,' Bajek said.

'And, being part-time, do you do anything else?'

'Help in the family business.'

'Which is?' Gil asked, all smiles.

'My dad's got a plumbing business.'

'Oh, so you're a plumber?' Gil asked.

'No. Tried and hated it. My dad has six plumbers working for him, plus mates. I'm more on the admin side.'

Gil nodded and sifted through some papers. 'Ordering, logistics, debt collection, that sort of thing.'

Nico's expression did not change from neutral.

'So, when you aren't in the gym, you get about?' Jess asked.

Nico narrowed his eyes and looked across at his solicitor, who sighed and turned to the officers. 'Mr Bajek is here voluntarily. He is a busy man. We'd both appreciate it if you got to the nub of what this is about.'

'Nub, is it?' Gil said. 'Very well, though we tend not to term the unnatural death of someone a nub. Disrespectful.'

Roebuck sighed again.

Jess continued the interrogation. 'We're aware of the fact that you visited Mrs Dobbs after her husband died, Mr Bajek.'

'I did. I wanted to do it for myself and for the team. Marc and I didn't always see eye to eye, but that doesn't change how the team felt.'

'When you say eye to eye, what exactly do you mean?'

For the first time, Bajek smiled. 'Common knowledge that Leah and I were an item. That broke apart. She ended up with Marc. I had trouble dealing with that to start with. But I am over it now.'

Jess smiled. 'Are you in a relationship now, Mr Bajek?'

'Nothing serious, if that's what you mean.'

Gil took a sip of water and shifted another sheet of paper. 'Visiting Mrs Dobbs to express your condolences must have been hard.'

'Not easy. But I have responsibilities.'

'When you say Marc and you did not always see eye to eye, did that ever end up in violence?'

'You know it didn't,' Bajek said. 'I was pissed off. We argued. Nothing came of it. It's years ago, now.'

'Indeed.' Jess sat forward. 'But did you ever come to terms with what happened? What Marc Dobbs did?'

'What did he do?'

'Some people have said he stole Leah from you.'

Bajek's eyebrows went up. 'Some would say that. But I'd ask Leah before you go around making remarks like that.'

'We will,' Jess said.

'Is that it?' Roebuck asked.

'Almost. Yesterday, a man was found dead in a lay-by in Cardigan after a fentanyl overdose.'

'What?' Roebuck squeezed his eyes shut and shook his head at the same time.

'A Leighton Sullivan. Does that name mean anything to you?'

'No,' Bajek said.

'Where were you at 10.55 yesterday morning?'

Crinkles appeared on Bajek's forehead. 'What's that got to do with Marc Dobbs?'

'Nothing to do with Marc Dobbs,' Gil said.

'I don't know. Out and about. I was in the gym that afternoon at two.'

'Does the coffee shop Domachi's mean anything to you?'

Bajek's expression hardened. 'I know it.'

Gil turned over a grainy printout of the interior of Domachi's revealing Nico Bajek in conversation with another man.

'Domachi's yesterday morning at 10.55. The man talking to you is Leighton Sullivan.'

Bajek leaned back and whispered something to Roebuck. Gil and Jess exchanged glances. This was the point in any interview where the interviewee turned turtle and withdrew into his or her "no-comment" shell. They were both surprised when Bajek started talking.

'I got a call on a phone I used to get supplies.'

'Illegal supplies?'

'Not always. But I work with a GP who does voluntary clinics for people addicted to anabolic steroids. Happy to give you his name. He's been worried lately because there's been some very dodgy produce appearing. Stuff that causes lots of problems for people. Even sepsis in one case. I get this out-of-the-blue text offering product, and I decide to follow it up, to see.'

Gil had his fingers steepled on the desk. 'Wow, let me get this straight. You were playing private investigator?'

'I was playing their game. At least, I thought I was. But, when this guy – and I did not know his name until you just told me – comes up to me, he thinks I'm there to sell him something. He says he knows nothing about Juice.'

'Juice?'

Bajek held his hand up. 'Steroids.'

'What did he think you were selling?'

'Some kind of fuckin' Spiderman shit.'

'Spiderman?' Jess asked.

This time, Bajek held both hands up. 'Look, you can believe me or not, but that's what happened. He was the right bloke 'cos I had his photo, and he probably had mine. But it was a cock up. Or he got spooked, I don't know. Either way, we parted ways.'

'Where did you go after meeting him?'

'I went to a site for my dad. There's an estate going up in Rhydlewis. They want plumbers. I said I'd drop in and see what was going on.'

'And someone saw you?'

'Yeah. I spoke to a site manager there. Got his number on my phone.'

Jess pushed across a piece of paper. 'Can you write it down?'

Bajek had his phone out.

Jess let her eyes drift down. 'Is this the phone you were contacted about Sullivan?'

He had his head down close to the paper and sent Jess a look that showed a lot of white under the irises. 'No. And we both know the number that sent the text won't be traceable.' He slid the paper back.

'We'd like that number, though, Mr Bajek.'

Nico folded his arms. Thought about it, and with a big sigh, grabbed the paper back and wrote down a number.

'Can you account for your movements over the twenty-four hours between midnight Thursday the sixteenth and Friday the seventeenth?'

'I was with a client in the morning and afternoon. Two different gyms. One in Carmarthen, one in Cross Hands. Loads of witnesses.'

Gil slid over more images. This time of the Daher brothers. 'Either of these men known to you?'

Jess watched Bajek closely for any telltale tics. But his mouth turned down, and he shook his head.

'No. Who are they?'

'You're certain?'

'Never seen them before.' Bajek sat back.

'You happy for us to speak to this doctor who does volunteer clinics?' Gil asked.

Bajek shrugged. 'Not a problem.' He grabbed the same piece of paper and searched again for a number on his phone. When he'd finished, Roebuck packed up his notepad.

'I think we're finished here, don't you?'

'Just one more question. Have you ever used fentanyl, Mr Bajek?'

'Jesus, you must be fuckin' kiddin'. Stuff's lethal. I wouldn't touch it with a barge pole.'

CHAPTER TWENTY-NINE

ROEBUCK STOOD and began to follow Bajek towards the interview room door. The solicitor had a smug look of triumph on his face.

'We may have more questions, Mr Bajek,' Jess said.

'Look forward to it,' Roebuck replied. 'But we'd need a bit more notice next time.'

Warlow held a quick debrief in the Incident Room.

'He wouldn't touch fentanyl with a barge pole?' Catrin commented.

'But he's willing to pump himself full of "Juice",' Rhys said. 'I know some people who've used that.'

'Anabolics?' Gil asked.

Rhys nodded. 'Big business. Last year, a kid from Bridgend died from loading up on the stuff. Had a heart attack at twenty-eight. They said all his arteries were blocked.'

Warlow listened, his expression stony. 'Right. And the link between roids and violence is established.'

'Chicken and egg, sir,' Rhys said. 'Is it the drugs that cause the rage, or is it that the people who want and use the drug tend towards aggressive behaviour?'

'Well, we'll leave that one for you and the trick cyclists to work out, Rhys,' Gil mused. 'But what happened to Marc

Dobbs wasn't an act of rage. It was all planned out. The kidnapping and ransom demand.'

'Hmm,' Jess said. 'He seemed pretty sure of his alibi.'

'I've already rung the gym in Cross Hands,' Catrin said. 'They vouch for Bajek. He was there the afternoon Marc Dobbs went missing.'

'Then if he's involved, it's not directly,' Warlow said.

'I'm still not willing to discount him altogether. Though, he didn't flinch when we showed him the Dahers,' Jess said.

'Could be a poker player,' Rhys said.

'Another bloody blank drawn,' Warlow muttered. 'I should go and speak to Leah Dobbs again.'

'Time for a cup of tea first, sir?' Rhys asked.

'Silly question,' Warlow answered. 'Jess, fancy a trip up to see Leah, since Gina is there, too?'

'Delighted.'

'Right. Rhys, tea as takeaways. I have that vacuum mug you all kindly gave me for Christmas.'

'The one with "It's Not Road Rage If You Have Sirens" logo?'

'No. Catrin gave that one to Craig. You lot got me one with "10-4 coffee that" on it. Nice and tasteful.'

'There were other choices,' Gil said. 'I particularly liked "Arsebadger", because it also had the definition on it.'

'I can't wait,' Warlow said.

'Medically, a rather large and hard stool that causes painful dilation of the sphincter when it presents itself for removal.'

'In other words, a pain in the arse?'

'Correct,' Gil said. 'But I was voted down.'

'I liked "Now We're Sucking Diesel" but you had to deliver it in a Northern Ireland accent,' Jess said.

'And then there was Charlie, Uniform, November—' Gil began.

'I'll bring the mug,' Warlow said quickly and sent Gil a quelling glare.

BY NOW IT was mid-afternoon as Warlow drove the Jeep back up towards Cardigan. Both his logo'd mug and Jess's shiny stainless-steel logo-free version sat in their holders in the centre console.

'Well, this is nice. A day trip out to Cardigan with my favourite DCI,' Jess said.

'We're probably only adding fuel to the fire by going up together.'

'Really? Or is that a smidgen of paranoia I see on your lip?'

Warlow wasn't convinced. 'Is there a rule about colleagues who are romantically involved working together?'

'Romantically involved? If you said that to Rhys, he'd say you'd stolen it from a Downton Abbey script.'

Warlow ignored her taunt. 'In the States, they're pretty strict. Different shifts or even departments.'

'Well,' Jess said, and opened her phone. 'I looked it up. Draft guidance from the College of Policing, and I quote. "Staff who are in a relationship should recognise when a conflict may be created and ensure that it does not negatively impact on the work of the service or its reputation." It's mainly about who wears the trousers. A power imbalance.'

'Will that apply to us?' Warlow asked.

Jess shrugged. 'Greater Manchester Police had more formal policies, but they were discretionary.'

'Such as?'

'Removing staff members from the decision-making process in relation to promotion, selection, or discipline. Requiring officers or staff members not to work on the same shift together, or even work on the same team. Redeploying one or both.'

'Oh, *cachu*.'

'I know what that means,' Jess said. 'And the *cachu* only hits the fan when a given "romantic relationship"—' She made rabbit's ears around the words with her fingers. '—

might cause significant conflict. We've worked together for long enough. Have you had cause to discipline me and not done it because you had me on a pedestal?'

'Disciplining you while you're on a pedestal? There's a website for that.'

'I'm trying to be serious.'

'Okay, being serious. The answer is no,' Warlow said without even thinking.

'There we are, then.'

'Okay. Let me mull it over. Maybe I should run it past Buchannan at some point. But there's no rush. I mean, I might be back out in the garden shed within a week.'

Jess hit him gently on the arm. 'Oh, and Molly got back to me. She's come up with a list of thirty words and phrases associated with Fern.'

'Thirty? Okay, I'll study that later. At home, over a glass of wine. But first, Leah Dobbs.'

Once again, when they got to the Dobbs's property, it was Gina who opened the door to the knock.

'Who is here?' Warlow asked.

'Only Leah, sir. Beca is having tea with *Mamgu,* and Emyr is at work.'

'Okay. I don't want her to feel this is an ambush.'

Gina smiled. 'We've discussed the possibility that you'd call. She's expecting you.'

Warlow sat in the same black armchair he sat in when he first came here with Rhys. This time, it was Jess who sat next to him while Leah took the sofa.

'Gina has been keeping you informed, I hope?'

Leah nodded. A smile fluttered over her lips like the wing of an injured bird. 'She's been great. I don't know what I would have done if…'

'But I'm here to answer any questions you might have.' Warlow spoke into the gap Leah left.

'Questions? They're the same questions I had the day Marc died. I want to know who took him and why?'

'I want those answers too, Leah.' Warlow nodded. 'How's Beca?'

'She doesn't understand why her daddy isn't here to read her a story at bedtime. I try, but that was his thing. Their thing.' She teared up again. 'I haven't had the heart to tell her it's never going to happen again.' She paused, her lower lip tremulous. 'I'm sorry.'

'We're all sorry,' Jess added. 'Sorry that we're here having this conversation. Finding out who did this won't change anything for Beca. But it's something we have to do. And we will do.'

Leah nodded.

Warlow and Jess hadn't planned the discussion between them, but it was she who posed the first hard question.

'The ketamine we found in the shed. You know nothing about that?'

'Why don't you believe me?' Leah said. 'Emyr doesn't believe me, either. But I swear to God Marc did not do drugs. He didn't take them, and he didn't sell them.'

'Okay,' Jess said. 'Okay, Leah. Does anyone have access to the shed besides you and Marc?'

'No. My mother-in-law possibly, but you surely don't believe she—'

'We don't. But did Marc keep anything else in there?'

'Your people have been through everything. He kept tools in there. And paints, and brushes. The usual.'

'There was some sports equipment,' Warlow said.

Leah nodded miserably. 'He has a net. He wanted to teach Beca to play football. They put the net up in the garden when it's dry. It's too wet now. There is a net and a soccer ball and his togs and hers. He insisted on buying her football boots.'

'You didn't keep the shed locked?' Jess asked.

'Only when we went away.' She looked up at them. 'What about those men you asked me about? Are they drug dealers? Have you found them?'

'No, not yet.' Jess waited a long beat before asking, 'Does the name Leighton Sullivan mean anything to you?'

Leah thought, her pale, pinched face struggling to concentrate. 'Gina already asked me that. Why? Is he a drug dealer?'

'No,' Warlow said, realising in the same instant he had no idea whether that was true or not. But he needed to calm things down. 'He's another name that's come up, Leah. That's all.'

Leah picked at the thread from one of the throw cushions on the sofa. A habit she'd adopted ever since they sat down in this room. 'How long is this all going to take?'

'We don't know the answer to that. I'll tell you what I tell everyone. It'll take as long as it takes,' Jess said.

Gina's phone chirped from the kitchen. A moment later, she came through with a look on her face that told Warlow he needed to hear what she had to say.

He got up. 'Excuse me.'

As he left the room, Jess asked a neutral question.

'How many hours a day is Beca in school for now?'

Warlow did not wait for Leah's answer. Instead, he followed Gina into the kitchen and through into the small garden without speaking.

'It's Gil, sir. He's texted me because he assumed you were talking to Leah. He's had a message from Vetch.'

Warlow's pulse ticked up a notch.

'Apparently, Vetch has a CHIS who's come up with a potential address for the Dahers.'

The drugs officers were insistent on using CHIS instead of informant. Covert Human Intelligence Source needed an acronym. Too much of a mouthful without it.

'Good. I'll ring Gil.'

He stayed in the garden and speed-dialled Gil. When he got through to the sergeant, he was in a vehicle.

'You got the message?' Gil asked.

Warlow stared across to the garden fenced off by wood

panels stained with creosote. He wondered which end Marc Dobbs had used as a goal.

'You're in transit?'

'Actually, it's a Ford Focus.'

'Let me guess. You're on the way to Swansea?'

'Top marks. But the address is in Clydach. I'm going down there to meet Vetch.'

'On your own?'

'It's late in the day. Catrin needs to get home and put her bulbous and swollen feet up. Rhys was champing at the bit, but I'll be with Dai Vetch. Too many cooks, etc.'

'I trust you're taking some Uniforms along.'

'Yeah. We're all meeting up in Ynystawe. You familiar with that neck of the woods, Clydach?'

'I went to school in the Swansea valley, remember?'

'Of course. And you survived. That's impressive.'

'Let me know what you find,' Warlow said, ignoring the taunt.

He finished the call and turned towards the house again and the grieving widow inside, hoping that this thread of Gil's, once pulled, might lead them to something concrete.

CHAPTER THIRTY

GIL WENT in convoy from the meeting point on the Clydach road off the B4603 at Ynysforgen. Vetch was in a Mazda, the Uniforms in a marked response vehicle. Quick words were exchanged, and they agreed to follow the marked car since the driver knew the address.

'Believe me, it's not exactly on the milk round,' said the officer as she slid into the driving seat.

Gil followed as they headed out north and west of the village of Clydach itself towards the smaller village of Craig Cefn Parc. The translation of Park Ridge Rock always seemed a bit prosaic to Gil. He knew of the village because the Lady Anwen had once bought him a book called The Death Ray Man that explored the fascinating life of Harry Grindell Mathews who set up a laboratory on the wild mountain moorland to the north of the village between the First and Second World War. The man and the laboratory had entered into science folklore. A veteran of the Boer war, he transitioned into electrical engineering and proceeded, on his own, to research the potential of radio and light waves.

Gil loved the idea of this man setting up on his own to invent and discover and provide endless hours of gossip for the little village. And he was successful, after a fashion, claiming to develop rays capable of deactivating an engine's magneto and bring down an aeroplane. Alas, his fear of industrial espionage fed into his paranoia. The fact that he ended up marrying a Polish American operatic singer whose aspirations rivalled those of Florence Foster Jenkins, made the entire story all the more idiosyncratically splendid.

Once they reached the village, they doubled back to head south and east, climbing steadily on Rhydowen road that gave way to concrete and gravel shortly after leaving Craig Cefn Parc. As was so often the way, soon they were on higher ground with the light sliding away from them as the afternoon sped on. This was an ancient lane flanked by a dry-stone wall demarcating farmland on the right and the open moor on the left dotted with bracken, scrub, birch, gorse, and cotton grass. This was Mynydd Gelliwastad, literally a plateau with groves of trees.

Lights appeared in the couple of houses as they passed along a three-quarter mile stretch. Then, at a gate which looked to have been fenced off with steel mesh, the response vehicle stopped.

Gil got out to join the others.

'Does not look promising,' he said.

Vetch shrugged and then a shout from one of the Uniforms reached them. 'Another gate.'

Twenty yards further along the lane, another farm gate, but this time the mesh had been removed. The Uniform jumped over and disappeared into the space behind, completely hidden by a line of conifers.

'There's a car in here,' came the shout from the now out-of-sight officer.

Gil and Vetch hurried to join the Uniform. The building here looked like it had once been some kind of half industrial unit.

'There were some kennels up here once,' said the older of the two Uniforms. 'Shut a couple of years ago.'

The car was locked. A black E-Class Merc. Vetch snorted. 'Much loved by the travelling salesman.'

'By that, you mean dealers?' Gil asked.

'I do.'

Vetch peered inside, and Gil joined him. The car was empty bar three energy drink cans with lurid artwork, a half-eaten giant crisp packet, and a crumpled Tesco bag.

Both men turned to the building. It would be a stretch to call the one-storey shed a house. Long and low, it had windows and a door at one end, nothing but faded white-washed breeze blocks as a wall for the rest of its length.

Vetch walked to the door and knocked. 'Police. Open up.'

No response.

Gil walked up to the dark window that looked out into the weed-strewn yard where grass was rapidly reclaiming the hardstanding.

'Think they're playing hard to get?' He turned back to Vetch.

'There's a door at the far end, sarge,' the intrepid Uniform who'd found the second gate called to them and rattled the door. 'Locked.'

'Do we know who owns this place?' Gil asked.

'Belonged to a farm. They sold the land. The business didn't survive Covid,' the older Uniform said.

Vetch, never one to waste words, turned away and headed back to his car.

'Something we said?' Gil called after him.

'I have a key,' Vetch called back without turning around.

The land fell away to the west. There, darkness was encroaching, while above, on the higher ground, the last thin ribbon of fading gold to the east crowned the hill.

They heard a car door slam, and Vetch reappeared carrying a crowbar.

'Ah,' Gil said. 'That key.'

'I know this is their car. It's the one we've been tracking. I believe that a crime has been committed here. Agreed?'

'Agreed,' Gil said.

'The back door has the flimsiest lock, sarge,' the younger Uniform said.

They walked around. It was a Dutch door, probably

bolted at the bottom with a handle on the top half only. It was this that Vetch attacked, prising the bar into the space that time and the weather had created between door and frame. And it was the latter that gave, splintering easily under Vetch's efforts. He swung the top half inwards and reached inside for the bolt that secured the lower half.

The young Uniform had a torch to hand and led the way along a dusty concrete walkway, past caged kennels, some still with blankets on the wooden crates at the back. The beam danced over the walls and caught in the thick swirls of dust their footsteps threw up. Gil coughed and sucked in a waft of dampness and decay.

At the end of the walkway stood a door with a frosted glass panel in the upper half.

'Gloves,' Vetch said.

The search party halted as nitrile gloves were donned. 'I'll go first,' Vetch said and switched on his own torch. 'Police,' he shouted again. 'Show yourselves.'

He knocked on the door.

No reply.

Vetch turned to the Uniforms behind him who'd already drawn their telescopic batons. Vetch nodded and opened the door. Gil followed him into the room, empty apart from cans and discarded takeaway wrappers scattered across the grimy floor. The cracked window struggled to let in a feeble light, their torch beams casting long shadows that danced across the walls like ghosts in the darkness.

Yet another door, also shut, guarded the final room. Vetch led the way, his face set in a determined grimace as he pushed. The door opened with a dramatic creak.

'Ah, Christ,' he muttered and slid a sleeve over his nose in a bid to modify the stink that clawed at his throat. Sweet and sickly, the stench of rot and decay.

Vetch's flashlight darted across the room, illuminating the gruesome tableau before them. The bodies of the Daher brothers lay sprawled on the cold, damp floor, their vacant eyes open and staring into the abyss. The beams glinted off the fentanyl patches on their necks, sending a cold tremor down Gil's spine.

He swallowed hard, his throat dry and constricted. The room seemed to close in around him, a claustrophobic grip that mirrored the sinister nature of the crime scene. He exchanged a solemn glance with Vetch before fumbling out the mints he always carried in his pocket and offered one to Vetch, who declined with a shake of his head. The Uniforms accepted one each. Polos wouldn't banish the smell and taste, nor erase the image of death this room contained. But they would help with the cloying stink.

Gil threw Vetch another glance.

Another twist in a case that already had them grasping at straws.

'Warlow is going to bloody hate this,' Gil muttered. 'Any clue what the heck is taking place here, Dai?'

Vetch was leaning over the first of the bodies. 'Bloody Dragon's Breath,' he muttered darkly.

'What?' Gil asked.

'Sorry,' Vetch muttered. 'Street name for Fent. But Christ knows what's happened here.'

He turned to look at the Uniforms standing together in the doorway. 'You two check outside. I didn't see any other buildings, but you'd better make sure.'

They both left, and Gil sensed a degree of relief in the way they did so without question or hesitation. Vetch directed his flashlight towards a side table. 'Car keys,' he said.

Gil picked them up, stepped over to a window, and activated a switch. The Merc chirped and lights flashed.

Both men retraced their steps out into the dark yard and to the car. Vetch opened the driver's side door, rummaged, and pressed a button. The boot opened. Gil shone his torch in. He looked through a couple of thin raincoats and found a pack of garden ties and silver duct tape, a lump hammer, and bungee cords.

'Anything?' Vetch called from the front.

'Enough to make me like the Dahers even more for the kidnapping.'

'It's clean up here,' Vetch said. 'I mean, it's not. They were messy eaters, but no drugs. The last time they were stopped, the vehicle was clean, too. They use lines of transport that keep their hands dirt-free.'

Gil stood up. 'Best we leave this to CSI.'

The Uniforms appeared. 'Nothing,' the older one said.

'Okay.' Gil took some steps away from the car. 'Nothing for it but to ring the boss and tell him the good news.' He walked back towards the gate they'd come through, holding his phone to his ear.

'Hello,' answered a familiar voice.

'Ah, DCI Warlow.' Gil opted for mock formality in an attempt at cushioning the blow. 'I hope you're sitting down because I do not think you are going to like what I've got to tell you.'

'I'm all ears,' Warlow replied.

WHEN GIL ENDED the call that had come through on Warlow's phone as he and Jess were driving away from the Dobbs's property, he sat in his parked car. Halfway through the call he'd pulled off the road to give it his full attention. Now he and Jess stared at each other.

'My God,' Jess said.

'What's going through your mind?'

'All kinds. But mainly that I don't like fentanyl. And that I don't have a bloody clue what the hell is going on.' Jess turned to stare out of the window at the darkness. They were on the way home. Back to Ffau'r Blaidd. At least they had been. 'Do you want to go back into HQ?' she asked.

'Nah. No point.'

'No. We need to wait for due process. See what forensics comes up with. Gil's already with the Dahers.'

'What I really want to do is go home and see my dog,' Warlow said.

'I'm starving, too.'

'I took some of Molly's risotto out of the freezer when you weren't looking. The salmonella-free kind.'

Jess laughed. 'I'll tell her you said that.'

Warlow's eyes crinkled. 'I'll feel better after I've eaten,' he said. 'Though better is a relative term.'

'I hate drug-related killings,' Jess said.

'When we get home, I will also drink to that.'

CHAPTER THIRTY-ONE

BRIGHT AND EARLY IN the dining room Rhys Harries and Gina Mellings shared, Rhys sensed that something was not right. Gina had soaked some oats with a little oat milk, yoghurt, and cinnamon. She'd eaten several spoonfuls without speaking whilst Rhys polished off eggs, a bagel, and a bowl of something that pretended to be healthy because it had a sprinkling of nuts in it.

He drained a glass of orange juice, emptied the dregs of the carton into the same glass, and then crumpled the carton. He noticed Gina looking at him as he did all of this, spoon poised.

'You do know that is full of sugar.'

Rhys put the glass down and pushed it away with a finger. 'Kombucha from now on, I promise.'

'I'll remember that the next time we're walking down aisle six in Morrisons as you put armfuls of juice into the trolley.'

Rhys dabbed his mouth with a paper towel and looked across the table.

'You okay, PC Mellings?'

Gina, caught out in a moment of mean-spiritedness, pushed away the last few spoonfuls of oats in her bowl and turned an unusually serious face up to her partner.

'It's Leah Dobbs.'

'Does she know something?'

'No, I… I don't know.' She huffed out a sigh.

'She must be in pain.'

'Of course, she is. And so is Emyr. Him even more so. Leah lost her husband, but Emyr was there. I mean, he watched his brother die. Difficult to imagine anything more traumatic.'

Rhys frowned and searched for something to say but couldn't find anything worth saying.

'I'm worried about Leah, and I'm worried about Emyr. He is so angry. At us and Leah… I dread to think what he'd do if he ever found out who did this.'

'He'd go after them?'

'He's so wound up he could do anything.'

Rhys sat forward. 'He's not a danger to Leah or the kid?'

'If Leah was implicated, then yes, he is.'

The small creases in Rhys's forehead, brought on by Gina's angst, deepened into furrows. 'You don't feel threatened, do you?'

'No.' But the dismissiveness in her voice came across as a little too forced.

'I'll talk to DI Allanby. She would swap you out in a heartbeat.'

'I can't do that. I can't let Leah down.'

Rhys got up and came round the table, reached down, and pulled Gina up out of the chair. 'Then we can talk to Emyr. I'll get Gil to do it, or the Wolf even—'

'No,' she interrupted him and pulled away. 'This is just me. I could be completely wrong.'

'You have great instincts, Gina. I mean, look, you're with me for a start.'

She thumped him. Not too hard.

'At least let me tell the boss what your gut feeling is.'

She shook her head. 'I may be reading too much into all of it. Maybe I'm getting early burnout.'

'I thought you like being a FLO?'

'I do. But it's draining sometimes. I see Leah and Beca—'

Rhys pulled her back into a hug. This time, she did not resist. She only said one more thing. 'And you can drink as much orange juice as you want to.' She whispered the words into his chest. 'If it keeps you as sweet as you are.'

Rhys laughed.

CATRIN LOOKED flushed when Warlow got in the next morning, five minutes after Jess. He sensed a frisson of excitement in the air.

'What have I missed?' he said before even taking off his coat.

'Something positive at last, sir,' Catrin said.

Gil came in from behind with a fresh tray of tea.

'Povey found something at the kennels.'

Warlow grabbed his other mug, one with Foxtrot Foxtrot Sierra written on it, and turned to watch Catrin hold court. She pinned up an A4 sheet.

'The Dahers were not big on tidiness, so it seems.'

'I can confirm that,' Gil muttered. 'Empty cans and wrappers all over the place.'

'Given the urgency—'

'And that Alison Povey doesn't sleep,' Warlow added.

'They found this crumpled bit of paper amidst the rubbish in a plastic bag.' Catrin had the sheet up in her hand. 'I suspect the Dahers would stuff everything into this before they left to cover their tracks.'

'They hadn't covered their tracks when Dai Vetch and I were there yesterday,' Gil said.

'Anyway, in amongst the crisps and sandwich wrappers was this.'

Everyone stepped closer to the Gallery to look at it. Povey's team had flattened off the wedge-shaped triangle of paper. It had a torn edge and next to it a yellow measuring tape showed it to be 70mm by 160mm at the thickest side, with a jagged tear cutting off one end to taper off at 212mm of length.

A series of numbers 07700 9167749.

'What happens when you ring it?' Warlow asked.

'Nothing. And it's unregistered, sir,' Catrin said.

'Right, well, we—' It was then he caught the look on Jess's face.

'What?' he asked.

She held up a different page of A4. 'This is the sheet Nico Bajek gave us yesterday. You remember he volunteered that he used a burner phone for his "Juice" contacts. It's the same number.'

'Bingo,' Gil said.

Warlow looked at Gil with eyes burning. 'I hope someone is on the way to Bajek's house?'

'Rhys is on the way with some Uniforms,' Catrin said.

Warlow took out his phone and dialled Rhys's number. 'How are you getting on?'

'Two-thirds of the way there, sir. The Uniforms have already knocked on the door. Bajek has a house but rents out a couple of rooms to some mates. He's effectively the landlord. They were happy to let the Uniforms in but no sign of Bajek. Though there was someone in his bed. A woman. I thought I'd keep going to have a nose around, chat to the woman.'

'Good idea. Keep me informed.'

Warlow turned a disappointed face towards the others. 'Not there.'

'And to think we had him here yesterday,' Catrin said.

'Get on to the solicitor. Tell him we need to speak to Bajek again. That we have fresh evidence that needs explaining. See what he says. Any word on when the postmortems are likely to be?'

'This afternoon,' Jess said. 'But Povey said there was not much sign of violence.'

'So, bloody Dragon's Breath again?'

'I suppose we'll have to wait to find out,' Jess suggested. Stating the obvious to try deflating Warlow's frustrations.

He sat in the nearest chair and stared at the boards. The Gallery now had four dead people on it. Marc Dobbs, Leighton Sullivan, and now the Dahers.

'What are you thinking?' Jess asked.

'That it's got to stop.'

'Then we have to find the link here before more people die.'

'Where the hell do we start?' Gil muttered.

'Where we always start,' Warlow muttered. 'Back at the beginning.'

RHYS CAUGHT up with the woman, Beth Kaper, on the upper floor of the house Bajek owned. A floor converted into a self-contained flat from the looks of it, with a separate entrance to hive it off from the tenants on the floor below.

The girl, a natural blonde dressed in leggings and a training top, sat in a modern kitchenette. A Uniformed female officer stood at the door leading to the rest of the apartment. In case of what, exactly, Rhys had no idea. But he was glad she was there because Kaper had the air of someone who did not want to be bothered with all of this … kerfuffle. She had a gym-fit physique, much of it on display under her spray-on leggings in an eye-catching pattern, puffed lips, and a perma-tan that would make the sun blush. Gil would probably have called her a firecracker, but not in polite company.

'Detective Constable Harries.' He introduced himself, skipping the pleasantries. 'We're looking for Nico. Any idea where he's gone?'

Kaper's eyes, a combination of defiance and mischief, locked onto Rhys's. 'He didn't enjoy yesterday's interview. He hasn't been himself since hearing about Marc Dobbs.'

'Kaper, is that Dutch?'

'Yep. But I've been here for twenty years. Came over with the 'rents and stayed. I can even speak Welsh.'

'Tell me about your relationship with Nico.'

'Love buddies,' she claimed, a mix of casual and coy in her tone. 'No strings attached, just muscles and fun.'

Rhys raised an eyebrow, sceptical of her nonchalant stance. 'Love buddies, okay.'

She folded her arms. 'Unless Nico attaches some strings.'

'Is that what you want?'

She shrugged, but her gaze lingered.

Shaking off the distraction, Rhys refocused on the case. 'You say Nico was upset by what happened to Marc Dobbs?'

Kaper snorted. 'He was obsessed with it,' she admitted, a shadow crossing her tanned features. 'But obsessed doesn't mean guilty, right?'

'What about his side business? Selling roids?'

She sighed. 'Nico did some shady deals, but I'm clean. I don't mess with that stuff.'

Beneath her confident exterior, Rhys detected a glint of anxiety at his line of questioning. 'Worried about something, though?'

'Nico's not a drug dealer. He didn't want this attention. He's not like those arseholes that sell to kids to get them hooked. If anything, he's trying to help. If you knew anything about gym culture, you'd understand...' She bit back the rant, eyes searching for understanding. 'Dobbs's death messed him up, and now he's not answering his phone. He has clients this morning. We both do.' She held up her watch with the face towards Rhys to indicate her impatience.

'Why was Nico so bothered by Dobbs's death?'

'You know why. Because of Leah and what happened between the two of them.'

Rhys pressed on. 'He went to see Leah—'

'I warned him not to. I said it was too soon. Just before the funeral would be early enough. But he's a stubborn man.'

'If you are worried about him, Beth, then the best thing he could do is not run away. We have questions—'

'So your shock troops said. About what?'

'About some bad things that are happening.'

Her sculpted brows clenched. 'He was over Leah. I mean, he had a soft spot, but that was because of how he reacted when they split.'

'We've heard.'

She leaned back, a pout forming on her plumped lips. 'What do you want from me? I'm not the bad guy here. And neither is Nico.'

Rhys shot her a knowing look, silently acknowledging the tangled web they were navigating. 'Find him, so we can figure out who the bad guys really are.'

There was no less defiance in the glare she sent him, but she added, 'I am trying.'

Rhys slid over his card. 'That's my number.'

She glanced at it and let a pair of large blue eyes drift up. 'Business only?'

'I'm afraid so.'

Rhys left, and the uniformed officer cast a raised eyebrow in his direction. He shook his head, silently responding to the half-smile on her lips.

'Tell me if she leaves,' he said.

The Uniform nodded.

CHAPTER THIRTY-TWO

Jess rang Bajek's solicitor, who remained very cagey when quizzed about his client's whereabouts.

'You realise we warned him to remain available?'

On the other end of the phone, Roebuck remained reticent.

'Can you hear me, okay?' Jess spoke into the static.

'You only questioned him yesterday.'

'Which part of fresh material evidence did you not understand?' Jess asked. 'Evidence that confirms your client was known to two more people relevant to the case.'

In the long beat that followed, Jess liked to imagine Roebuck loosening his tie in order to get a little more air into his lungs. 'Can I ask what kind of evidence?'

'You can certainly ask. But we present that evidence to Mr Bajek, and you are more than welcome to be present.'

'Bloody Carmarthen is fifty miles from my office.' Roebuck sounded petulant.

'Okay,' Jess said. 'The next time someone dies, we'll try to make sure it's closer to you. How about that?'

The sardonic barb elicited no obvious reaction, but Roebuck's next sentence suggested he had heard the word 'dies' well enough. 'I told him not to do anything stupid.'

'And has he?'

'He's incommunicado.'

Incommunicado. A top five word on Warlow and definitely Gil's hate list along with Chrimbo, holibobs, and bants. The last time someone had mentioned it in front of the sergeant, he'd growled out, 'Well, no problemo, get them a ticket out of bloody communicado and straight here, pronto.'

'And you do not know where he is?' Jess asked.

'No.'

Jess pressed home her point. 'It would definitely be in your client's interest to volunteer to answer these new questions.'

'I am aware of that.'

'Good. Unfortunately, the SIO in this case is not known for his patience in regard to someone obstructing an investigation.'

'That's a bit extreme, isn't it?'

'That would be up to the CPS.'

Roebuck sighed. 'I'll keep trying, but my guess is he's switched off his phone to lie low.'

'Hardly a sensible move in the middle of a murder investigation.'

'It's not on my suggestion.'

'Glad to hear it. When you do find him, unless he cooperates, tell him that our next step will be a warrant for his arrest.'

'You don't have any good reason to—'

'We have. Four very dead reasons, Mr Roebuck.'

JESS RELAYED this information to the team later when Rhys announced he had the preliminary toxicology screen from the postmortem urine and blood on the Dahers.

'Positive for fentanyl, sir. The final report will give us blood levels.'

'Why am I not surprised?' Warlow growled. 'Trail of bloody destruction.'

'Is that what killed them?' Catrin queried. She was eating a banana as she asked this. No one commented. She was eating for two.

Rhys walked up to the board. 'I had a long chat with Sengupta about this, sarge. We have the blood levels for Marc Dobbs. No levels for Sullivan, or the Dahers, yet and the length of time the Dahers had been dead—'

'Best guess?' Jess asked.

'Three days at least.' Rhys wrinkled his nose. 'Anyway, there's something called an agonal state. We have rapid timelines on Dobbs and Sullivan. But for the Dahers, it's more difficult. Sengupta says that the drug might have caused suppression of respiration such that they were brain dead but kept on breathing, dying slowly. The drug might have been metabolised for longer in their case. We'll know when the results come through, but she's saying it will be less reliable.'

'*Mam fach*, this stuff is a nightmare,' Gil said. 'Fancy giving me a refresher course, Rhys?'

The DC smiled and nodded.

'The short version,' Catrin qualified Gil's request. 'I'm sure your discussions with Sengupta were… extensive.'

Rhys wrote fentanyl up on the board. 'This is the stuff used in humans. Some of the nonpharmaceutical derivatives are much more potent.'

'You mean, the illicit stuff cooked up in labs?' Jess asked.

Rhys nodded. 'As it is, fentanyl is eighty times more potent than morphine. It's used for analgesia, through patches, but used too in anaesthesia during ops.'

'The patches are only for analgesia?' Gil asked.

'Yep. Slow release. They come in dosage per hour, 12.5 up to 100 micrograms per hour.'

'Micrograms?' Gil was keen to understand.

'One millionth of a gram, sarge. And the level that gives you in blood is 1 to 2 nanograms per millilitre.'

'And a nanogram is how much?' Catrin asked.

'One billionth of a gram. You need higher doses for anaesthesia, but that's given via IV. Even then, the blood levels are about 10-20 nanogram per millilitre. Depending on how much fat there is in a body.'

'Gil would be on the higher dose, then,' Catrin said.

That earned her a scathing look. 'Pot, kettle, black,' Gil said.

'This isn't fat,' Catrin pointed at her abdomen.

'The camera doesn't lie,' muttered Gil.

'Rhys, how convinced is Sengupta that fentanyl is the cause of death in all these cases?' Warlow asked.

'Ah, right, sir. So, three tests need to be met, she said. First, history and circumstance. And all our cases had fentanyl patches still on the bodies, or, in Marc Dobbs's case, the residue of a patch as in sticky glue. So, that fits. Second, no disease or injury as a cause of death. And third, the blood levels of drug are consistent. And in Dobbs's case, despite the exposure, they are. He had 87 nanogram per millilitre in his blood. That's four times the level needed for anaesthesia.'

'And what would the symptoms be?' Jess asked.

Rhys didn't even have to consult his notebook. 'Extreme drowsiness, difficulty with balance and walking, slurred speech, difficulty thinking, confusion, irrational actions, shallow and slow breathing, and heart rate. Basically, everything stops, ma'am. It's like unplugging someone from life support.'

Catrin put down the last third of her banana. It would remain un-eaten on her desk until she pushed it into a bin.

'Do we concentrate our efforts on finding Bajek?' Gil asked with grim resolution in his voice.

'Looks that way,' Warlow said, but grunted something else incoherent under his breath.

'What are you suggesting?' Gil asked.

'I'm thinking I should start practising what I preach and go back to the beginning. Marc Dobbs. We have one witness who was with him when he died.'

'His brother?'

'Yes. Marc Dobbs may have been confused and drowsy,

but perhaps he said something that hasn't registered as important to his brother. Rhys, text Gina, ask if he's about today.'

Rhys's fingers danced over the screen of his phone. A minute later, he came back with, 'It's a yes. He usually gets up around ten after a late shift.'

Warlow glanced at his watch. 'Right, Rhys, with me. Let's hit the road. But I don't want to speak to him with Leah present. It'll be too much for her. Anywhere we could chat up there?'

'Ooh, Aberteifi,' Catrin gushed, using the Welsh name for the town of Cardigan. 'It's got some cool credentials now. We had some uni friends down over the summer and it was on their bucket list. Bit of an arts scene, good food, independent shops.'

'Somewhere quiet,' Warlow said.

'I'll give you a couple of choices.'

Later, in the Jeep, Rhys opened up about the Dobbs's case. 'It's funny we're on the way up to see Emyr, sir. Gina and I had a chat about him and Leah over breakfast.'

'Oh?'

'She's pretty tough, sir, normally.'

'You don't need to remind me of that.' Warlow toyed with the idea of revisiting the case where he and Gina had dodged a bullet, literally, from a rogue officer who'd gone over to the dark side in another drug-related crime.

'She says neither of them, Leah nor Emyr, are coping very well.'

'Hardly surprising. Coping is such a crap word, anyway. It's all too raw to start coping.'

'That's what I said, sir. But then, Gina is not exactly a novice when it comes to being a FLO.'

Warlow glanced across at Rhys's unusually serious face. 'All the more reason to sit up and take notice, then.'

'Either that or she needs a break from it.'

'Does she want a break from it?'

'I think she was just talking out loud. But she is worried about Emyr gaslighting Leah a bit. She's pretty vulnerable and I can tell it's getting to Gina. DI Allanby thinks she needs a break.'

'Have you got any holidays planned?'

Rhys scowled. 'We don't exactly have the funds, sir.'

'No,' Warlow said. Hardly anybody did these days.

THEY MET with Emyr at eleven in a café next to the market hall that served its coffee with a milky swirl in the cream. The thing that struck Warlow as they walked from the car park was that this town was alive. It had a proper high street with shops, and not every other one was a charity outlet.

Emyr was already seated in a corner, his coffee on a low table beside him, with two empty black upholstered tub chairs waiting to be used.

Warlow ordered flat whites for him and Rhys.

'Thanks for meeting us,' Warlow said when he sat. 'Mind if we record this?'

Emyr nodded. He looked tired and drawn. He looked like someone who had been through hell.

Rhys took his phone out and put it on the table. The café was quiet, the corner quieter.

'I'm not going to insult you by asking how you are,' Warlow began. 'I've seen too many of these cases to know you're not in a good place. And you will not be for a while.'

'I appreciate that. People don't know what to say to me.'

'Of course, they don't. And you can't blame them for that, either.'

Emyr nodded, eyes down. The barista shouted the name, 'Evan.'

Rhys got up to fetch the coffees and came back with chunky black cups on saucers, full to their brim.

'Do you have any updates?' Emyr asked.

Warlow appreciated that there would be no small talk here. No discussion of how work was. Emyr was a single man. They'd learnt that from previous discussions. He used work as a distraction from the horror of the circumstances he'd been thrust into. Asking how that was would be an insult.

'We've made some progress,' Warlow said.

At this, Emyr's expression sharpened. 'How?'

'Parts of a puzzle that don't quite fit together yet. That's why we're here.'

'What can I do?'

'That night that you found your brother, I know it must be hard for you to revisit it. We have your statement, and that's been very helpful. But is there anything he said that you've remembered since we last spoke?'

Emyr sipped his coffee. The cup clinked when he put it back down to the saucer, and he needed both hands to steady it. 'I've thought about it a lot. I've tried not to, but I can't help it. I wake up at three every morning, and I'm still there with him on the mountain. He was out of it. Didn't know where he was. Mumbling and gabbling all sorts. When I tried to wrap him up in the blanket I had, he kept saying that he'd been stupid. I said he wasn't stupid. He'd never been stupid.'

Warlow leaned in. 'When you say mumbling, can you remember the exact words he used?'

A ghost of a smile flickered on Emyr's face. 'I knew you'd ask me that at some point.' He took out his phone. 'I made notes. He mentioned Leah and Becs. Said Becs needs stories…' He paused, stared at the screen to gather himself.

'Take your time, Emyr,' Warlow said softly.

Emyr made a noise like a silent whistle. He had another sip of coffee. 'There isn't much. He said sorry a lot. Sorry for the mess. But then he'd go off and talk rubbish. Stuff about work, I think. The Peniel job. Mitchell, and then just nonsense.'

'We'd like to hear it, anyway.'

'Spoke my name, our parents' names. He asked where Rollo was. He used to be our dog. But some of it was just weird, you know? Second fixing, PIR, Minty, Minty's K, L, and M, a lot of it makes no sense.' He looked up at the officers.

Warlow caught Rhys's expression change in his peripheral vision. Had something clicked? But Rhys said nothing. 'That list of things you've remembered, we'd like to see it,' he said to Emyr.

'Of course …' He paused and then asked, 'What pieces of the puzzle have you found?'

Warlow didn't hesitate. 'There have been more fentanyl-related deaths, Emyr.'

'What?'

'Three more.'

'Jesus.' A look of shocked horror dragged down the corners of Emyr's eyes. 'What the hell is going on? Have you found out who's doing this?'

'Not yet. But we will. And thank you. This has been useful.'

'How? He was out of it. Marc, I mean. He was spouting rubbish. In a way, I'm glad he didn't know what the hell was happening to him, but—'

'It doesn't matter. We'll put our heads together. If you remember anything else that you think might help, get in touch.'

They talked for a bit longer, but not about that night. Warlow finished his coffee and he and Rhys left Emyr, who had a day off after a late shift, in the café.

'Right,' Warlow said when they were in the street. 'You heard something there, didn't you?'

'I did, sir. It might be nothing, but… Nico Bajek has a nickname in the football club he captains. A stupid nickname from school days. His parents are Polish. So, with a touch of casual racism, they call him Minty from Polo Mints.'

'Minty's K,' Warlow muttered. 'Nico Bajek's ketamine.'

'That's what I thought, too, sir.'

Warlow grinned at Rhys. 'And you had the good sense not to say anything. Remind me to get a gold star out when we get back to HQ, DC Harries. I might even let you eat a packet of crisps in the car.'

CHAPTER THIRTY-THREE

By the time Warlow and he got back to the Incident Room, Rhys had relayed the gist of their conversation with Emyr Dobbs. Catrin and Jess had been busy looking at Bajek's family connections in the UK with an uncle in Scotland. There were also cousins in Krakow. Gil had initiated an ANPR search. And it was Gil who, over a working lunch, got a hit on the missing man's hatchback.

'He's come up as travelling north on the A487, just south of Machynlleth.'

'Not far from your Shepherd's Hut, sir,' Catrin said.

'No,' Warlow agreed and immediately put a brake on his mind revisiting that little episode. 'But that is also the only road north on this side of the country.'

'What time?' Jess asked.

'A little after 6 pm yesterday.'

'Is that significant, ma'am?'

'Time enough for him to get home, pack a bag, and make a run for it.' Jess had a bowl of salad on her desk, and she picked out a leaf and ate it.

'Did we spook him at the interview?' Gil said.

'The Dahers were a ticking bomb. Only a matter of time until we found them. My guess is he's wondering what to do next. Run or give it up.' Jess dabbed the corner of her mouth.

'To where, ma'am?' Rhys asked.

'The A487 leads to all points north and east. So, he could be heading across to Birmingham, north to Manchester. Places with big enough airports to get him abroad.'

'And there's the Irish ferry at Holyhead,' Catrin said.

Warlow sighed. His half-eaten sandwich had lost all of its appeal. 'To think we had him here only yesterday.'

'He was very cool at interview, though, sir.' Rhys looked confused.

'The real sociopaths always are,' Warlow muttered. 'Let's alert Border Control. I don't want this bugger sliding across the channel or the Irish Sea.'

Warlow got up, but Jess remained seated, staring at the boards with her arms folded. He stopped and took a step back before tilting his head. 'What are we not seeing?'

'What if he is spooked, but not by us?'

Warlow sat down again. Jess's eyes hadn't left the boards as she continued. 'Yes, it's reasonable to consider he's bolted because we know he's connected to Sullivan and now to the Dahers. But what if he isn't responsible for their deaths and simply a part of whatever convoluted mess this is? Some kind of drug deal gone west.'

'You think he's running scared?' Gil asked.

'It's another scenario to consider.'

'I agree,' Catrin chimed in. She had a yoghurt pot in her hand and had to take a spoon previously laden with Skyr out of her mouth to speak. 'It doesn't change the fact that we need to find him.'

'But it changes other things,' Jess said.

'Like what, ma'am?' Rhys asked.

'Like, who else might be in danger if Nico is running? If this is a bad drug deal, in whatever sense, and if it has any link to organised crime, they are not known to be considerate or discriminatory when a vengeful act is in play.'

'In other words,' Warlow said, 'other people could be in danger.'

'By other people, you mean Leah and Emyr Dobbs?' Gil asked.

'I do.' Warlow nodded his head and looked to Jess for confirmation. She flattened her mouth in resigned agreement.

'Do we warn them?'

'I'll speak to Gina,' Jess said.

'And I'll talk to Emyr. He's still staying at Leah's house,' Gil said. 'Perhaps just as well to have them both in the same place. I'll get Uniforms to make sure there's someone about.'

'We're not talking about moving them to somewhere, are we, sir?' Rhys asked. Warlow sensed the concern in his DC's voice. It was a fair enough question, especially where his partner was part and parcel of the at-risk group by dint of being a constant presence in Leah Dobbs's daylight hours for the moment. But that would not last forever.

'No. This is just us thinking out loud.'

Rhys nodded, but Warlow wasn't sure his words had reassured him completely.

When the dust had settled, Jess walked out into the stairwell of secrets and called Gina.

'Three reasons for the call,' Jess said. 'Firstly, a heads up. We've lost Bajek. His car was spotted yesterday, heading north, and he is not answering his phone to us, nor to his solicitor. If that is to be believed.'

'Do you believe it, ma'am?'

'I do. Bajek isn't a fool. If he has his phone on, we can trace it.'

'So, Bajek is running because he's guilty?'

'That's one school of thought. But there is another. That he's running scared because he does not want to be another victim.'

Gina stayed silent.

'Rhys has told you we found the Dahers?'

'He did, ma'am.'

'So, four dead. Accidentally or deliberately, that's for us to find out. But Bajek might have woken up with the realisation that there was a target on his back and wanted to get out of the firing line as soon as possible.'

'I can see that. But if he's in the firing line …'

'Then Leah and perhaps Emyr could be, too.' Jess finished her sentence for her.

'Oh.' Gina's voice was flat.

'DCI Warlow is going to speak to Uniforms. But Leah should not be anywhere on her own. We can't put a leash on Emyr, but a quiet word might be in order there, too.'

'No one seriously believes Leah and Bajek are in this together?'

'All options are on the table,' Jess said. 'We have to take account of them all.'

'Personally, I hope that Bajek and Leah are not involved. Emyr would … I dread to think what he'd do.'

'You're stuck in the middle there. It can't be easy.'

A pause, and then Gina said, 'I hope Rhys hasn't been worrying you over this, ma'am?'

'We discuss this case regularly, Gina. If we believe that Leah or Emyr Dobbs are under threat, then we also need to consider the risk your presence there might pose to you.'

'Today, we're going to see the funeral directors about Marc. Emyr is coming too.' Another pause before Gina asked, 'But you don't know for sure that Leah is in any danger from persons unknown, do you?'

'No, but we'd be idiots for ignoring it.'

'Rhys will not be happy about any of this.'

'Are you?'

'I'm not whistling on the way to work, ma'am. It's a horrible case. But it's what I'm paid to do.'

'It is, but none of us signed up to get hurt. Physically or emotionally.'

'I still don't want to move from this case, ma'am.'

'I wouldn't expect you to. But sometimes, talking about it

helps. And that brings me to the other two reasons for the call. What are you doing on Thursday evening?'

When Jess got back into the Incident Room, Rhys looked up. 'Gina okay, ma'am?'

'You do not need to worry about PC Mellings, Rhys. Other than the fact that you will have to do without her company on Thursday night.'

'Oh, why? What's up?'

'I'm arranging a night out for our bride to be.'

'A hen do?'

'Not quite. The time for an overindulgence in Prosecco is well past. But I'm sure Gina and I and the others who are not thirty-something weeks' pregnant will do our bit.'

'Good of you to ask Gina, ma'am. Did she say yes?'

'Do owls hoot?'

Gil walked back into the room just at that moment. 'Did I hear you ask if owls hooted, ma'am?'

'You did, sergeant.'

'They were certainly making a noise in Llandeilo last night,' Gil said.

'At the hootenanny?' Rhys asked.

Gil sent him an old-fashioned look. 'I see. It's like that, is it? When are you and Gina getting engaged?'

'Wow, sarge, that's a bit random.'

'Not really, it's only so that I can send you a card that says, you twit, to who?'

'Oh, God,' Jess said.

'I do like owls, mind.' Rhys had a faint sparkle in his eye that engaging with Gil always seemed to bring out. 'In fact, I brought two in for questioning last week. Both from Peru.'

Gil grinned. 'Ah, yes, they were Inca hoots, right?'

Rhys looked crestfallen. 'Oh, sarge. You stole my thunder.'

'Oh, come on, I had the same Christmas cracker. And I'll thank you for keeping your thunder to yourself. Or at least open a window. I've heard about that irritable owl of yours.'

'All I said was do they hoot,' Jess muttered.

Gil shook his head. 'You should know better than to tempt Rhys with such statements, ma'am. He can't help himself.'

'What did I do?' Rhys objected.

'Not much, judging by the paperwork yet to be signed off on your desk.' Gil cocked an eyebrow.

Catrin, who'd been on one of her frequent visits to the loo, walked in, stopped, and surveyed her colleagues. 'Am I missing something?'

'Not a great deal,' Jess said. 'But we're on for Thursday night.'

'Girls only, I hope?'

Jess glanced first at Rhys and then at Gil. 'One hundred per cent.'

'None taken, ma'am,' Gil said. 'Though I am sure a case could be put for lack of inclusivity if Rhys and I were ever to take it to arbitration.'

'Really?' Jess eyed him suspiciously. 'You want to come?'

'Good God, no. But we have feelings, too, I'll have you know.' Gil kept up the false umbrage.

'Then why don't you two take Craig out?' Catrin rose to the challenge.

'Good idea. I'll run it past the head-honcho. Craig free on Thursday night, is he?'

'He is now.' Catrin smiled sweetly and eased herself back into her seat, which was a good twenty-four inches further back from her desk than it usually was. 'I'll text him, shall I?'

'Already done it. The good news is there's a game on. We can watch it in the pub,' Rhys said.

'Let's hope your waters don't break before then.' Gil eyed Catrin warily.

'Me too. I'm looking forward to it now.' Catrin sent him an appreciative smile.

'I'm not concerned about it spoiling the celebrations. Judging from the size of you, I'm more worried about drowning.'

He barely dodged the banana skin that came sailing through the air towards him.

CHAPTER THIRTY-FOUR

GINA HAD to confess to not having been to many funeral director establishments before. In fact, she'd never been to one. All the people close to her, except for one grandfather who died two years before she was born, were alive and kicking. Sober was the word that sprang to mind as she entered the premises of Mansel Garmon and Daughters on the edge of Cardigan Town.

On the way there, it had felt like they were off on the worst shopping trip ever.

Gina had even offered to pick up Beca to allow Leah's mother to come, but Leah had declined the offer and had asked Gina to come instead. Emyr had offered to drive them. He parked the car and walked with them towards the corner building with the Garmon company name in silver letters on black above the bay windows of the funeral parlour.

Now they sat in a little room off the reception area with the biggest surprise of the morning. They were being attended to by a young woman, Medi Garmon, clearly the fresh face – and one of the daughters – of the business. She was not much older than Gina, dressed in black, obviously, gently guiding Leah through the entire process.

'I've been told there will be an inquest,' Leah said.

'Of course,' Medi replied. 'If there's been a postmortem,

the coroner will usually allow a burial or cremation once that side of things is settled, but the only thing is the death can't be registered.'

Leah nodded blankly.

'How does that affect things?' Emyr asked.

'It won't affect us, but it will delay registration and therefore all the technical aspects of probate.'

'I don't even know what that means,' Leah wailed.

'I'll give you some literature. But you're doing the right thing, Leah,' Medi said. 'Best to start thinking about the funeral arrangements as early as possible. It's a process.'

'What do I need to do?'

'You'll need a medical certificate for the cause of death to register it. But since the coroner is involved, you'll need to contact their office. But, for now, have you decided if you want to bury or cremate?'

Leah sucked in a breath. They were not harsh words. It was why they were here, but they hit home.

'I … cremation,' Leah said. 'We only ever talked about it once. He didn't like the thought of being in the ground, slowly…' She swallowed loudly.

Medi made a note.

'Where is Marc now?'

Emyr had said nothing, but seeing Leah flounder, he said, 'Still in the Heath after the postmortem.'

These were not usual circumstances, but to be fair to Medi Garmon, she didn't flinch. 'Once the coroner gives his permission, we can arrange for the body to be brought to the Chapel of Rest here.'

'Won't he … I mean, how long can someone be kept–'

'We have refrigeration facilities, Leah. We can also arrange for viewing.'

'No,' Leah said. 'I've done that once. I don't want to … I don't want Beca to …'

Medi put up a hand. 'We always offer. As for where for the cremations, there are two choices, Narberth, or Aberystwyth.'

Leah blinked.

'But you can think about that. Don't worry for now. Would there be hymns?'

Leah shook her head.

'Not religious, then?'

Another shake.

'Is there anyone you had in mind to direct the service?'

Leah swivelled to look at Emyr. 'No, I couldn't. I won't be able to hold it together.'

Another understanding smile from Medi. 'We have a list of people, humanists, who offer their services.'

'Thank you.' Leah's voice had shrunk.

'But some people like to have music. Perhaps Marc had something he liked to listen to. For when people walk in and the casket is taken away …'

Leah nodded again. 'I can do that.'

'And as for the casket and the urn. We have many choices. From classic oak to decorated cardboard, or wicker, willow, or seagrass. More sustainable options these days. They're all online with us.'

Gina sat back and let Medi do her thing. That fine line between sympathetic inevitability and, just like any other service industry, offering a practical shopping list of what could and could not be done. Urn or scatter tube? Newspaper notices? Charity donations? Private or public? How she wanted Marc dressed? When it came to asking if someone would speak again, Emyr shook his head. But Leah had a name written on a piece of paper. Eifion Mitchell, the man that Marc often worked for, had offered. He'd been chairman of the local rugby club and would do a great job. Then Medi handed over checklists of things to do, the agencies that needed contacting when someone died, Mansel Garmon and Daughter's price list.

Finally, it was over. A shell-shocked Leah got up.

Medi opened the door to the reception area. Someone else was already waiting there. Another appointment. Death, it seemed, was a lucrative business.

Three people sat on chairs upholstered in blue velvet. One elderly woman and a younger man and woman. The older woman looked up as Leah, Emyr, and Gina came through, and her face broke into a broad smile. Gina fought to recall if they'd met, but the woman immediately stood up and made for Emyr.

'What are you doing here?' she asked in a shaky voice.

For a moment, Emyr's expression took on the look of a rabbit facing a ferret, but then he reddened and took her hand.

'Hello,' he said, but his smile of recognition faltered.

The woman saw his discomfort and frowned. 'Oh, of course, Marc Dobbs.'

Emyr bowed his head.

'I'm so sorry,' said the woman. She still had Emyr's hand.

'Thank you,' he muttered. 'I…' He blew out air and took back his hand, turned, and hurried away without another word.

'Emyr?' Leah hurried after him, leaving Gina alone with these people she had never met. She offered a brief and toothless smile.

'Difficult time,' she said.

The woman nodded. 'I didn't think,' she whispered. 'Dobbs, of course.'

She let out an open-mouthed exhalation of regret. 'I only know him as Emyr. Took my Gwilym to hospital in his ambulance at least three times when he had bad turns. So kind. He even came afterwards to sort things out for us. Pick up the equipment and everything else. I think everyone who works for the NHS should get double whatever it is they're paid, don't you?'

Gina nodded. 'You'll have to excuse them.'

'Of course. Different for us. Gwilym had been ill for so long with the cancer. A blessing in the end because the medication wasn't touching his pain and—'

'Sorry for your loss,' Gina said. She did not have a name

and didn't want one. But this was not the time nor the place for an introduction.

'Thank you,' the woman said and reached for a handkerchief. The younger woman stood up and put a hand on her arm.

Gina excused herself and hurried after the Dobbs.

The journey home began in silence. Leah sat in the back, studying the leaflets Medi Garmon had given her. Gina had been tempted to get in the back, too. But it would make Emyr look like a chauffeur, so she'd opted for the passenger seat.

'There's such a lot to think about,' Leah said in a tearful voice.

'I can help you,' Gina said.

'The biggest thing, the worst thing, is deciding whether to take Beca to the funeral or not. She won't understand.'

She won't, Gina thought. 'That's a difficult one, Leah. You're right, she probably won't understand but, you know what, these days, with everything on video, someone might tape it and, in the future, she might wonder why you didn't take her.'

'Take her to say goodbye to her dad,' Emyr said in a voice that was drained of emotion.

'Oh, God. She's still asking me when he'll be home,' Leah said.

They drove on, silence like a poison gas snuffing out any conversation in the car. The tension was palpable. But Gina had been here before and distraction was called for. She turned to Emyr.

'The woman in the funeral home remembered you.'

'Curse of the job. You meet dozens of people, and most are instantly forgettable because there's always the next one to get to. But for them, you're the lead in a major production. We show up, and it's just another call for us, but for the patient and their family, it's a major life event.'

He was right. She had seen it many times in her line of work, where you're constantly in the public eye.

'I don't even remember her name,' Emyr said. 'Is that bad?' He glanced across at Gina.

'No. The important thing is you left a good impression. She remembers you, that's what counts.'

He shrugged.

From the back seat, Leah asked another question. 'Did you think I should ask the football boys?'

Gina turned. 'The club was important to Marc, wasn't it?'

'It was. He loved his soccer.'

'Then I don't see why—'

'Not Bajek, though, right? You can't ask him,' Emyr said.

'I …' Leah sounded flummoxed.

'Oh, come on, Leah. Something was going on between the two of them.'

'Was it?'

'Christ, they found drugs in your bloody shed. Bajek is a bloke that deals in juicing up his gym mates. Those are illegal drugs. Why did he come and see you after Marc died? Did he come looking for stuff? Did Marc tell you where he kept them—'

'Stop it. Stop it,' Leah brayed.

Emyr pulled in and screeched to a halt. No one spoke until Gina said, 'I think you need to calm down, Emyr.'

He turned a face contorted with rage towards her. He looked just about capable of anything at that moment as he gnashed his teeth and thumped the steering wheel hard three times, his breath heaving in and out of his chest. Then he opened the car door, got out, and walked away with the engine still running.

'Emyr.' Gina leaned across and called to him. But he took no notice and kept walking.

'He hates me,' Leah said from behind her. 'He blames me for it all.'

Gina turned and reached towards the woman, who was slumped in the corner. Gina rubbed a hand on her arm. 'No, he doesn't. He's confused and hurt. He'll calm down.'

'I swear I know nothing about Nico and drugs, Gina. You

were there when he called. You know we didn't talk about anything except Marc.'

Gina turned back and opened the passenger-side door.

'Where are you going?' Leah wailed.

'I'm going to drive you home, okay?'

'Okay.'

Gina walked around the car and got into the driving seat. Emyr was hurrying down a side street. Just as well, Gina thought. Give him time to calm the hell down. She put the car in gear and drove off.

This case … she couldn't remember one where things were such a complete mess. But she'd need to tell Warlow about this. About Emyr's state of mind.

The conversation she'd had that morning with Jess Allanby seemed like a month ago. But she was now looking forward even more to being able to talk to her and Catrin about all this crap. Rhys was a good sounding board, but he wasn't one of the girls.

Most definitely not one of the girls.

That had its good and its bad points.

She glanced in the rear-view at Leah Dobbs's face. 'Once we get home, I'll make us a cup of tea, okay?'

Leah caught Gina's eye and offered up the faintest of smiles that, as she turned away, dissolved into bitter misery.

CHAPTER THIRTY-FIVE

VESPERS.

Though in terms of its content on this late afternoon, it made for slim pickings.

Warlow and Rhys reported back on their visit to Emyr Dobbs and the Minty's K revelation.

'Well, that puts friend Bajek right in the middle of all of this, doesn't it?' Gil asked.

'Seems that way.' Warlow tapped a pencil on a file on one of the desks. 'I've been reflecting on where the ANPR cameras picked him up. Someone made a quip about the Shepherd's Hut, but it might be worth getting a response vehicle out to the farm. Uh, Bryn Teg. Why he'd want to go back there, though, I have no idea.'

'Fox returns to his lair?' Rhys suggested. 'Or he has something hidden up there?'

'Povey's lot went over the place, though,' Jess pointed out. 'But yes, we should get someone along there.'

'Why don't you ask the people who owned the Shepherd's Hut, ma'am?' Rhys asked. 'Didn't they have a key?'

'We could,' Warlow said. 'And they will probably need to provide a key, but what if Nico is there?'

'Ah,' Rhys grimaced. 'Best not ask her to check, then.'

'No. Keep it in house,' Gil agreed. 'But I doubt he'll be there. It's somewhere he knows we'll look.'

'So, how do we see him fitting in, though?' Rhys posed the question. 'DS Vetch had him down as a supplier of IPEDs, and he as good as admitted that. Fentanyl isn't in that bracket, sir.'

'Let's ask the man. He needs to know about the ketamine, anyway.'

Gil dialled Vetch's number and this time, they set up a group call on everyone's monitors. The DS's background was also an office, with people moving around behind him.

'I see you're out on your fishing boat, Dai,' Gil quipped.

'Chance would be a fine thing. What can I do?'

Warlow explained about Minty's K and the new information from Emyr Dobbs. Vetch shook his head. 'Okay, that's not what I expected.'

'Right, so that's why we needed to talk to you. Rhys rightly pointed out that Bajek's background is in IPEDs. He mentioned working with some health workers.'

'Yeah, Bajek is part of a group. He's a user, or at least was, but also an advocate for support for bodybuilders. This is complicated. Everyone knows IPEDs are used, but a lot of users are pretty ignorant. There have been various projects tied into NHS Trusts across the country. Dedicated outreach clinics in sport supplement stores or even gyms. Usually, voluntary workers, sometimes GPs, but not always.'

'To what end?' Gil asked. 'If their use is so widespread, I mean?'

'Put simply, there are needle and syringe programmes. Like any other injected drug, users are at risk of Hep C or worse.'

Warlow was delighted when this did not draw a glance from anyone else in the room. His own adventures with blood-borne viruses were well known to all here. But they were too polite or well controlled to apply the parallels.

'Look,' Vetch launched into an explanation. 'There is the criminal side of things and there are the health concerns to users. They're not exclusive. And, like any addiction, we have a holistic approach. This is a predominantly male problem and associated with psychological dependence. There are subgroups who use alcohol and other psychoactives. And that can spill over into eating disorders, muscle dysmorphia, you name it. The clue is in the term, Image, and Performance-Enhancing Drug. People want to look and to feel better. But that carries risks. And because it's criminalised, half of what's injected isn't what it says on the label because it's cooked up somewhere. And because this stuff is used in excess. People may look better, at least in their own minds, but there are long-term consequences. Heart problems, high blood pressure, possible neurodegenerative. People need to know.'

'If I was a cynical man,' Warlow said after listening to Vetch, 'and there are rumours that I have a tendency, I might conclude that Bajek's apparent altruism might be a front for finding new customers. And providing a new product such as fentanyl.'

Vetch pondered the idea. 'I'd like to say that sounds farfetched, but nothing in this job surprises me anymore. Any progress in finding him?'

'Not yet,' Gil said.

'If I hear something, I'll get back to you immediately.' Vetch signed off.

'Gil, get on to Aberystwyth and get someone out to the farmhouse in Machynlleth.'

'Any point going public with a search for Bajek?' Catrin asked.

'Not yet. I'll speak to Buchannan, but he'll say it's too soon. How are we getting on with a list of his contacts?'

Catrin looked up. 'Work in progress.'

Warlow glanced at his watch. The day had a sell-by time, and they were rapidly approaching that. He'd call it a day in half an hour, go home, get some rest, and pray that no one else died overnight.

Leah's phone buzzed in her hand.

Probably her mother, she thought. Asking if she should return Beca immediately. There'd been no sign of Emyr since he'd walked off. She had no idea where he was and was quite glad of that. Leah wanted to tell him he could leave. That she would be better on her own. Or at least with Gina. But having him in the house at night, even if they didn't communicate all that much, provided a degree of security. Since Marc's death, a nameless fear had hung over her. But she was gradually coming to realise that this was just a fear of what was to come. Of life on her own with her daughter.

Leah glanced at the message and frowned. It wasn't a number she recognised. Could it be the funeral directors?

The message, when she read it, made her catch her breath:

Leah, I need to speak to you. Find somewhere quiet. Send back an OK and I will ring then. NaBa.

Naba.

The stupid name she used to call Nico by when they were…

So, it *was* him.

Shit. What should she do? Should she tell Gina?

She checked the number again. He'd contacted her a couple of times after Marc's death. Messaged her before he'd turned up that day, but not on this number.

Gina would want to know. But she'd gone to grab some groceries. Leah was alone in her bedroom… resting.

She texted back:

OK

The phone rang almost immediately.

'Nico?' Leah said.

'Leah. Is there anyone there?'

'No.'

'Leah, I had to phone you. I had to speak with you. The police, they—'

'Did you put drugs in my shed, Nico?'

'What?' Nico's voice sounded almost comically high.

'They found ketamine in our shed. They think it was Marc. But Marc didn't touch drugs.'

'Do you know that for sure, Leah?'

Silence, and then Nico apologised. 'Sorry, that was stupid.'

'Oh, God. I don't know what to believe anymore.'

'Nor me. There's stuff happening. I… they want to talk to me about things. There's a guy I was supposed to meet in Aber, and now he's dead.'

The noise of a car pulling up outside reached Leah. She hurried back into the living room and glanced out of the window in time to see Gina opening her car door from the shopping trip.

'Nico, I can't speak. The police are here.' Even though she could not be overheard, Leah dropped her voice. 'You need to talk to Emyr, Nico. Please talk to him. He thinks I'm involved in all of this. He thinks I put the ketamine in the shed. That Marc and me—'

'That's bullshit, Lee. I know Marc didn't do drugs. I know you don't.'

'Tell Emyr that!' It came out as a wailing plea.

The doorbell rang.

'Nico, I have to go.'

'Lee, this is a mess. This is such a mess—'

She wanted to believe him. The doorbell rang a second time. 'Speak to Emyr. Just tell him… please.'

She put her phone away and opened the door to a smiling Gina. 'Got the strawberry flavour one and two chocolate ones.'

'Thanks.'

Gina must have noticed something on Leah's face. 'All okay, Leah?'

'Yeah. Fine. I'm going to text my mother to bring Beca back now.'

Gina smiled and glanced at her watch. Almost five-thirty. 'Sounds like a plan.' She hesitated, and then asked, 'Anything else?'

'Can you ask Emyr to go back to his own home for me?'

LATER, at Ffau'r Blaidd, Warlow and Jess sat over two glasses of red at the kitchen table. They'd agreed not to discuss the case for the rest of the evening. Instead, Warlow was studying the list of words Molly had sent him from her app. Things related to Fern. It was a long one. He began reading them out for Jess.

'Botanical, lush, frond, greenery, forest, nature, foliage, woodland, moss, bracket, sports, reed… the list goes on.'

'Ringing any bells?'

'Not yet. I think I'll print them out and stick them on the fridge so I'll see them now and again. I have a feeling this will come to me when I least expect it. When I'm doing something else.'

'Like fetching milk from the fridge?'

'That sort of thing, yes. But be sure to thank Molly for me.'

'Oh, I will.'

Cadi got up from her basket, stretched, and ambled across towards Jess, who was sitting on her stool in jeans and one fluffy slipper, the other having slipped off. Cadi duly retrieved the slipper and waited for Jess to say something.

'What is it with this dog and footwear?' Jess said, shaking her head.

'Soft, warm, and full of aroma. What is there not to like? If you're a dog.'

'Less of the aroma, thank you. These are relatively new.'

'I know this game.' Warlow looked at the dog. 'She wants to swap. Slipper for a biscuit, right?'

On hearing the trigger word, Cadi's tail sped up. Warlow slid off the stool, fetched one of her treats and went to the back door. 'Go on, then, out you go.'

Cadi dropped the slipper as Warlow threw the biscuit out

onto the little stone patio at the rear. The dog munched away and then wandered off into the garden to do her ablutions.

'I know we said we wouldn't, but I've been thinking about Nico Bajek.'

'I'm listening,' Warlow said.

'The possibility he's on the run because he thinks he's a target, too. From whatever OCG is behind all this.'

'One of many theories, I agree. If he is, he'd be better off with us.'

'Really? These sods have long arms. Even in jail.'

'Agreed, but I think he'd be okay in the custody suite in Aberystwyth.'

'Can you swear to that?'

Warlow thought about it and then shrugged.

Jess finished her wine. 'I'm going to check out what's on TV for half an hour. There's something new on.'

'UK based or US?'

'Not sure. The Sunday supplement has it as pick of the week. "Tub thumping finger on the pulse cop drama with no quarter drawn." And then its chief critic calls it, "yet another ponderous domestic thriller where the cultural tick-box messaging overwhelms the plot to such an extent that pace and tension gets sacrificed on the altar of agenda within ten minutes".'

'Okay, well, that's both sides of the fence right there. And it's the same no matter what side of the pond you're on. Let's see if this one manages not to make every male of my persuasion a complete bastard, or a bigoted, run-down, morally corrupt has-been.'

Jess laughed. 'You feeling hard done by, Chief Inspector?'

'I'm just biding my time until the world turns enough for my particular spot on the cultural wheel of fortune to come full circle.'

Jess dropped her chin. 'I do not see you as an oppressed victim in any scenario.'

'Probably because I refuse to be. Maybe we should get Molly in on this discussion—'

'Don't even say that in jest. She's in uni now. I can't wait for her take on … things.'

'She has a mind of her own. I wouldn't worry.'

'Besides, that kind of trope sounds okay to me. Like being at work.'

Warlow's nodding smile had touché written all over it.

CHAPTER THIRTY-SIX

ANOTHER 8 AM start the next day fizzled and drifted into a long day of frustrations and lack of progress. The team was searching for those little threads that connected Marc Dobbs, Leighton Sullivan, and the Dahers, and now probably Nico Bajek, together. They had fentanyl, but that was not enough.

Fentanyl was the instrument.

What Warlow wanted was the sods who'd played the tune. Still, he'd been in the game long enough to realise that things rarely played ball in an investigation. You observed, asked, filtered, phoned, and let the information flow in until, like the panhandlers of old, you poured out the murky water and there, with a bit of luck, sat a little nugget.

They'd found no nuggets by six that evening. And so, at 7.30 pm, Warlow sat in the Players Room in the Quins Club on Morfa Lane. Rhys, who knew the staff there pretty well, having played as a junior, had suggested it as a sensible compromise in terms of accessibility. Plus, the fact that, apart from Gil, the men were acting as chauffeurs for their partners. Though Warlow was keen to avoid going anywhere near that term for the moment. He still daren't consider Jess on those terms. Not yet. It had only been a matter of days.

They'd been good days, he had to admit.

Wake up with a smile days, even.

But still.

And, if any of the others had felt the urge to comment on that, they sensibly stayed quiet. As far as they were concerned, the Allanbys, mother and daughter, were Warlow's tenants.

The big screen TV had a Champions League game playing, Manchester City vs Roma, and the room was half full. The Quins were a rugby team, but its members needed no excuse to enjoy a soccer game, especially of this calibre.

'So,' Warlow said as he sipped his zero-alcohol lager, 'to Mrs and Mrs Peters, then.'

They lifted bottles and drank.

A near miss on screen brought a few groans from the clutch of thirty punters invested in the game. But it fell away as the game progressed. The room was big enough for Craig, Warlow, Rhys, and Gil to have found a corner table while the game was on.

'I asked Catrin if she was going to keep her own name, Craig. She didn't answer.'

Craig was in his early thirties. Clean cut, short dark hair. Fit and good at his job in Traffic. 'She's not. She'll be DS Catrin Peters when she comes back to work after the baby.'

'Always the hyphenated option,' Gil dangled the suggestion.

Craig bobbed his head. 'Peters-Richards? Too awkward. And some wag would no doubt shorten it to PR.'

'Public relations?' Rhys asked.

'Per rectum,' Craig corrected him. 'My grandad knows all about that. He had his prostate removed ten years ago. And you don't get that done without becoming an expert in medical jargon. Especially medical jargon related to that part of the anatomy.'

'How is your grandad, Craig?' Warlow asked.

'Not bad at the moment. In good form, actually. He isn't in pain.'

'Is he looking forward to the wedding?'

'He is. He'll be first at the bar, no doubt.'

'Ah, us men of a certain age,' Gil said with feeling. 'I've had the misfortune of the old slippery finger of fate.'

'Me too,' Warlow said. 'Very emotional experience. Brought tears to my eyes, anyway.'

'Don't,' Craig winced.

'I knew a surgeon once,' Gil said. Everyone tuned in. It was usually worth a listen. 'Huge he was, put the fear of God into his patients just looking at him. Six-six, shoulders like tallboys, hands like shovels, and fingers like bananas.'

'Is he still working, sarge?' Rhys asked.

'No, got too close to the chimpanzee enclosure, and one of them bit his hand off.'

Craig groaned out a laugh. Warlow shook his head. Rhys merely bunched the muscles between his eyes. 'Because of his banana fingers, right, I get it.'

'No.' Gil rounded on him. 'Because chimps can be vicious little bastards.'

The commentator on screen became animated as a City winger got chopped down by a Roma player who, by his actions, clearly saw nothing wrong with a tackle that bordered on GBH.

'Anything we can do for the day, Craig?' Warlow asked.

'If you could sort this Dobbs case out beforehand, that would help. It's the only way Catrin will relax. She can't until a case is sorted.' Craig looked them all in the eye and, seeing not much in the way of humour, back peddled. 'If you could, like. No pressure. I'd be grateful.'

'We'd all be grateful,' Gil muttered.

'Have I touched a nerve?' Craig asked.

'Not really,' Warlow said. 'We've stagnated, that's all.'

'We'd be arresting someone now if Rhys could only pull his finger out,' Gil teased.

'Are we back on the banana hand now, sarge?' Rhys held up a single finger. The middle one.

Craig laughed.

Which was the point of the whole exercise.

'Don't bloody encourage him,' Gil warned. He finished his bottle. 'My round. More pretend beer or are we going to have half a real one each?'

'Go for it,' Craig said.

'What time's the table at the Raj?' Rhys asked.

'Eight-fifteen. We have time,' Warlow said. 'It's only a five-minute walk.'

'Great.' Rhys called after Gil, 'See if they've got any prawn cocktail crisps, sarge?'

'Only if they have noise suppression,' Warlow called at equal volume.

'Oh, come on, sir. We're off duty.'

'And I'm half deaf with an auditory crunch neuropathy.'

'That's not a real thing, is it?' Rhys asked, perturbed.

'Pardon?' Warlow replied.

Craig laughed again. 'You lot are worse than my family. They hate each other one minute and in a bloody group hug the next.'

'That's what families do, isn't it?' Rhys said and then shot both arms up in triumph as the Blues scored a cracker on screen.

'Yes,' Warlow said in a low voice. 'And, in families, there's always one you wished you'd left on the bus.'

'Heard that, sir,' Rhys said, feigning hurt.

'How do you know I'm talking about you?' He sent his eyes back towards the bar where a dance arcade machine was on trial. Sergeant Gil Jones had put money into it and was now attempting to emulate the on-screen instructions.

'Someone take a video of that,' Warlow said. 'So that I know I am not hallucinating. Please.'

NOT TOO FAR AWAY, but in another part of town, Jess, Gina, and Catrin, each one of them brushed up with some extra makeup, and wearing glittery tops, were also sitting at a table in a place that sold alcohol. Although, Catrin was not drinking for reasons obvious to anyone who looked at her.

There were few places in town with any glitz. Covid had put paid to the few that had existed. But Caesars would do for three women who wanted a chat and a drink with some background music. The bar wasn't big but lit up in neon with all the bottles on display. The servers wore braces. The women sat in a booth as the place slowly filled up with Thursday night revellers.

Gina finished her wine before Jess was halfway through hers.

'Wow, looks like you needed that,' Catrin said.

Gina sighed. 'It's been a tough one. Leah wanted Emyr to leave, so I had a chat with him. He didn't like it, but in the end, he saw sense.'

'So, he's definitely gone?' Jess asked.

'Yeah. Her mother is staying over tonight.'

'Did he make a fuss?' Catrin sipped at a mocktail called Dark Harvest. Angostura bitters, blackcurrant cordial, mint, blackberries and a lime wedge, and ginger beer. It wouldn't get her merry but was halfway to her five a day.

'Not as much as I was expecting,' Gina answered. 'He's a difficult one to gauge. He lost it in the car earlier. But he's angry and depressed about his brother.'

'PTSD?' Jess asked.

'There must be some of that,' Gina agreed. 'But I'm with Leah on that one. I got the impression he could blow a fuse any time. And I'd rather he blew it somewhere else, not at Leah's.'

'Does he still think she's involved?' Catrin sipped her drink through a straw.

'Yes, and no. I mean, he's a deep one. We met someone at the funeral home today—'

'Sounds like your day has been full of fun,' Jess said, eyebrows raised.

'Long story about Leah not wanting her mother there,' Gina explained. 'Anyway, this poor woman was there to talk funeral, and when she saw Emyr, she recognised him. Said how wonderful he'd been to her partner, who probably had some sort of chronic disease. How he'd taken him to hospital twice and even helped collect stuff after he'd passed.'

'That's nice,' Catrin said.

'Yeah, but Emyr was in one of his moods and just brushed her off.'

'Ah well, he's out of your hair,' Jess said.

Conversation then moved quickly on to what they were wearing to the wedding. The men would probably wear suits. 'It's so easy for them, isn't it?' Gina complained. 'I mean, their biggest decision is a tie.'

'Yeah, but you don't need to go overboard,' Catrin protested. 'It's as much a party as a wedding.'

'So, party frocks, then,' Jess said.

'Good idea,' Gina's eyes lit up, and the little spark of mischief that glinted was there for all to see. 'Will you and Mr Warlow be coming in one car, ma'am?'

'We're in a cocktail bar, Gina. Ma'am gets left at the door. It's Jess.'

'Same car, Jess?' Gina repeated the question.

'I expect so. Unless we book a taxi. I will not drive for sure.'

'It would make sense,' Catrin said.

Jess looked down at her drink. She might have missed the pointed look between the two younger women had it not been so deliberately obvious.

'Have I missed something?' Jess's eyes narrowed.

'No.' Catrin's protestations were a little too quick and way too over-egged.

Jess kept her eyes as slits and waited.

Gina took up the baton. 'It's just, with Molly away, and then the Shepherd's Hut…'

'That was Storm Frida.'

'Absolutely,' Gina said, her eyes wide. 'So, nothing happened…'

Jess paused, and then said, 'Am I under oath?'

'Only if you want to be.'

'Something may have happened.'

'What?' The word, emitted as a duet and in high soprano by both Catrin and Gina, drew stares.

'Oh God, it feels good having said that,' Jess said. 'How did you know?'

'We didn't,' Gina said. Though it was more a delighted squeal when all was said and done.

'We just wanted it to be,' Catrin added.

'Right, but you are sworn to secrecy. Evan would literally kill me. There are workplace and HR issues. Please, you have to swear. Not even to Craig and Rhys. God, not to Rhys.'

Gina held both hands up. 'I swear.'

'I won't even be at work after another week, two at the most. But your secret is safe.'

'I… we… need to work things out.'

'Does Molly know?' Gina asked.

'She does. She was more excited than I was.'

'Are you? Excited?'

'A little bit.'

'The wedding will be a double celebration,' Gina gushed.

Jess sent her an admonishing look.

'Only kidding,' she said, adding a theatrical batting of eyelashes.

Catrin laughed. 'Thank you for this,' she said.

'Well, we ought to have done a proper hen.'

'We still can do before the wedding proper.'

'I think it's a wonderful thing you're doing for Craig's grandad,' Jess said. 'I'm looking forward to meeting him.'

'It's just the right time. He gets very tired but for now he's still able to do everything just about.'

'You and Craig will do him proud.'

'Thank you,' Catrin said, her eyes moist.

'Stop it now, you two,' Gina sniffed. 'I spent ages on my eyes, and I do not want to cry and ruin them. I'm fully expecting to before the night is over, but I want to delay it as long as.'

'Right.' Jess got up. 'Best we get you another drink.'

She walked to the bar. When she glanced back, her two colleagues were deep in giggly conversation, and when they saw she was looking, they both gave her a mouth-wide-open, silent scream of delight.

Jess smiled back and, through her broad smile, whispered to herself, 'Shit.'

CHAPTER THIRTY-SEVEN

THE FOLLOWING MORNING, as Gina surreptitiously swallowed a couple of paracetamols with her morning tea and Jess stood in the shower thanking the stars that she'd had the good sense to stop at just three glasses of wine, Emyr Dobbs got a text.

He was at home, a couple of miles outside Cross Inn, when his phone chirped. Still dark outside the bedroom window. The number that came up was not one he was familiar with.

Leah says we should talk.

Who is this?

Nico. Nico Bajek.

Emyr toyed with not responding. From what Leah had told him, the police were running around, trying to find Nico Bajek. But the bigger part of him was all too aware of unfinished business here. And unanswered questions.

Where?

You say.

I'll drop you a pin. I'm here alone.

He did just that. Not for one minute did he feel anxious or fearful about it. He was scheduled for a night shift with the ambulance service, and his plan was to try to get some sleep this afternoon. But all thoughts of that had now fled. He wandered through the bungalow to a kitchen at the rear of the property with views over open fields. The kitchen was neat. Nothing out, or on display, that did not need to be. A reflection of the man. His brother had been like that, too. Unlike Leah, who was messy and careless. Maybe Bajek was the same.

Time to find out.

THE EIGHT-THIRTY BRIEFING in the Incident Room had a morning-after-the-night-before feel about it, even though no one present, bar Jess, had drunk more than half a pint of alcohol. And Jess's three glasses of wine, though more than her normal school night amount, did not seem to have had any effect on the way she looked, or her abilities.

Rhys, meanwhile, stood staring at the boards as if he was searching for inspiration.

'You look like you're solving the crime of the century,' Catrin said, handing him a tea and looking up at him. At 6 foot 4, he towered over her. Towered over most people.

He managed a weak smile. 'Just thinking about the sergeant's exam. I'm seriously considering pushing the button.'

'Ah, the dreaded legal knowledge test.'

'Application deadline's mid-January for the March exam.' He sipped, wincing at the heat. 'Not sure I'm ready, though.'

'I'll let you in on a secret. You'll never be sure you're ready, Rhys. But I think you are, so does the Wolf. You are good at this.'

Rhys let out a breath. 'Being good operationally doesn't always translate to exam success.'

Catrin nodded, understanding in her eyes. 'True. But you've got time, and you're still able to study. By that, I mean you've already got a degree, so you know how to handle the academic side. That's what trips a lot of people up. They wait too long and forget how to learn. The rest is just preparation.'

'Easy for you to say. The curriculum is massive. You aced

it first time, didn't you?' She laughed. 'Hardly. I passed, but it wasn't a walk in the park.' Catrin leaned in, lowering her voice. 'Want to know the secret?'

Rhys raised an eyebrow. 'There's a secret?'

'The pass rate is always 55 per cent. They adjust the mark to make sure of it.'

He groaned. 'That's supposed to help?'

'Just be in the top half. Look, do the prep course. Get Blackstone's manual.'

'Got it. Tough read.'

'Check frequent topics. Watch for syllabus changes. Do practice Q&As, but don't rely solely on them.'

Rhys nodded, scribbling mental notes.

Catrin's eyes flashed. 'Knowledge is crucial, but practice passing the exam specifically. Question structure. Spotting tweaked repeats.'

'Thanks. That helps a lot.'

'I've got loads of online resources. I'll email you the lot. You've got this. Just a formality.'

Doubt clouded Rhys's eyes. 'Imposter syndrome is no joke, though.'

'Nobody feels ready. I didn't.'

Rhys wrinkled his nose.

'You can do it. Put in the work and you'll be fine.'

Warlow, dispirited by lack of progress, growled out a question, 'Anything new come in overnight on Bajek?'

Break over.,Rhys and Catrin turned back to the case at hand. 'Nothing on Bajek, sir, but we have had an update on the toxicology report for Leighton Sullivan.'

'And?'

'He had 74 nanogram per mil in his blood, sir.'

'That's less than Marc Dobbs, isn't it?' Gil asked.

'It is, sarge,' Rhys concurred. 'But it's still a lethal dose.'

Jess stood up, her frustration echoing everyone else's. 'I have no evidence, but I can't help feeling that Sullivan holds the key to all this. Where exactly does he fit in?'

The woman who came in through the door to the right had a hand up in apology. 'Sorry. Got held up.'

'Alison, good of you to come.'

No one needed an introduction to Povey.

'Tea?' Rhys got up.

'No, thanks. Just had one. Did I hear mention of Sullivan's name?'

'You did,' Jess replied. 'He's our dark horse.'

'You saw the tox report?' Povey had a bundle of papers under one arm, and she plonked these down on the nearest desk.

'We did,' Warlow answered. 'Same as Dobbs and I suspect the Dahers.'

'We finished up at Sullivan's place last evening.'

'Find anything?' Gil asked.

Povey swung around towards the sergeant. 'If by anything you mean drugs related, no. Sorry to disappoint.'

'But, from the expression on your face, you did find something?' Gil wore a suspicious grin.

Povey nodded. 'Sullivan was, as you probably noticed, a bit of a nerd. A gamer and a collector.'

'The Superhero action figures?' Jess asked.

'Indeed. But not just any superhero action figures. These are collector's pieces. Limited editions. Some of them eye-wateringly valuable for bits of plastic.'

'To whom?' Gil asked.

'Other collectors,' Povey said. 'I spent half an hour last night trawling eBay and now know much more than I need or want to about Iron Man, Boba Fett, and a variety of other vaguely remembered comic heroes. At least a dozen of the boxed figures there are worth over a thousand and one over five thousand.'

'Which one?'

'Ghost Rider.'

'Who?' Gil asked.

'Rides a bike, has a skull,' Rhys explained. 'Nicolas Cage was in the film.'

'Some of the more obscure ones are worth even more. Luke Cage anyone?'

'Who?' Warlow said.

'Any relation to the actor?' Catrin asked.

'Uh, no. Not unless he's suddenly been wrongfully accused and imprisoned, is black, and has super strength and unbreakable skin. According to my research, that is.'

'I think there was a TV series, wasn't there?' Rhys asked.

'There was,' Povey agreed. 'I looked it up. Anyway. This is the Luke Cage chap in a silver shirt.' Povey slid out a crime-scene photo of a display box with Super Poseable in yellow letters next to a black plastic figure in an open silver shirt under a moulded plastic wrap.

'Looks like you didn't waste your evening, then, Alison,' Warlow said.

'My point is, Sullivan had a collection worth at least forty thousand pounds. His car was also new. Bought with cash six months ago.'

The detectives frowned en masse and looked at one another.

'What was his salary at the hospital?' Warlow said. He'd sat up, following Povey's train of thought like a greyhound after a hare.

'Thirty thousand pounds,' Gil said.

'How could he afford all of that stuff?' Rhys asked. 'And a new car.'

'My thinking exactly,' Povey replied, with eyebrows raised. 'I guessed you'd want those little details.'

'That's useful stuff, Alison.' Warlow bobbed his head slowly.

'If we come up with anything else useful, I'll get back to you. His phone and computer are with our techs. Might be worth giving them a ring.'

Povey left.

'Drug dealing as a source of funds?' Rhys asked.

'Most likely.'

'We need a close appraisal of Sullivan's financial history,' Warlow said with a nod at Catrin.

'This makes his link to Bajek even more bloody suspicious,' Gil muttered.

Jess was frowning.

Warlow picked up on it. 'You've got that faraway stare, Jess.'

'Something someone said.' Jess looked up at Gil. 'You spoke to Sullivan's supervisor. What was her name?'

'Niamh.'

'At Glangwili? Let's go and see her again.'

Gil didn't argue.

NICO BAJEK PARKED his car outside the bungalow that stood in its own grounds half a mile south of the village of Cross Inn. The place looked bare. All around were fields, with only the roof of the nearest neighbouring building visible where the land dipped half a mile away. On his left, beyond a double garage, sat a dilapidated barn, its stone walls topped by old wooden boards for the upper floor.

Nico looked around. Only one other vehicle to the side of the garage.

The building might have been a longhouse once but had been converted into an ugly twin-bay bungalow. The door opened before Nico could knock.

'Emyr.'

'Nico.'

'I don't know what you've heard, but I came to explain.'

'I'm listening.' Emyr hadn't moved from the doorway.

Somewhere above them, the drone of a helicopter a dozen miles away met their ears. Nico looked up at it.

'Is that out looking for you?'

'It's possible,' Nico said.

'You want to come inside?'

'Good idea.'

Emyr had not smiled, but now he stood back and let Nico in.

'This your place?' Nico asked.

'Yep. Fifty acres and the ugly bungalow. And, before you ask, left to me by an uncle. I'm doing it up bit by bit.'

They went through to the kitchen. Nico took in the polished concrete floor and sleek units. 'Is this you doing it up?'

'Yep.'

'Pretty high-end.'

Emyr didn't answer. 'Why did you want to see me?'

'To explain. The cops are all over me for this shit. They're going to try to fit me up for something I definitely didn't do.'

'Like?'

'Like kidnap your brother or kill some dealers.'

'I'm listening.' Emyr didn't offer Nico a seat, so he stood in the echoey space.

'Something really odd is going on.'

'No kidding.' Emyr barked out a bitter laugh.

'I was as shocked as anyone to hear about what happened to Marc, man. I mean, what the fuck is that all about? You were with him, right?'

'Yes, I was.' Emyr's expression gave nothing away.

'I'm sorry about that. Then there's me and Leah. But that was before Marc.'

'I know that too.'

'Okay, so I visited Leah. Out of common decency, man. Nothing else. The next thing is I'm being asked all kinds of shit by the cops.'

'And why do you think that is?'

'Because I used to sell Juice. I was a user. But I don't anymore. Now I work with support groups for kids getting into body building.'

'So, you've got a halo, is that it?'

'I never said I was an angel. But here's the thing. I'm on the lookout for people peddling the crap stuff. Then I get a call from someone who says they have Juice. I go along because if they are, it would need testing. Thing is, users will get it from anywhere, so if someone is selling, I go in and get some to see what kind of crap is in it. I'm not the cops, and I'm not a dealer.'

'Superhero, then. Why are you telling me this?'

'To explain why the cops are after me. The bloke that I assumed had messaged me asking if I wanted Juice… when I approached him, he acted like I was from fucking Mars. He'd been sent a message, too. It was a setup to make it look like I knew him. Then this poor bastard winds up dead.' Nico dropped his head and blew his cheeks out. 'I tell you; it's screwed up.'

'Did you do ketamine?' Emyr asked.

'Juice. Only Juice, and not for like six months. I swear. I told the cops this. All they had to do was talk to the outreach guys. I can give you a number, too. I have no knowledge of anything involving your brother. That's what I came here to say.'

'What about the cops?'

'I'm talking to my solicitor. I'm going to hand myself in. But I needed to get my head straight, that's all.'

'And Leah?'

'I've spoken to Leah, like, once or twice only in the last two years. And one of those times was at hers last week when I came to give my condolences. She thinks I'm in this, too. But she's wrong.'

Emyr turned and walked to a cupboard. He took out two glasses and a bottle of vodka. 'Took some guts to come here,' he said. 'You look like you could do with a drink.'

Bajek stared at the bottle and shrugged. 'That's good stuff. My dad drinks it. It's his mid-morning hit. But you're not Polish.'

'No. But I've worked with a few. On building sites before I became a paramedic. They had this stuff for breakfast.'

Nico gave a curt nod. 'I've got uncles who do the same.'

Emyr held up a glass. 'Well?'

'Yeah, why the fuck not?'

Emyr poured the vodka into two shot glasses. 'Marc called you Minty.'

'That's an old nickname,' Nico said.

'Let's drink to Marc.'

They threw the vodka back. Emyr immediately choked and turned to the sink, where he coughed violently, head low over the bowl. He turned back, red-faced, his voice a rasp. 'I'll never get used to the stuff.'

'But it means you have to do it again.'

Emyr reached for Nico's glass and filled it. Took the bottle to the sink to refill his own. But, with his back to Nico, used water from the tap in lieu of the alcohol.

'Do it quickly or it'll catch in your throat,' Nico said.

'*Na Zdrowie*,' Emyr said, and this time threw the contents of the glass down in one as Nico did the same.

'Want a coffee?' Emyr asked, voice high from the spirit.

'I should go.'

'Have a coffee. I want to ask you about Marc's mates in the club. I need to know who to ask to the funeral.'

Nico sighed and pulled out a chair while Emyr turned to his espresso machine.

CHAPTER THIRTY-EIGHT

NIAMH MONAGHAN WAS EXPECTING THEM.

'Thanks for seeing us at such short notice,' Jess said.

'No problem. What can I do for you?'

'Couple of questions.' Gil sat in the same chair he'd sat in the last time they'd met in the prefab offices. 'First, a confirmation that Leighton Sullivan's salary was about thirty thousand pounds?'

'Thirty-one eight hundred. Incremental increases year on year or unless he got a promotion.'

'And was he freelancing as well?'

'I don't know. But I'd be surprised,' Niamh said. 'Can I ask why?'

Catrin had spoken to Gil just before they'd pulled up in the hospital carpark. The nerds found emails from a big online investor, a confirmation of a deposit of ten thousand in a high-interest, three-month-notice cash account and some emails relating to issues with a cryptocurrency account requiring certification and authentication hoops to be jumped through.

'All to do with categorisation and appropriateness assessments,' Catrin had explained.

'What?'

'Apparently, if you have Bitcoin or anything like it, new

Financial Conduct Authority rules require everyone who has such investments to reconfirm if they are a seasoned investor or a new investor. You need to do an appropriateness assessment to ensure you are equipped to make informed decisions.'

'*Bois bach*, what does that mean in plain English?'

'It means he has cash accounts and cryptocurrency.'

Gil, in light of this, considered his answer to the Digital Services team supervisor. 'We're looking into Leighton's background and finances. Checking for anything that might help.' As nebulous a response as he could muster. Gil had done this before.

'Well, I can't help you there.'

'And there's no other suggestion you can think of that might assist us?' Jess asked.

Niamh replied with a startled glance that gave Jess a little jolt. There was something in that look.

'Well, I'm not sure, but after you came to see me—' She glanced over at Gil. '—and you had those odd questions about links to pharmacy and the fact that your people came and took the contents of Leighton's drawer away… did you find anything, by the way?'

'Not so far,' Jess answered.

Niamh nodded. 'Well, I reviewed his recent work schedule and logins.' She sighed.

'What did you find?'

'I found that Leighton had accessed our Palliative Care Community Pathway database over three-hundred-and-fifty times over the last two years.'

'Why haven't you told us this?' Jess asked.

Niamh wriggled in her chair. 'I wanted to double-check. It looked so odd. I thought it must be a mistake.'

'And?'

'No mistake.'

'What is Palliative Care Community Pathway?' Gil asked.

'Exactly what it says it is. It's shifting End of Life care to the community. It's how we allow people with end-of-life needs to experience their illnesses at home instead of in a hospital or a hospice using overall responsibility from a Palliative Care consultant and community palliative care teams.'

'In other words,' Gil said, 'letting people die at home.'

'Yes. With dignity and proactive management of pain and support for the family and patient.'

'Right. You seem surprised that he's accessed this database.'

'I am. Because we had no reports of any issues with the data handling or access from the end user … but then Sergeant Jones asked me if Leighton had any links to pharmaceutical or pharmacy-related systems.'

Jess's antenna twitched again.

'Something like 90 per cent of the patients on this list require significant pain medication. Opiates and the like. And this list is for the whole of the Health Board, that's four counties since we cover half of Powys, too.'

'How many patients?'

'Several hundred,' Niamh said.

'But he could access no drugs this way, right?' Gil asked.

'No, not at all. Distribution of drugs would be via the hospital pharmacy or retail pharmacists. On prescription. I truly have no idea why he'd want to examine this particular list so frequently—'

'He wanted to see who was dead,' Jess said abruptly.

'What?' Niamh did a double take.

'The list is dynamic, right? People coming on and off it. By definition coming off it means that patient has died.'

'Well, yes,' Niamh said.

'I don't suppose there is any point in me asking for a copy of that list?' Jess asked.

Niamh's expression hardened. 'There's a data protection issue—'

Jess pursed her lips. 'We will request it through the usual channels. But by then it might be too late.'

She got up. A single rapid movement that took Gil and

Niamh Monaghan by surprise. 'Thank you for your help,' Jess said. 'Gil, we need to go.'

Gil got up. 'Obviously.'

'We'll be in touch again,' Jess said at the door.

Gil had to trot almost to keep up with the DI as she hurried to the car. 'I hope you know what's going on, ma'am, because I don't have a bloody clue.'

'I will explain,' Jess said. 'But I need to speak to Gina first about a funeral.'

In the Incident Room, Warlow hovered, watching Catrin work and waiting for Jess to get back to him.

'Dare I ask what was discussed last night?' He stood, arms folded, staring at the boards, now full of images and pasted-up notes.

'Come on, sir. I can't tell you that. What goes on in Caesar's…' She turned from her screen. 'How about you? The four musketeers. What was the goss?'

'If the world is not put right by the discussions we had, then there is no justice.' Warlow's smile was a lopsided one. 'Has Rhys shown you the video of Gil attempting a dance-off?'

'Not yet, though Craig did tell me about it. I lost five minutes cleaning up the porridge that sprayed out of my mouth when he did. And thank you for not letting him get totally legless. Lucky he has a day off today.'

'He had a lot to celebrate.'

'He asked me to say thank you, too.'

'For what? A couple of pints and a meal?'

'For making him feel at home, he said.'

'He's had a bloody troubled existence if he thought that was like home.'

Catrin sent him an indulgent smile. 'You know what I mean, sir. One of the team.'

'He is. By dint of being your partner. Besides, he's helped

us out more than once, has he not? Mainly in trying to find you since you manage to get lost on a regular basis.'

'Something he keeps reminding me of, be reassured.' Catrin turned back to her screen. 'The computer techs are finding more stuff on Sullivan's laptop, sir. Incidental things he forgot to delete. There's an email from a mortgage company about a deposit on an off plan flat in Cardiff. I mean, that's not a small amount of money.'

'No, it is no—'

Warlow did not get to finish as Rhys yelled out from his desk. 'Sir, ANPR has just flagged a notice on Bajek's car.'

Warlow hurried over. 'Where?'

'It's the same camera that picked him up last time, sir. Up near Machynlleth only travelling in the opposite direction. Should I get someone over to his property, sir?'

Warlow pondered that. 'Think he'd really go home? He knows we're watching. No, my guess is he's heading somewhere else.'

'Do I need to warn Gina, then?'

'Yes, you do. And get a response vehicle over to the Dobbs's house.' That was a belt and braces necessity, but Warlow's order fell short of being an absolute emergency. 'Again, I can't see him doing that. It's too obvious. He knows we have a presence there.' Warlow was leaning on Rhys's desk. He tapped his middle finger idly on the cover of a file.

'Why don't we ask his solicitor?' Catrin suggested.

Warlow shot her a glance with his face lit up and a pointed finger. 'Good idea, Sergeant Richards.'

Catrin reached for the landline, dialled Roebuck, and handed the phone to her boss.

'Ah, DCI Warlow, to what do I owe the pleasure?' Roebuck's voice oozed sarcasm.

'Your client is on the move,' Warlow said.

'Is he now?'

'Either he told you, or he didn't. Has he contacted you?'

'This morning, early. I suggested that his best course of

action was to return to the fold and offer to help you in any way he could.'

'And?'

'And… he said he'd consider it. But that he had something to do first.'

'What?' Warlow barked.

'Interestingly enough, he didn't say. The implications being that it might be something I would not approve of.'

'Leah Dobbs?'

'I don't think so. Your FLO is there, is she not?'

'She is.'

'Nico says she's a tiger. He'd rather stay away.'

'He's showing a rare streak of good sense there, then.'

'Look. I honestly don't know what he's doing. I took some consolation in knowing he was heading down this way. I'm sure he'll do the right thing.'

'Are you, though?'

'I am not his keeper, Detective Chief Inspector. And he is at liberty to take my advice or not.'

'That makes you pretty bloody pointless, then, doesn't it?'

'As I say, Nico is his own man.'

'If he rings again, tell him not to do anything stupid. Use your barrow-loads of charm.'

The line went quiet for a beat before Roebuck spoke again. 'Like you, I do not want to see Nico self-destruct. Our firm knows the family.'

'Put me on speed dial. I want to hear as soon as he contacts you.'

'I work with the police a lot—'

'No, you don't. You work against us a lot.'

'Alright, I'll rephrase. I come across a lot of police officers. And I have to say that you are not the easiest I have dealt with.'

'I'll send you some flowers.'

Warlow ended the call and turned to Rhys. 'Grab your coat. We're heading north.'

'You know where Nico is, sir?'

'No, but he'll be closer to Cardigan than he is to us here. Let's pretend we're an ambulance and head for a holding pattern until he's spotted.'

'Great.' Rhys grinned.

'No crisps. But if you're good, we might call in for a coffee somewhere.'

'Yay,' Rhys said, by way of a joke. But he only got a smile from Catrin. The DCI was already striding out of the door.

CHAPTER THIRTY-NINE

Warlow let Rhys drive the job Audi.

'Is there anywhere special we need to head for, sir?'

'Cardigan. That's Bajek's stomping ground. If you step on the gas, we'll get there in time for an early lunch.'

'We could call in on Gina, sir?' Rhys suggested.

'We have nothing new to tell Leah Dobbs. Might make for an awkward stop-off.'

'Gina says it's a better atmosphere in the house now that Emyr Dobbs has moved out.'

'Ah, yes. He went yesterday, right? Remind me where he lives?' Warlow asked.

Rhys was passing the Quins' Club where they'd had a drink the night before. 'Good question, sir. Gina would know.'

'Of course, she would.'

Warlow dialled Gina's number and got an engaged signal. 'Busy,' he said as they negotiated Water Street and drove out of the town, past the Fire and Rescue Service HQ and the smattering of houses that eventually petered out into open countryside.

Warlow let his thoughts bounce around as the fields and forests sped by. There would be a fixed point in all of this mess. A commonality from where everything else flowed. But he was damned if he had a clue what that was at present.

They were passing the cemetery on the hill at Bwlch-newydd when Gina phoned back.

'Sorry, sir. The phone's been red hot.'

'I won't keep you, Gina. Do you have an address for Emyr Dobbs?'

'Not offhand, but I can get it. Leah would know.'

'Fine, can you text me it?'

'I can, sir. I'll do it now.' She sounded a little breathless.

'No rush.'

'Isn't there, sir? DI Allanby gave me the impression there might be.'

'DI Allanby?'

'Hasn't she rung you, sir? I've been on the phone with the funeral directors for the last half an hour at her request. I thought—'

Warlow's phone signalled a second caller. He glanced at the screen and saw Jess's name.

'Gina, that's DI Allanby now. Text me that address.'

'I will, sir.'

Warlow took the call.

'Evan, where are you?'

He sensed an urgency in her voice.

'In the car with Rhys, heading up towards Cardigan. Where are you?'

'Still in the car park at the hospital. Gil and I have been busy making calls.'

'So Gina said. I—'

'No time, Evan. Just listen.'

'I'm putting you on speaker for Rhys as well.'

'Fine. Gil is with me, too. We spoke to Sullivan's boss at the hospital. She confirmed his salary. Catrin also dug into his background. Three years ago, he had a twenty-nine-thousand-pound student loan debt.'

'So, how can he afford toys worth thousands of quid?' Rhys asked.

'Exactly,' Jess answered. 'But Sullivan's boss was spooked enough by Gil's last visit to do some digging of her own. She found that he'd accessed their PCC pathway database literally hundreds of times.'

Gil came through with the acronym before Warlow could ask.

'PCC is Palliative Care Community Pathway. For terminally ill patients to receive care at home.'

'I'm listening,' Warlow said, trying to make sense of all this and failing miserably at present.

'These are patients who might receive treatments at home. Pain relief included,' Gil explained.

'Like the fentanyl patches,' Rhys whispered.

'Exactly.'

'So, was Sullivan stealing this stuff?' Warlow asked.

'No. I don't think so,' Jess continued. 'Drugs are issued by prescription only.'

'Then how does it help?' Warlow asked.

'This is where it gets really interesting,' Gil said in a low rumble.

'When we were out last night,' Jess explained, 'Gina told us that while she and Leah and Emyr visited a funeral director, another visitor recognised Emyr. She sang his praises as a paramedic. Said how good he'd been with her now dead partner. How he'd even called after the partner died to collect what she termed "equipment".'

'And?'

'I've just got off the phone with that woman. Her name is Elsie Vaughan, and her husband, Gwilym, passed away last month. From the funeral director, Catrin also got the name of four other people, cancer victims mainly, all of whom passed over the last six months, and Gil and I spoke to their relatives, too. And guess what? Every one of them knew Emyr the angel.'

'I don't understand, ma'am?' Rhys asked. 'What's wrong with all that?'

'What's wrong is that only one of those grieving people, three widowers and one widow, had come across Emyr as an ambulance driver. But they all met him when he called at their houses.'

'Sullivan was giving him the names on the database,' Warlow said, his voice now a harsh whisper.

'Giving, or selling,' Gil said.

'And top of the list of the "equipment" he was calling to collect after death were residual drugs,' Jess added the icing on the cake.

'Fentanyl patches,' Rhys muttered.

'Bingo,' Gil said.

'Two of the people I spoke to said Emyr Dobbs, dressed in scrubs and wearing his NHS lanyard, had also called with a yellow box for patients who were legitimately on fentanyl patches to use for disposal. He'd then collect those at the end of a week or two.'

Warlow let that one sink in. 'I can understand him collecting unused patches, but why used patches?'

'Catrin's been on that one, too,' Gil said. 'Something like 20 per cent of the fentanyl in a patch is still there after it's been used. You can extract what's left by something called a fentanyl patch boil-up. Just punch it into a search engine. You simmer the patches in a bit of boiling water for fifteen minutes. The extract can then be used any way you like. And it'll be full of fentanyl.'

'Sullivan stole the list and sold it to Emyr Dobbs,' Jess said. 'Dobbs then used it to collect used and unused patches once the patients passed. A lucrative little side-hustle, as Molly would say. And now Dobbs is adopting a slash and burn clean up approach.'

Warlow felt the car lurch as Rhys took a bend a little too fast.

'Sorry, sir.'

'Pull over, Rhys,' Warlow ordered. But in truth, it was more like advice. If the DC's heart was racing half as fast as his own was, he needed to take a breath.

Rhys found a spot and pulled up. 'But Emyr Dobbs? He's been so mad about his brother's death.'

But Warlow didn't answer. He was too busy joining dots. And the picture they were revealing was of a dark and heartless monster.

'Jess, this … this is brilliant work.'

'I don't have it all yet,' Jess replied.

'Maybe not, but it's enough. Shit.' The word hissed out of Warlow's mouth. 'To think he's been there all this time, right under our bloody noses.'

'But sir… Emyr Dobbs?' Rhys kept up the objection. 'I mean, he's the one that found his brother on the mountain. Are you saying there weren't any kidnappers?'

Warlow turned to Rhys, and for a moment there was dead silence inside the vehicle as all four officers considered the implications. But it was Jess that spoke. And rightly so. It was she who'd made the leap, put all this together, broken the case. 'No, the Dahers were involved. I'm thinking, what if Emyr Dobbs was trying to make a deal with the devil? What if he thought he could supply the Dahers, but something went wrong? Maybe what he'd cooked up was poor quality. What we know about them is they were just soldiers. Sent to do a job.'

'But—'

And then Jess dropped the real bombshell. 'What if the Dahers messed it up?'

'And got the wrong Dobbs,' Gil finished the harrowing suggestion in a low growl.

'Oh, shit,' Rhys whispered.

Warlow's insides did an impression of a capsizing kayak just as his phone buzzed and he read another message.. 'Gina's sent us the address we have for Emyr Dobbs. We're almost halfway there,' he said.

'We're leaving Carmarthen now,' Gil replied. 'Right behind you.'

'I'll forward Dobbs's address, Jess.' Warlow's pulse was thrumming in his ears. Jess had seen the connection that no one else had, all thanks to Gina's keen eyes and ears. Rhys brought him back down to earth.

'So, where does Nico Bajek fit in to all this?' he asked.

'He doesn't,' Warlow replied, frowning. 'It's only Emyr that wants us to think he does.'

'And if he ends up the same way as the Dahers and Sullivan …'

'He'll just be another scapegoat. Another fentanyl victim. Another death to muddy the waters.'

'Do you think Nico might want to talk to Emyr? To apologise for what happened between him and Marc. Set the record straight?'

Warlow didn't like those words. But they explained why Bajek might head back towards Cardigan. 'Only one way to find out. I suggest you put your foot down, Rhys.'

THE ADDRESS GINA had given Warlow was really a small farm. Warlow wondered, as they pulled up in the overgrown yard, whether the original property might have been divvied up and the bungalow built as a retirement home. It looked … unprepossessing and utilitarian enough. There were no cars parked outside.

'There's a double garage with closed doors and a barn fifty yards to the left, sir. Want me to check those out?'

'Let's see if there's anyone home first.'

Warlow exited the vehicle and crunched over the stoned yard to the front door. He got no reply after three knocks. 'Go around to the rear. I'll go left, you go right.'

The curtains on the windows of the two wings were open. Warlow peered in by cupping his hands on the glass. A bedroom, the bed made. One old wardrobe, an ugly patterned carpet on the floor. He met Rhys coming the other way towards a back door. It, too, was locked, but the kitchen window revealed an extraordinary picture. A polished concrete floor, expensive fixtures, and fittings.

'Doing it up, sir?' Rhys asked.

'Looks like it. See anything else?'

'No,' Rhys said.

'Look at the sink.'

Rhys squinted. 'Two upturned shot glasses, sir.'

'And the draining board is still wet. Someone has been here and recently.'

Rhys turned towards the garage and the barn.

'Yes, you now have your wish, DC Harries. But let's first of all gear up with stab vests and batons.'

'On it, sir.'

CHAPTER FORTY

Warlow and Rhys picked up their gear, slipped off their coats, and slid on the vests.

Rhys looked up for it.

'If you say Starsky and Hutch, I swear I'll ban crisps from the Incident Room forever.'

'I wasn't going to say anything, sir. Just having a bit of déjà vu. I wear this more when I'm with you than at any other time.'

'Seems that way, doesn't it?'

Rhys walked over to the garage block. Two identical up-and-over doors with concrete ramps leading up from the yard and a rough stucco rendering of dirty grey. Compared to the weathered wood on the barn beyond, they appeared modern, ugly, and not at all in keeping.

Rhys tried the handle.

'Locked, sir.'

Warlow glanced down at a three-inch gap between the base of the door and the ramp on the far left. 'See if you can get a butcher's.'

Rhys got down on his knees and used his phone torch.

'It's a blue Hyundai, sir. I can see the reg. I'll get Catrin to run it.'

While Rhys texted, Warlow observed the barn from fifty

yards away. They should have used it as the model for the new buildings—it had an original, authentic charm. But, as so often happens, practicality trumped aesthetics, leaving them with something far less attractive.

Rhys's phone made a buzzing noise.

'That's Catrin, sir. It is Bajek's car.'

'Right, get some Uniforms out here. Tell them we've found the car.'

'Are we going to wait, sir?'

'No. If Jess is right, people who come into contact with Emyr Dobbs do not do well. Bajek, I have no doubt, is in danger.'

Rhys made the call. Warlow began walking towards the barn. This was West Wales. No untreated wood did well in this wet a climate. And so, previous owners had treated the outside of the barn with something that had turned the wood almost black. Oil or creosote probably. Now gaps had appeared between the weathered boards, and the window on the upper floor had a broken pane. But the doors were closed.

'On the way, sir.' Rhys waved his phone.

'Okay, let's go.'

Last night's rain had blown off and a mild, blustery day had come in from the west. More rain was forecast but, for now, at least, the ground underfoot remained puddle free, the wind not too chilly.

'How many acres did they say?'

'Fifty, sir.'

'And Dobbs owns this?'

'Bought at auction last year for five-hundred-and-fifty-thousand pounds.'

'Most people would think it was a bargain,' Warlow said. Glancing around at the empty fields on all sides.

'Most of the people I know would think it was a dream to be able to afford a place at half that price.'

'So would your average paramedic, I'd guess.'

They got to within a few yards of the door. The black-iron, heavy-duty, T hinges looked old, the door closed only with a rusting latch. Warlow walked around the outside. Two bigger doors at the side had a large chain and padlock.

'Only one way in,' he announced.

Both officers returned to the small door in the stone wall of the first floor. Rhys lifted the latch and pushed the door open. It slid smoothly.

'Someone has oiled the hinges,' Warlow muttered as they stepped through into the building. The only light came from the top window in the gable ends. Above them, dusty boards formed a roof that also served as the floor for the upper story, which stretched out as a gallery along both sides and a mezzanine at the far end—presumably where hay had once been loaded through a sealed-off hatch. The gallery's walls were warped, rotting planks of wood.

On both sides at ground level, old tools and iron implements had been haphazardly stacked, leaving the central area clear. And in that central area sat a building on wheels. Not a caravan as such because the windows were too small, and the thing had been painted white. It looked almost clinical. More like a laboratory than a mobile home.

Warlow approached. He called out as he did.

'Emyr, this is the police. If you are in there, show yourself.'

He got no response except for the wind rattling a loose board somewhere above them.

He sent Rhys a nod. The DC, baton unfurled, walked towards the door of the white vehicle. He climbed up the two steps and opened the door, flicked on a switch, and the vehicle lit up.

'Empty, sir,' Rhys called back. 'But it has a Breaking Bad vibe about it, sir.'

Warlow knew little about fentanyl, but he'd seen news reports about police officers being overcome from contained fumes or even dermal exposure. He'd even seen the video of an officer falling over after opening the boot of a car. 'Careful, Rhys, you don't have a mask.'

Rhys turned around with a grin. 'Common misconception, sir. It won't poleaxe you by touching it or breathing it in. But that's got into the hive mind. There have been studies—'

'Right, save the lecture until later. Let me have a look.'

Warlow took the steps. Inside, definitely a lab. A rudimentary work surface, lit from flat LED lights in the ceiling. Flasks and water jugs littered the surfaces along with a microwave and a gas-fired burner. He picked out three yellow NHS style hazardous waste bins. He used his baton to slide back a lid. Inside, he saw a pile of folded over opaque rectangles. He could not be sure, but they would do, he suspected, for fentanyl patches.

From outside, Rhys called in a whisper.

'Sir, I can see something.'

Warlow came back down the steps. Rhys pointed towards the first-floor gallery to the left of where they'd come in. Dust fell through gaps in the boards.

Warlow raised his voice. 'Emyr, if you are here, best you give up now. Other people are coming. Tell us where Nico Bajek is.'

No reply.

Warlow pointed towards a ladder under the far gable end. Rhys nodded.

Warlow stood next to the laboratory and watched the DC climb the ladder.

'We know, Emyr. We know what you've been doing, the list of terminally ill patients on fentanyl patches. There is no need for Nico to die. No need for anyone else to get hurt.'

Rhys had gained the mezzanine now, working his way around towards the location where they had observed the dust.

'Old bales up here, sir. It's a mess,' Rhys called down.

'If you cooperate with us now, Emyr, it will look better for you in court.'

Warlow walked slowly across to where they'd seen the dust, peering up into the upper floor between the gaps.

'You have nowhere to go, Emyr.'

It all happened quickly after that. Warlow didn't see the

bale until it tumbled. He scrambled away as it fell, but it hit his leg and erupted in a volcano of dust and dry and rotting straw that almost choked the air out of him.

More footsteps then. Two lots, running.

Rhys yelled a warning, Warlow followed the progress of the steps above as he went around the gallery towards the hatchway.

Warlow guessed Dobbs might be trying to lure Rhys away from that spot. And he'd succeeded as Rhys took the long way around in pursuit. He might even have got out of the barn if the floorboards, rotten and petrifying, had not collapsed under Dobbs's pounding feet.

Another shout. This time of surprise, and then halfway along the other gallery, Dobbs crashed through the floor.

It was not a long way. Only ten feet. But it was what lay beneath that caused the damage.

Later, Warlow would be told that the vicious-looking iron screw was a posthole digger, and the thing on iron wheels was a hay rake. Dobbs's foot hit the screw, and his leg twisted. Both Rhys and Warlow heard the crack as bones snapped.

But the second noise was a duller thud as Dobbs's skull hit the hay rake's rusty metal wheel.

Warlow rushed over. There was not much blood, but even in the few seconds it took to cross the barn floor, Dobbs had gone very pale.

'Lie still,' Warlow ordered.

'Ah fuck… ah fuck… I feel sick…'

'Where's Nico, Emyr?'

'Jesus, my leg… Jesus, it hurts…'

'Nico.'

'Wasn't supposed to be like this,' Emyr said through gritted teeth. 'Wasn't supposed to…' He turned his head and vomited. 'Oh fuck, I feel awful… my head.' He put a hand up to a large and expanding lump on his left temple.

'Nico—'

Dobbs wiped his mouth with a trembling hand and missed.

Warlow half turned to see where Rhys was, but Dobbs's hand clutched at his coat. 'Marc had figured it out. They messed up. It was me they wanted. Marc figured that out when they let him go… he was going to blab. Fucking Marc…' Dobbs made an odd keening noise and grimaced in pain. 'I gave him some patches. Lots of patches… and then I let him sleep in the water… what a mess…'

A sick feeling billowed in Warlow's throat. Rhys arrived at his elbow. 'Phone for an ambulance,' Warlow ordered. 'Emyr, where is Nico?'

Dobbs looked at Warlow, an odd, startled expression suddenly on his face, and managed one last word before he lost focus. 'Car…'

'He's passed out,' Warlow said. 'Rhys, get that garage door open. Take whatever you can find and get that bloody garage open.'

Warlow stayed with the injured man but got no more answers.

By the time help arrived, Rhys had somehow opened the garage door wide enough to crawl into.

Bajek was in the back seat, five fentanyl patches on his neck, but still breathing.

So was Dobbs when they got him in the ambulance.

But only one of them made it through the night.

Emyr Dobbs never regained consciousness and died before dawn from intracranial bleeding.

Warlow was at home when he got the news. Jess held out her arms to him. He accepted her embrace, a much-needed hug.

All he managed to say was, 'What a bloody tragic waste.'

CHAPTER FORTY-ONE

Five days later, Warlow and Jess sat in the same chairs they'd sat in previously in Leah Dobbs's living room. Gina made them tea, and this would be the last day she'd be there as a FLO.

Beca was with Leah's mother on this bright December day. At ten in the morning, the sun shone, but with it came an easterly wind. Leah did not look any better than she had the last time Warlow saw her. If anything, she looked even thinner, her cheek bones rendering her face bony, the dark circles under her eyes a deeper shade than he remembered.

'I've come to explain what we think happened, Leah. You deserve that. All I'd ask is that you keep it to yourself, or at least to those close to you for now, as it's a complex case that is still under investigation.'

'Okay.' One unemotional word uttered through a barely moving mouth.

'We now know that the kidnappers, the Daher brothers, worked on their own initiative. They bought drugs in the big cities like Liverpool and Birmingham, bringing those drugs into Aberystwyth and Machynlleth to sell. They might have been stepping on other suppliers' toes, but they were small fry.'

'What about Emyr?'

Warlow glanced at Jess to continue. 'We now also know that Emyr supplied drugs. Stealing from ambulances, perhaps for his own use, perhaps for profit. But then he hit on an idea.'

'What idea?'

'Another man, Leighton Sullivan, accessed lists of patients being treated with fentanyl. We've found hard copies of those lists at Emyr's farm. He abused his position as an NHS employee to call on these patients and their relatives, posing as some kind of official drug disposal service. He collected fentanyl patches, took them to the farmhouse he'd bought, and extracted residual fentanyl.'

Leah shook her head. 'Was Marc...'

Warlow was waiting for the question, but the words he spoke next remained difficult to get out. 'Emyr tried to make his extracted drug into a powder or crystals. We found something like that, but in doing so, it looks like it lost its potency. My guess is the Dahers got angry at that. We think they came down intending to kidnap Emyr Dobbs and getting their money back. But they got the wrong Dobbs.'

'How? How is that possible?' Leah sat frozen, her dark-rimmed eyes wide with horror.

'From what we understand, many of these drug deals take place via encrypted messaging. It could be the Dahers had never met Emyr,' Jess explained.

Warlow ensured that what he said next came across as his own opinion, 'My guess, and it is a guess, is that the Dahers realised their mistake and let Marc go. They took him to somewhere remote, like the shore of Llyn y Fan. That's when he phoned you. They'd tried injecting him with heroin to make him compliant. That was a botched job. When Emyr found him, he decided he could use the scenario to his advantage.'

'In what way?'

'This is going to be hard to hear, Leah.'

'I want to know,' she said firmly.

'Before he died, Emyr told me that Marc worked out what

had happened. Perhaps the Dahers told him once they twigged. He might have told Emyr all this. But Emyr couldn't afford to let Marc tell the truth. And so, he put fentanyl patches on his brother, which made him even more confused and disoriented. I think he then marched Marc across the moor towards Llyn y Fan Fawr, the bigger lake, and stayed with him, put him in the cold water, and waited until he died before calling the rescue services.'

Leah's breath had become ragged. Once more, Gina sat with her arm around her shoulder.

'She's hyperventilating,' Jess said.

Warlow went into the kitchen and found a paper bag. Gina held it over Leah's mouth as a rebreather, keeping her head-down. After a few breaths, Leah looked back up.

'Emyr killed Marc?'

Warlow nodded. 'He also killed the Dahers. We found bottles of beer and vodka laced with fentanyl. Enough to knock people out. My guess is Emyr contacted the Dahers again and offered money or more product. Maybe shared a beer with them. Gave them booze laced with fentanyl, waited for it to take effect, and then doubled down with more patches.'

They could drive a bus through the enormous gaps in the story. They had yet to work out how Emyr Dobbs had overcome Leighton Sullivan. Perhaps with a replica gun or a knife after a clandestine meeting in the lay-by. But they might never find out that truth. Yet, he, too, had succumbed to the Dragon's Breath.

'So, Marc wasn't dealing drugs?' Leah asked, tears forming streaks down her face.

'No.' Warlow told her straight.

'But what about the ketamine?' She poked holes in his conviction. Wanting to trust him, needing certainty.

Jess answered this time. 'One of the terminal patients Emyr visited had been a vet. It's possible he got ketamine from him.'

'Emyr put it in the shed?'

'That would be my guess,' Warlow said.

Again, they had no evidence, but Emyr had access, and they'd found a stash of other drugs at the farm.

'Then Marc…'

'Is a completely innocent victim in all of this, Leah.'

'And so is Nico Bajek,' Jess added. 'Emyr tried to implicate him, too.'

They didn't tell Leah they'd found a packed bag at the farm, a lot of cash and tickets to Portugal on a flight due to leave the day after Warlow and Rhys visited Emyr Dobbs. Their reason for being here was to try to bring some solace to this grieving woman.

'None of this will bring Marc back, I realise that,' Warlow said.

'No, but it's important. For Becs as well.' Her expression had changed. Instead of the nameless fear, relief flooded in and brought a real and grateful smile. 'Thank you.'

Warlow shook his head. 'It isn't me you need to thank. It's these two.' He pointed at Gina and Jess. 'If it wasn't for them, we'd still be chasing our tails.'

Leah stood up and gave Gina a hug, then she turned to Jess, who stood, too, and gave her a hug as well.

Warlow held out his hand. Leah shook it.

'Nico texted me. He said that the football club was raising money for us. Marc made sure there was insurance, too. He was always thinking about me and Becs.'

Warlow could only nod. Little enough compensation for a family ruined by drugs and greed yet again.

At 5.30 pm on the Friday of that same week, as Warlow sat in the room at the registry office used for the marriage proceedings, there were more tears. Catrin's mother and sister made significant lacrimal contributions, as did Craig's mother, Gina, and Anwen. If any of the men felt moved enough, they hid it well under itchy eyes and the odd blown nose.

But these were tears of joy and celebration, and they were outweighed by the show of grinning teeth on view. And the biggest smile came from Iorrie Peters, Craig's grandfather. Not a big man, a wiry frame perhaps the only hint at his underlying illness, he was smart in a new dark suit and gave them all a rendition of *Myfanwy* at the little reception in a function room in Nant Rugby Club that brought more tears, this time even from Gil.

But then *Myfanwy*, a song of unrequited love, was written very much with tears in mind.

Jess listened with rapt attention and moist eyes and asked Warlow for a translation of the first two lines.

'*Paham mae dicter, O Myfanwy, Yn llenwi'th lygaid duon di*? Why such anger in those dark eyes of yours?'

'Wow,' Jess said.

'I know,' Gil leant over. 'Guaranteed shiver with that one.'

Warlow made a point of chatting with Craig's parents and his grandad who, remarkably enough, seemed happy and one of the most contented there.

'Glad you came,' Iorrie said, his tie a loose knot below an undone top button of his shirt. 'Thank you for what you've done. For Catrin especially. It was you who found her when that bugger kidnapped her, right?'

'My dog did most of it,' Warlow said with a wry grin. 'She's an honorary Dyfed Powys Officer now.'

'Craig and the family will never forget that. They think a lot of you.'

'They think a lot of you, too.'

Iorrie grinned. This one more wistful. 'You a grandfather, Evan?'

'I am.'

'It's a privilege, isn't it? And the good kind,' Iorrie said. 'Be great if Catrin hurried up and had the baby now. I'd be a great-grandfather, then. That would be an achievement.'

They drank to that.

More people came to the dancing later at around eight.

The DJ read the audience well and played mainly floor fillers – Abba, obviously – and Motown.

Warlow let the youngsters do their bit. But when they played Chaka Khan's *Feel for you*, Jess saw him chair dancing and came over to where he was sitting from where she'd been boogying with Gina.

'One for you?' she asked, her eyes reflecting the lights from a glitter ball.

'On my top ten list.'

'Fancy it?' she asked.

'Should we?' Warlow glanced around. But the alcohol in his system emboldened him.

'Everyone else seems to be.'

'Why not?'

He moved to the music. Jess's eyebrows went up. 'You can dance, Mr Warlow.'

'Misspent youth.'

They danced. If he noticed the whoops and cheers from Rhys and Gina, Gil and Anwen, and Catrin and Craig, he put it down to them seeing him in a new light.

Come to think of it, he was seeing himself in that light, too.

It was carriages at eleven-thirty. The lights came on in the room. There were hugs and thank yous. Gil and Anwen were being picked up by one of his daughters. Jess and Warlow booked a taxi.

It was as Gina, merrier than most, was giving Catrin one last hug, that Gil, who'd been discussing the misfortunes of the Welsh rugby team with Iorrie, looked over at Catrin and yelled out a warning.

'*Arglwydd*, careful there, Catrin. Looks like someone has spilled their beer. Mind you don't slip.'

But Catrin didn't move. Instead, she stared in horror at Gil.

'That's not beer,' she wailed. 'That's my waters breaking. Craig!'

Gil looked at Iorrie, who was grinning broadly.

'All that dancing, see. Shaken her up like a bottle of pop.'

CATRIN GAVE birth to a healthy baby girl at 4.27 am. They called her Betsi.

Warlow woke up to that text on his phone and made Jess a cup of tea after he'd fed Cadi. He told her the news, and she smiled and took the tea from him.

'See, Evan. Sometimes the stars align.'

'They pick their bloody moments alright.'

He left her to let Cadi back in. What he did not tell Jess then was the name that had popped into his head as he'd waited for the kettle to boil and his mildly hungover brain was off on a jolly of its own somewhere.

He took his phone from where it was charging and looked again on the fridge door at the list from Molly's synonym word cloud app.

Denise had used the word "Fern" in her letter. A name that had shifted and twisted in Warlow's mind, like steam swirling from the kettle as it heated, taking shape and then vanishing before he could grasp it. Not Fern, but something close. Almost there—then gone.

It gnawed at him. The name lingered just beyond reach, like a shadow slipping out of sight. He felt it was something from his past, a thread connecting to a memory buried deep. A name? He clenched his fists, forcing himself to think. Was it a case? One of those old, half-forgotten ones from when he'd been transitioning from London to Wales? Or was his mind playing tricks, weaving some fabricated connection after Denise's written deathbed confession?

But what if she'd got it wrong? Her mind had been scattered in those final days, and yet... something tugged at him now, an instinct sharpening as he opened the door to let Cadi in after breakfast. A quiet certainty settled over him, pulling at his gut, telling him there was more to this. He was close—so close to unlocking it.

Or was he fooling himself? Maybe it was nothing at all. Denise's muddled thoughts could've easily confused things, mixing memories and meanings. But that feeling, that pull, wouldn't let go.

Damn it all.

Warlow sighed, frustration flickering inside him. He could be completely wrong. It might be something else entirely. But still, the name haunted him, elusive and teasing, like the steam that vanished into the morning air.

'Evan,' Jess called out. 'I'm just nipping into the shower, okay?'

Hearing her call him shattered all his other ruminations like the crack of thin ice on a lake.

He was still hopeless when it came to Jess Allanby subtext. Telling him she was about to have a shower might be simply be her keeping him informed of the days's events unfolding.

Then again, it might mean something else altogether.

He set aside fern for now and took his tea, and Jess's, back to the bedroom.

Learning subtext was hard.

But he was a very apt pupil.

ACKNOWLEDGMENTS

As with all writing endeavours, the existence of this novel depends upon me, the author, and a small army of 'others' who turn an idea into a reality. My wife, Eleri, who gives me the space to indulge my imagination and picks out my stupid mistakes. Sian Phillips, Tim Barber and other proofers and ARC readers. Thank you all for your help. Special mention goes to Ela the dog who drags me away from the writing cave and the computer for walks, rain or shine. Actually, she's a bit of a princess so the rain is a no-no. Good dog!

But my biggest thanks goes to you, lovely reader, for being there and actually reading this. It's great to have you along and I do appreciate you spending your time in joining me on this roller-caster ride with Evan and the rest of the team.

CAN YOU HELP?

With that in mind, and if you enjoyed it, I do have a favour to ask. Could you spare a moment to **leave a review or a rating**? A few words will do, but it's really the only way to help others like you discover the books. Probably the best way to help authors you like. Just visit my page on Amazon and leave a few words.

A FREE BOOK FOR YOU

Visit my website and join up to the Rhys Dylan VIP Reader's Club and get a FREE novella, *The Wolf Hunts Alone,* by visiting the website at: **rhysdylan.com**

The Wolf Hunts Alone.

One man and his dog… will track you down.

DCI Evan Warlow is at a crossroads in his life. Living alone, contending with the bad hand fate has dealt him, he finds solace in simple things like walking his neighbour's dog.

But even that is not as safe as it was. Dogs are going missing from a country park. And not only one, now three have disappeared. When he takes it upon himself to root out the cause of the lost animals, Warlow faces ridicule and a thuggish enemy.

But are these simply dog thefts? Or is there a more sinister malevolence at work? One with its sights on bigger, two legged prey.
A FREE eBOOK FOR YOU (Available in digital format)

Only one thing is for certain; Warlow will not rest until he finds out.

By joining the club, you will also be the first to hear about new releases via the few but fun emails I'll send you. This includes a no spam promise from me, and you can unsubscribe at any time.

AUTHOR'S NOTE

I was secretly please, and mildly disturbed by the outpourings of concern as to whether The Last throw was, indeed, that last of DCI Warlow's cases. As you will have noticed, it was not. And by this time, everyone, bar Warlow himself, needed him to take a long hard look in the mirror and tell Jess how he felt.

So that's done.

At long last.

And the case, the theft of pain medication, is a real thing. Quite often I use actual cases as a jumping off point. Dragon's Breath was no exception. And it allowed me to utilise one of my favourite places, LLyn Y Fan Fawr and Fach. If you get the chance, you ought to go. Really.

And when you stand on the edge of that body of water, remember, not everyone here is a murderer. Not everyone … Cue tense music!

All the best, and see you all soon, Rhys.

And do not forget that for those of you who are interested, there is a glossary on the website to help with those pesky pronunciations.

READY FOR MORE?

DCI Evan Warlow and the team are back in...

The Bowman

When two bodies are discovered in the remote Cambrian Mountains, slain most horribly, DCI Warlow faces a chilling echo of unsolved murders from the past.

The Bowman has returned—or has he?

As fear grips the Elan Valley, Warlow must unravel decades of mystery to stop the killer before the wilderness claims more victims. In a land where secrets lie hidden in every crevice, no one is safe

Made in United States
North Haven, CT
21 November 2024